M000086163

THE BANKSY EXCHANGE

Kim Rowland

Kim Rowland Media LLC

FOR BEN AND SKYLA,

my partners in crime.

CHAPTER 1

Everybody needs a partner in crime. A wingman. A side-kick. Someone to hold you accountable for your actions. Somebody to reign you in when you're about to do something dumb. Moronic even. But what if that person, your person, is Lark Kingsley?

Georgia native, Lark Kingsley, hops down from a beer bike trolley into the heart of Savannah. Tourist season is alive and kickin' first thing this morning. A hot mess after last night's debaucheries, Lark's still wearing her indigo sequin mini dress, with the addition of gently smudged mascara and tousled hair.

"Sorry, this is as far as I can take you. Gotta have the trolley back by nine o'clock sharp," declares the driver, who incidentally appears to be at least five years her junior. Sweat slicks his mutton chop sideburns and man bun.

Footloose and fancy-free herself, Lark recognizes a fellow lone wolf when she sees one. The germination period for her romantic relationships lasts at most a few days and yields no true leaves. While the evening had been just what she was looking for, he wasn't. Their carbon copy feelings create a clean break for both parties, which makes her respect him all the more. Lark blows him an exaggerated kiss. "No worries. Had fun — err — Trolley Guy."

Much to Lark's dismay, she flew solo last night. Her roommate, Darbie, a bit of a goodie-two-shoes, doesn't mind cutting loose on the weekends, but a work night is out of the question. Darbie insisted she needed to get a jump start on her day to prep for a graffiti exhibit opening. Lark doesn't see why anyone would prioritize someone else's art over their own livelihood or lifestyle. After all, life isn't about grownup responsibilities. While turning thirty this year is going to be a major bummer in Lark's book, she isn't about to let it slow her down. She plans on squeezing twenty-nine for all it's worth.

With her shoulders back and chin up, Lark steps up onto the bustling sidewalk, proud as a peacock. Teetering for a moment in her stilettos, she catches her balance on a passerby's arm. The gentleman starts to object but takes one gander at her prominent doe eyes and sumptuously compact figure and tips his Panama hat instead. Not the first time her looks have saved the day, Lark won the genetic lottery in that department.

Sending the gentleman a wink, she straightens her dress and runs her fingers through her long honey highlights. Most women would kill for some dry shampoo right about now but not Lark Kingsley. She couldn't possibly care less. Removing her heels, Lark begins her strut home.

A brass shopkeeper's bell, hanging above a door, dings as a patron enters the establishment, releasing a cool breeze of bought air. The blast sweeps over her, chilling the perspiration between her shoulder blades. Albeit breakfast time in May, the temperature on Abercorn Street steadily climbs to a toasty eighty-six degrees. Coupled with the stifling humidity brewing from the brackish water of the Atlantic Ocean and Savannah River, the downtown air is thick enough to curl a cat's whiskers.

Swinging back an iron gate, she cuts across a quaint private courtyard. Without missing a beat, Lark seizes a turn on a hopscotch board. Already in mid-game, two adorable little girls with bouncing pigtails pay her no mind. When her round ends, without so much as a word, she promptly departs, boasting an innocent grin.

Heading south, Lark passes a darling little cafe. Mr. and Mrs. Barfield, an elderly couple who go together like church on a Sunday, are seated under the awning at an outdoor bistro table. The savory aroma of freshly baked pastries makes Lark's stomach growl. Mrs. Barfield sets her delicate teacup down.

History bonds these three; Lark grew up in the penthouse next-door to the Barfields. Roughly five years ago, the pair relocated to an upscale retirement community in Richmond Hill. Suffering from Parkinson's disease, Mr. Barfield could no longer navigate the treacherous stairs to their third-floor walk-up.

They say it takes a village to raise a child; this was most assuredly the case with Lark Kingsley. "Getting a little old to be doing the walk of shame, aren't you, Lark?" asks Mrs. Barfield, with an air of politeness and pleasantries. The weight of her clip-on earbobs tug on her stretched out earlobes.

Lark doesn't even flinch at the paper cut left on her thick skin by Mrs. Barfield's verbal knife. It's not over, though; the real sting comes later. Mrs. Barfield always pours lemon juice over the wounds she inflicts. Lark steals a bite of Mrs. Barfield's scrumptious jam-covered buttermilk biscuit, dropping crumbs on her dress. "Mmm-mm. There ain't no shame in my game, Mrs. Barfield."

"I'd be delighted to share a few pointers on discretion and etiquette with you, my dear. Perhaps, it may help silence any idle chatter and allow you to rise in social graces," advises Mrs. Barfield, fluttering her hand up towards the heavens.

"Yawn. Sounds positively medieval. Besides, everyone knows I'm a lady," replies Lark, licking marmalade from the corners of her lips.

"A lady of the night," teases Mrs. Barfield, sipping her chamomile tea.

There's the lemon juice. Sluggish and not on her A game, Lark walked right into that one. "Hey, I'm a good girl," she lightheartedly opposes.

Mrs. Barfield nearly spits out her warm refreshment at the preposterous notion. Always the empress of propriety, she removes the folded napkin from her lap and daintily pats her creased mouth while maintaining a straight face. Her soft, delicate flesh drapes and hangs loosely from her prominent cheekbones. Poking fun, she clears her throat and inquires with a raised eyebrow, "Please do illuminate us — is 'good girl' some sort of slang auto-en-autantonym verbiage?"

Before Lark can conjure up a rebuttal, Mr. Barfield, leaning back in his chair, pipes in, "Ahh, I believe the simple term you're looking for, my love, is a contronym. What was the one that youngster on the skateboard said to me the other day — when critiquing the animal interlace carving on my cane?" He removes the handle of his walking stick, hooked to the armrest of his seat, and taps it three times on the table's leg.

"Vicious," states Mrs. Barfield.

"No, no, not vicious. Very close, though... hmm... wicked," recalls Mr. Barfield.

"Yes, wicked," agrees Mrs. Barfield, nodding along.

"It means righteous," relates Mr. Barfield, taking an unsteady mouthful of his grits. A little dribbles off his lip. Mrs. Barfield leans over and wipes his chin with her napkin.

"Wicked means cool. Nobody has used the word 'righteous' since 1979," interjects Lark, schooling them. "You two crack me up," she says, shaking her head side-to-side. She pours a small glass pitcher of maple syrup in a spiral motion onto Mr. Barfield's pancakes, helping him out.

Appreciative, he grins fondly.

For as long as Lark's known Mr. Barfield, he's been bald. As a child, she imagined Mr. Barfield polishing his round head to perfection with a microfiber towel like a bowling ball every night. "At any rate, I was being literal. I'm a good girl. I just like to cut loose and have a little fun is all — no harm, no foul," Lark reassures, cutting Mr. Barfield's stack of saucer size pancakes into wedges. "You oughta try it sometime," she suggests, eyeing Mrs. Barfield. "You haven't reached your expiration date yet, ya know." Lark breaks a piece of Mr. Barfield's bacon in half, spins it in the overflowing syrup, and helps herself to the sample.

A look of disapproval seeps from Mrs. Barfield's feeble face. She opens her mouth to say something, but Lark beats her to the punch this time. "And even though I appreciate the thought, I'll pass on the civility chit chat. After all, decorum is no more a substitute for virtue than a stick of butter is for a cup of olive oil," finishes Lark, nipping in the bud any reproach Mrs. Barfield might hurl her way.

"I'll make an honest woman out of you," flirts Mr. Barfield.

Narrowing her eyes, Mrs. Barfield picks up the folded *Savannah Morning Chronicle* newspaper on the table and playfully swats him. "You're taken," she scolds. The lead headline on the paper reads, "Banksy's Manhole Cover Visits Savannah."

With a blatant disregard for what Mrs. Barfield or civilized society may consider socially acceptable, Lark smiles warmly and continues her journey. The marmalade and syrup spiked her blood sugar, increasing her energy and giving her step a giddy-up. She skips by countless opulent residences in an array of nostalgic architectural styles varying from Victorian Gothic, Regency, Second Empire, Italianate, Greek Revival, and Georgian. Up ahead, two men set a moss green, velvet, pied-a-terre sofa down. It's blocking most of the sidewalk in front of a brownstone row house currently defaced with scaffolding. Sidestepping, she ducks under a renovation ladder to pass. "Nice couch. I have one just like it," shares Lark, skirting around them. Darbie's mom gave it to them when they moved out of the dorms and into their first apartment. It's made multiple moves all over town with them. She's never seen one like it before. On that note, with little warning, a small yappy dog chases a cat out from under a full bloom Azalea bush. A puff of pollen escapes the jostled shrub, tickling her nose. Thinking fast, Lark leaps over the jet black feline just as their paths cross.

Crossing the street, she enters historical Columbia Square. Basking in its painterly setting, Lark strolls along the brick walkway to the square's ornate centerpiece. Nonchalantly, she hops up on the ledge of the Wormsloe fountain and drops down into the water with a small splash. Quenching her tootsies, Lark wades ankle-deep, relishing the way the cold water feels on her tired feet. On a whim, she bends, scooping up change and hops out, tossing it in the cup of her loitering comrade, a teenage street performer, Mary Beth.

Mary Beth, a true bohemian, continues strumming her classical guitar and gives Lark an appreciative, "Thanks!"

Lark locks eyes with her. "Tighten up that G string, Mary Beth."

"If that dress were any shorter, I'd be able to see your g-string," ribs Mary Beth.

Giggling, Lark exits the park and proceeds several blocks. She rounds the corner to a view of a loft apartment complex with well-maintained flowerbeds and a tiny patch of fresh diamond-cut grass. Monarch butterflies flutter around enticingly sweet gardenias and a family of brown thrashers nests in a dogwood tree. In the foreground, a large flatbed trailer with lawn equipment obscures the left side of the greenery.

Lark's sugar high has crashed. She can think of nothing more satisfying than the comfort of her cozy bed. Lark longs to curl up under her sheets and sleep the day away until Darbie gets home. Yawning, she steps into the street to jaywalk and whispers to herself, "Home sweet home."

Hector, Lark's middle-aged landlord, walks out from the other side of the lawn truck. His potbelly jiggles over his belt buckle with each stride. "Lark Kingsley!"

Caught off guard and flat busted, it's too late to backtrack now. It's time to pay the piper. She resolves her best line of defense is a preemptive strike. "I've got that rent check for you, Hector. Let me just run up and-"

"Why? So it can bounce like the last one? Or the one before that?" he interrupts.

"Whoopsie. You know, Hector, you oughta wear green more often. It really makes your eyes pop," flirts Lark.

Hector's stony face softens. He glances at his reflection in the large side mirror on the lawn truck. Marveling at himself, he licks his hand and smooths his cowlick down.

Fabienne, fresh-faced and stylishly handsome in a polo shirt, skinny jeans, ten of Lark's bracelets, five of Darbie's necklaces, and designer shoes, sweeps by admiring his new jewelry. "Girl, the only thang that ever popped on Hector is his gut."

Lark's eyes widen as they study Fabienne's ensemble. She starts to object when the landscape truck pulls away, revealing most of her and Darbie's possessions. Lark's jaw drops. Staring at Hector in raw disbelief, she yelps, "You're evicting us?"

Off-kilter, a crushing avalanche of shock engulfs her. Intense dizziness, paired with a wee bit of nausea overcomes her senses; she ponders if this is how individuals inflicted with vertigo must feel. Positively dreadful, she surmises. Focusing, she spots a pitiful looking woman, skinny as a rail, with a shopping cart loaded to the gills with their stuff. "Shoplifter!" Lark denounces. Without hesitation, Lark grabs a mirror out of the cart. She and the woman play tug of war with it until the mirror slips and falls to the ground, shattering.

Hector, a pull-yourself-up-by-your-boot-straps kinda guy, is eager to enlighten Lark with a relevant life lesson. He lectures, "Oh, Lark. You can't walk around with your head stuck up in the clouds all the time. Ignorance is bliss, but we all have to face the music sooner or later. I've had this conversation with many people, many, many times. You don't pay your rent; I take the apartment back. You know, when you didn't show up for your shift last night at Angelo's, they sent someone to check on you." It wasn't a far hike. Angelo's is located across the street. "Mrs. Mathis told them she saw you leave at nine o'clock looking like that," he chastises, pointing his finger up and down at her skimpy frock.

Mrs. Mathis, the neighborhood busybody, lurks in her apartment window leisurely crocheting an afghan. Once a week, Mrs. Mathis spends four hours at the beauty parlor passing out and consuming salacious gossip like candy on Halloween. She looks up from her occupation and waves at Lark as if they're long lost best friends. Exposed, Lark returns a rather sad half-wave. Through her gritted teeth, she whispers, "That old bag couldn't keep a secret if her life depended on it."

"They said to tell you not to bother coming in today. My niece would kill for that job, and you just threw it away," continues Hector, smugly. Maintaining a lucrative and viable income for him and his large family is a task he doesn't take lightly. He's become desensitized to the traumatized state his tenants land themselves in on eviction day. Those first few evictions had been tough early on in his career. As he quickly learned, compassion typically paved the way for them to take advantage of his generosity, which inevitably led to lost earnings and caused a strain on his financial state. He can't afford the luxury of being an empathetic proprietor. Hector never compromises or gives an inch when it comes to his tenants. For him, this is a business, plain and simple; they signed a contract, and they're going to honor that legally binding agreement, or by golly, they'll find themselves out on the streets.

Hector hands Lark a considerably tall stack of previously opened bills. "Bet you want us hardworking folks to pay these students loans off too."

"Hey! It's against the law to read other people's mail, ya know!" Biting her nails, she mumbles to herself, "What am I gonna tell Darbie?"

"You'll be okay," reassures Hector. "You're hot ladies. You'll land on your backs. I mean feet."

Animal control officer, Ada Mae Williams, a strong, quietly beautiful woman, exits the apartment building with Rufus, a highly resistant redbone coonhound.

Lark's heart sinks when she spots them. "Hey! Stop! What are you doing?"

"The property owner reported this dog as neglected," responds Ada Mae, matter-of-factly.

"Neglected?" Lark sends Hector a wounded look.

"I found him abandoned in a vacant apartment with no food or water, howling a blue streak," Ada Mae vilifies.

"Hector, honestly! Did they discontinue your favorite brand of pickled pigs feet or somethin'?" fumes Lark. Frantic, she searches for the food bowls and locates them on a nightstand. She waves the handmade ceramic bowls at Ada Mae. "Here they are. That's my dog, Rufus! Come here, sweet boy."

Hector coolly pets Rufus. "Rufus is a good boy. He deserves a roof over his head," he says, laughing at his joke.

Ada Mae authoritatively tugs on Rufus. "Do you have a new address?"

Two overzealous ten-year-olds brush by them carrying away a plasma screen. Lark appears visibly torn that she can't pursue them; Rufus takes priority. "Not yet, obviously," she admits flabbergasted.

"Then you're homeless. That violates penal code 597," concludes the no-nonsense woman.

Lark steps in front of Ada Mae, roadblocking her. "Wait. I have a new place. I just meant I don't know the address by heart yet. It's the Harrington house."

"The Harrington House?" Ada Mae asks, stopping abruptly. "On Oglethorpe?"

"Yes, that's the one," confirms Lark, reaching for the leash.

"The fully restored 1930s grand estate with a brick facade, stately white columns, carriage house, and gardens that overlook Vetsburg Park?"

"Uh-huh."

"The Harrington House that's perfectly situated between Savannah's historic and commercial districts and its myriad of islands with sandy white beaches?"

Taken aback, Lark agrees, "Yeah. That's it."

Ada Mae possessively holds the leash out of Lark's reach as she steps around her. "Yeah, right, lady. I don't have time for this. You need two forms showing proof of residency. Which we both know you ain't got," she jabs, getting feisty. She gives her the once over and loads Rufus in a white cargo van. Lark catches Ada

Mae's not so subtle body check. This morning's reactions are a stark difference from last night's approving, come-hither stares. As she recalls, her dress killed last night. Lark's whole demeanor shifts; she looks altogether defeated.

"No, really! It's my roommate's childhood home," she pleads, grasping at straws. "Honestly, you have to believe me. You just have to."

After closing the back doors, Ada Mae hurries around the van. Lark shadows her right on her heels. Ada Mae softens, "I was real sorry to hear about Mr. Harrington's passing last Fall. Look, I suppose I could list him under 'lost' to buy you some time. You've got one week to show two proofs of residency and pay the five-hundred-dollar fine."

"Five hundred dollars!"

Climbing into the van, Ada Mae slams the door behind herself. She leans out the window and hands Lark a business card. "Here. I just started moonlighting as a realtor. Lemme know if Mrs. Harrington decides to sell. I could get her multiple offers well above asking price. And remember you've got one week. After that, all bets are off. He'll be put up for adoption." The van speeds off. Lark turns the card over. It reads: *Sold by Ada Mae Williams, Realtor.*

Lark returns to what's left of her belongings. Hector has movies pinched under his armpit as he wraps a cord around Lark's Blu-Ray player. "Hector, what in the heck are you doing?"

"That's how this works, Lark. You don't pay rent; we move you out for free, people take your things. Consider this collateral for the money you owe me. My children will love this movie player. Gracias!"

Hector's children stand shoulder to shoulder in front of the apartment complex. One holds a laptop, another a camera, another a set of speakers, and another Lark's cell phone. She snatches her cell phone away from the eldest. Ready as she'll ever be, she decides to face the music and dials Darbie. While the phone rings, she casually strolls by Hector's blue utility wagon. No longer giving a hill of beans what he thinks, with the flick of her wrist, she knocks her LED monitor over. It falls to the ground smashing the screen.

"What did you do that for?" asks Hector, waving his hands in the air.

Placing her hands firmly on her hips, Lark responds with an undertone of resentment, "If I can't have it, no one will!"

CHAPTER 2

Impeccably dressed in business attire with little makeup, Darbie Harrington props dual doors open by the loading dock entrance to the Savannah Seaside Art Institute Gallery. Cute as a button, she nervously giggles, struggling to get the stopper on one of the doors to catch, wedging it with the tip of her shoe into the locked position. The stopper momentarily catches before inevitably sliding on the uneven concrete floor, collapsing the door shut with a resounding thunderous bang. After several failed attempts, she throws in the towel and manually holds the door open.

A duo of robust male movers in navy jumpsuits shuffles by her, wrestling a cumbersome pine crate. Darbie is anxious to unveil the provocative street art packed inside. In her haste with her eyes on the prize, she turns to close the doors and smacks right into the new Banksy security guard, Jack Walker. He's hotter than hell and looking more like he should be one of Britney Spears's bodyguards. It's written all over his face that he's enjoying their predicament a little too much. Sweet on Darbie, he chivalrously apologizes, "Pardon me, Darbie."

In a daze, her heart somersaults while she remains pressed up against his firm body. "My fault entirely," she professes, pulling away and tucking her side-swept bangs behind her ear — her neat hair fixed in a chic bun.

Darbie's cell phone's rings. It blasts "I'm Too Sexy" by Right Said Fred, breaking their mutual gaze. Beyond mortified, Darbie's eyelids close as she sucks in a chest full of air. Walker takes a step back, fighting a grin. "Excuse me," she says, trying to downplay the absurdity of the untimely music as she scurries by the movers to retrieve her phone from the reception desk.

A guy in his forties wearing a t-shirt for the band The Clash enters the gallery. His Converse shoes are splattered with paint. He dillydallies near the reception area ambiguously, flipping through a brochure. Raising an eyebrow, he gyrates his head and shoulders to the rhythm of the unceasing music billowing forth from Darbie's phone.

Generating an obnoxious distraction in the otherwise painfully quiet environment, she takes the wrap for her unruly work faux pas. Her boss, Bernice Musko, who has the personality of a dishrag and is wound tighter than a clock, lowers her coke-bottle glasses and shoots her a dirty look. Darbie snatches her phone up off the reception desk, recognizes the number at once, and answers. "Lark, Gah. I told you to stop messing with my ring tone. It's not funny. I'm at work. This better be an emergency," she whispers at warp speed, revealing her stressed-out high-strung nature. Darbie sends Bernice a forced smile and motions 'one minute.'

"I'd say this constitutes an emergency," gulps Lark.

"What did you do?" Darbie is in no mood for any melodrama.

"I was just a tiny bit short on rent."

"Again? How much?" From the reception desk, Darbie directs Walker and the irritated movers where to go. Tilting her head ever so slightly and releasing a low, drawn-out sigh, she checks out Walker's tight butt as he passes.

"Seven hundred and fifty dollars. The student loan folks started stealing money out of my paycheck," she explains, bracing herself for Darbie's wrath. Lark grimaces as though she's waiting for Darbie's hand to reach through the phone and flick her on the forehead.

"Seven hundred and fifty dollars!"

"Times three," confesses Lark, cringing. "Hector evicted us," she adds, ripping the metaphorical band-aid off.

"We're evicted!" Darbie yells too loud. Everyone looks.

Bernice's eyes bore into hers while she shakes her head in judgment and gives a 'this way' wave to Walker and the movers. She ushers them out of earshot and into the Banksy exhibit room.

***

Without warning, the irrigation system activates. Sprinkler heads pop up out of the ground and in a well-choreographed and synchronized waltz spin about dousing Lark and their belongings. "Ugh... Not our lucky day, I guess," says Lark into her phone as she locates an umbrella lying on top of the clothes hamper. She mentally curses the device when she pinches her thumb in the metal catch opening it.

"Luck has nothing to do with it. How can you be so irresponsible? I swear, lately, everything you touch goes to hell in a handbasket. I can't believe you haven't even started paying those loans off," scolds Darbie, growing tired of Lark's unapologetic attitude. She'd find it refreshing if Lark showed even the slightest hint of remorse or owned up to her role in their current crisis.

Using the umbrella as her shield from the incoming water pellets, Lark fights her way through the piles of personal possessions. Distracted from Darbie's comments, she rushes to grab a trash can and cast iron pot; she purposefully places them upside down over the sprinkler heads, stacking books on the trashcan. "Say, you never liked that dingy old mirror of yours, did ya?" asks Lark, winded.

"The antique mirror that hung over my dresser?"

"Yeah. That tarnished hunk of junk."

"The nineteenth-century French Rococo mirror?"

"Um. I suppose so."

"It's an heirloom — belonged to Nanna. Why?"

Hesitating before she answers, Lark swallows hard and responds in as calm a voice as possible, "No reason."

Looking up from the reflective shattered shards, Lark witnesses Hector lallygagging near the sprinkler's nozzle snickering and grinning like the Cheshire cat.

Holding the phone away from her mouth, she intentionally yells loud enough Hector can also hear, "Hector's laughing 'cause he caught a glimpse of his teeny weeny in the mirror this morning." He counters the hostile smear campaign by cranking up the water nozzle to full blast. Outsmarting him, she foils his plan when her barricades hold up, and the sprinkler heads in closest proximity to him pelt him, drenching his pants. Lark smiles victoriously.

"What's happening?" asks Darbie, envisioning pandemo-
nium.

Little does she know, the situation is worse than she
imagines. Everything is soaked, including a stacked collection of
watercolor paintings Darbie's been slaving over since Christmas.
The cool colors of the ocean are all running together with the
warm colors above the horizon line, creating a jumbled up mess;
a series of once stunning seascapes now look as though they
should be titled "Ode to a Mud Puddle." Lark picks up the top
cold-pressed paper, and the liquid brown results of mixing complementary colors drip off the edge onto a white linen blouse of
Darbie's.

A burly man, 2B, stands ten feet away from her, fondling the
girls' underwear and sniffing a handful. Revolted, Lark flinches.
"2B just put a pair of my Victoria's Secret panties in his pocket.
No secret what he'll do with them."

"Ew!"

A tow-truck with a *The Repo Man* decal noisily cruises by
hauling Lark's car. Her yellow Chevrolet Camaro shakes and
clammers with every dip and shift in the road. Overwhelmed, she
throws her free arm up in the air. "I need your help moving our
stuff," she barks at Darbie.

***

In the first phase of an all-out panic attack, Darbie can feel
her chest tightening. Before the mind-boggling sensation of an
elephant sitting on her materializes, she takes action. She opens
the reception desk drawer. Inside is a miniature sandbox-style
zen garden with gnomes, mushrooms, and a tiny rake. She picks
up the rake. "I've got that Banksy exhibit installation today. Just

move anything of value. I'll help you move all our big stuff when I get off," explains Darbie to Lark on the phone.

Darbie notices that the peculiar guy wearing a t-shirt for the band The Clash starts roaming towards the still restricted Banksy gallery room. It's roped off with a "NOTICE: AUTHORIZED PERSONNEL ONLY BEYOND THIS POINT" sign. Dropping her hands, she promptly conceals her phone and the rake behind her backside. "Sir, I'm sorry. The Banksy exhibit doesn't officially open until next week."

Squinting, he intently reads the exhibition sign. "Right you are," he agrees with a British accent. The man promptly returns to the front of the gallery and admires an abstract painting near Darbie. A tad eccentric, he tilts his head side-to-side and then almost upside down.

Immensely entertained by him, Darbie returns the phone to her ear while maintaining a watchful eye. There's something mysterious and aloof in this quirky stranger's demeanor. Neat as a pin, she methodically rakes the sand into consecutive rows. "Where are you moving it?" Darbie asks Lark.

**

Contemplating her answer, Lark quizzically glances from the lady's shopping cart to Darbie's beach cruiser bike. Furrowing her brow, she takes a few steps backward, examining its frame. Touching the bike's rear basket, she exaggerates her Southern belle accent, "Why the Harrington House, of course, Miss Darbie," answers Lark into her phone.

"Absolutely not, Lark!" protests Darbie.

A homeless guy blissfully kicks off his shoes and stretches out on Lark's bed, moving his body like he's making a snow angel.

To say Lark is disgusted to the nth degree would be an under-statement; those sheets are officially dead to her. "Just meet me at your mom's house after work!" she retorts before abruptly hanging up the phone.

***

Darbie putters down Oglethorpe Avenue, slows, and parallel parks her beloved microcar, a cherry red and white 1958 BMW Isetta. Long ago, she fittingly nicknamed her prized bubble car, "Isetta." She opens the one and only door, which doubles as the front end of the vehicle. In doing so, the attached hydraulic based steering wheel and instrument panel swing out with it. She closes the door turning the silver handle in the same way an old Frigidaire refrigerator opens and shuts. A new black Lincoln Continental with dark tinted windows passes her as she locks the door.

Up ahead, Lark rounds the corner so wide that it puts her on the wrong side of the road. The Lincoln swerves to avoid hitting her. Afflicted with a severe case of road rage, she squeezes the bike horn and shakes her fist. She pedals towards Darbie, canopied by oak trees and Spanish moss, wearing half the outfits she owns. The front wheel and handlebars are missing from Darbie's bike. They sit in a jam-packed, filled to the brim, overflowing shopping cart. The front of the bike's frame is attached to the cart with two leather belts. The shopping cart is acting as the front axle and wheel; her hands grip the cart's push bar. She pants and sweats as she shutters to a halt. The rear bike basket is stuffed full of shoes, mostly high heels. One falls out as she drags her feet, coming to a complete stop.

Dumbfounded, Darbie unable to believe her eyes forgets to blink. "Is that my bike? Where is your car, my clothes, and the rest of our stuff?" she asks.

"Yes, repossessed. No worries, I grabbed everything of value." Lark rummages through the buggy and removes a hand-made broken ceramic mug that reads *World's Best Dad! (heart) Darbie* and an alien shaped stress ball. She performs a Vanna White impression in front of the disassembled bike.

Darbie's shoulders slump. She holds the pieces to the broken mug as if trying to reassemble them. "Score. This will be the focal point on the mantel at our next place."

"Look on the bright side; you've donated so much to those in need today that you'll get money back on your tax returns."

"You're unbelievable," quips Darbie.

Lark strips several outer layers of clothing off, tossing them aside onto the mailbox. "Thanks."

Darbie squeezes her alien head-shaped stress ball. The alien's eyeballs bulge out as she does so. "Let's just get this over with."

CHAPTER 3

Just as Ada Mae had described it, the Harrington House sits prettier than a picture. Red and purple garland lay draped across the front porch rails and between the center columns. Several tables enjoying the shade are set up on the expansive front porch and quaint lawn. They are dressed with red linens, Waterford Chrystal, Wedgwood china, and antique Baroque sterling silver flatware. White folding chairs encircle them.

Gazing up at the Harrington's house, Lark's soul glows. She relishes the way the home hugs her, the columns enfold her. Over the years, Darbie's house represented all the things hers lacked growing up. Two parents who offered stability and unconditional love. The Harringtons were her favorite family in all of Savannah. She knew they loved her too, warts and all, even Mrs. Harrington, Darbie's momma, who often referred to her lectures as tough love. Lark craved the attention. She gobbled it up, every bit of constructive criticism, licking her plate clean because it meant Mrs. Harrington cared, and that's all Lark ever wanted.

The girls spot Mrs. Harrington in the side garden. Her red flowing Dolce & Gabbana dress sways gracefully with her every movement. She knows how to accessorize, ornamented with a wide brim red floppy hat accented with a purple ribbon and a pair of red wedge sandals on her feet. Her immaculately manicured hands arrange freshly cut hydrangeas and red roses in mason jar vases.

On the front porch, an orange tabby cat sleeps peacefully on a rocking chair cushion. Bittersweet nostalgia tugs at the inner corners of Darbie's heart. There's one thing missing from this picture, her daddy.

Mrs. Harrington smiles with her graceful arms spread wide. "Good evening, my queens! To what do I owe the honor of your intrus... err... visit?" Not a touchy-feely kind of woman when she's all gussied up in a dry-clean-only garment. She embraces them both as though she's hugging two rose bushes rather than loved ones.

Darbie kisses her on the cheek, mindful not to mess up her flawless makeup. "Hey Momma, how are you?"

"Busier than a one-legged cat in a sandbox."

Darbie takes a deep breath. "Momma, I'm just gonna cut to the chase — we need a place to stay," explains Darbie, praying her momma doesn't notice the bike-buggy parallel parked on the street. Darbie's never been any good at lying or even fabricating half-truths. The few times she attempted to pull the wool over her parents' eyes, she'd failed miserably. Her lies were so outlandish, they read more like tall-tales. Even if she is miraculously able to conjure up a believable white-lie this time, there's no point in trying; her momma can read her like an open book. She recognizes all of Darbie's tells from a mile away. Like the time in seventh grade when she got busted sneaking out of the house to meet Lark at 11:00 p.m. to attend a Black Crowes concert. She claimed she was going to watch a meteor shower for science class. A dedicated student completing an assignment under the guidance of an esteemed teacher, Mrs. Culpepper. All the while, twitching her nose and grinding her knuckles into oblivion.

It's too late to fabricate a whopper now anyways. Mrs. Harrington cuts eyes at the bizarre yet quite ingeniously designed contraption. "I see. I'd love to help you girls out, but I'm hosting my Red Hats Society meeting tonight. And well, you can't be here." She's been meticulously orchestrating this social gathering for well over a month.

"Why?" inquires Darbie.

"I told everyone you're a big-time art curator in New York City."

"Momma!"

"Everyone embellishes a bit about their children. It's a perfectly acceptable thing to do," she says, fussing over a floral arrangement. "Why Joanna Adcock, for instance, said her son graduated top of his class from Berkley. And I saw him selling boiled peanuts in the parking lot of that convenience store, over on Fifth and Main, just yesterday."

"That's hardly embellishing. These are your friends. You shouldn't have to lie to each other about your children's accomplishments."

"Indeed, we shouldn't have to," she replies in a condescending tone.

Lark grins from ear to ear. "What did you tell them I do, Mrs. Harrington?"

"Oh darlin', everyone pretty much assumes you've reached your full potential."

Lark, unfazed, eats some cucumber sandwiches off the sublimely organized buffet table. Mrs. Harrington shoots her a dirty look. Lark flashes an apologetic smile and holds a sandwich out at arm's length. "Oh, sorry. How rude of me. Did you want one, Mrs. Harrington?"

Mrs. Harrington ignores her and climbs the stairs to the side porch, garnished with a 4-piece white wicker settee and hanging ferns. She pulls back on the squeaky screen door.

Avoiding eye contact, Darbie pleads, "Momma, we promise not to overstay our welcome," hoping her momma will bend the rules just for a week or so. They need time to formulate some sort of game plan.

"Darbie, honey, that ship has sailed. My party is in thirty minutes, and I can't have you here embarrassing me."

Lark sucks ripe raspberries off the ends of her fingers, one by one. "Please, Mrs. Harrington. We'd go to my parents, but my father's new wife is a raging — B-word."

"'B' better stand for beautiful. I declare you'd call a lizard an alligator. Dottie is one of my dearest friends. I set them up."

"Thanks again for that, Mrs. Harrington," praises Lark, cranking up her sarcasm.

Allowing Lark's words to shoot right past her, Mrs. Harrington turns her attention back on her daughter. "Darbie, your daddy made me promise not to continue bailing you out of your financial obligations. He felt we were clipping your wings."

And there it is, slapping her in the face, the stipulation her daddy made on his death bed. It saddened her to think that his biggest regret in life may have been how he raised her. Her daddy had done a fine job in her eyes, and any disappointments he'd had in how she measured up as an adult should lie squarely on her shoulders, not his. He'd spoiled her all right, but it was with his infinite love, not his monetary aid. To her, there was no finer man than her daddy.

Mrs. Harrington reaches inside the screen-door and detaches a set of keys from the tail of a mermaid shaped hook. "But he did leave this for you in his will. I've been waiting for the perfect moment to give it to you."

"Daddy left me something?"

"These are the keys to your daddy's most prized possession, his lake house."

Darbie and Lark both jump up and down and squeal with glee like piglets in mud, embracing each other and Darbie's momma, who stands frozen like a statue.

Darbie crinkles her forehead and cocks her head to the side. "Daddy had a lake house?"

Mrs. Harrington straightens her hat and dress. "Yes. Well, it was his man cave. He bought the place after you went off to college. It has a boat, too."

Darbie and Lark gush in harmony, "A boat!"

Once again, Darbie and Lark both jump up and down and squeal with glee, embracing each other and Darbie's momma, who stands perfectly still growing increasingly agitated. She straightens her hat and runs her arm down the front of her dress, smoothing the delicate material. "Yes. Yes. A boat. Gracious, you girls are happier than a tick on a mule's butt. Virgil will take you there." Extending her arm, she gestures towards an elderly handyman, Virgil, in faded overalls raking hedge trimmings, and then to Darbie's bike.

"I'm sorry, but I'm gonna have to insist that you both skedaddle now. And take that — newfangled contraption with you."

Lark snags one of Mrs. Harrington's mason jar vases, dumps the flowers out, and empties the contents of the plate she fixed for herself into the container. She tops it off with a handful of nuts. Holding up a pastry, she yells, "No worries, Mrs. Harrington. We'll get out of your hair. Thanks for supper." She chugs a crystal flute of strawberry Dom Perignon and hurries off towards Virgil.

Mrs. Harrington shoos a wave and whispers to Darbie, "If you gave that girl two nickels for a dime, she'd think she was rich. I've loved her since she was knee-high to a grasshopper but mark my words, Dar Dar; she is your kryptonite."

Seeing her point in this particular instance, Darbie gives her a knowing nod. Mrs. Harrington grabs her by the shoulders and looks her lovingly in the eyes. "You're turning thirty next month. It's time you both grew up, sugar."

Darbie refrains from inducing an argument, recognizing deep down that her mother is right as rain. That's why she didn't wish to seek refuge here in the first place. Furthermore, Darbie's proud of the way her momma has handled the unspeakable sadness of losing her husband. Maybe it was because she'd had time to prepare herself for the loss. At least, as much as someone can prepare themselves for such a blow. They were high school sweethearts. In plain sight, their righteous 1972 prom picture hangs proudly in their entry hall for all to see. She knows it wasn't easy for her momma to fall asleep without the man she'd shared a bed with for thirty-six years. Her momma has worked hard to establish a new routine and a schedule. One which she adheres to religiously. Darbie doesn't want to infringe on that, only to leave her alone again. She's just grateful to have a roof over her head tonight. Darbie hugs her and takes in a whiff of her sweet aroma. She always smells like lavender and jasmine, but mostly she just smells like home.

She kisses her earnestly on the cheek and turns to walk away. Mrs. Harrington playfully spanks Darbie's bottom as she does so. Darbie smiles and catches up with Lark and Virgil to assist in loading Lark's creation in the back of his old Chevy pickup truck.

"Thanks again for the ringtone mishap. I've had that song stuck in my head all day," quips Darbie.

"It is a catchy little ditty, isn't it?"

As they approach the sidewalk, an unnoticed Lincoln parked across the street cranks its engine. Lark thoughtfully pulls a napkin-wrapped sandwich out of her pocket and hands it to Darbie.

Peeling back the honey wheat bread, Darbie studies the contents of the roast beef sandwich; her eyes suddenly go wide, and she promptly inquires in a panic, "Lark, where's Rufus?"

"Rufus. Uh, yeah. Um." Lark's face falls flat. "So, funny story…"

CHAPTER 4

A choir of cicadas harmonize; a green tree frog ribbits, and a red-bellied cooter turtle resting on a rock takes a dip. *Splash!* The term lake is used a little more loosely in this neck of the woods than it is north of here. Folks that live on Lake Oconee in Greensboro or Lake Lanier in Cumming or even Lake Allatoona in Canton might say this here body of water is a pond at best, a mud puddle at worst. The vast Atlantic Ocean, rich riverbeds, and the abundant wetlands of the Okefenokee Swamp bless Savannah and its surrounding areas. Unlike those bodies of water, you won't find this here lake labeled on any atlas, but to the natives, it's a lake nonetheless.

Virgil helps Lark unload the bike-buggy and hands her a box. He tucks a bag of his homemade deer jerky inside, sets down a gas can, and unstraps his large water cooler. Lark hugs him, "Thanks, Virgie."

"Now, don't you go falling in love with me, Ms. Lark. I'm not the marrying kind," he kids.

"Ah. Just my type," seductively chimes Lark with a wink and a hair toss.

Darbie's heel gets stuck in the soft clay as she exits her car. She pulls up, but the pump doesn't budge. Then, she steps out of the shoe and yanks the heel out of the thick sludge, generating an odd suction sound. The force propels her back into a sitting position on the car's bench seat. Her side-swept bangs fall over her face, draping her eyes. "Ow. Yeah, thanks, Vigil. I don't think we could've found this place on our own. You weren't exaggerating when you said it was out in the sticks," she says, lifting her head and retucking her loose hair behind her ear.

"T'was no trouble at all, darlin'. This here is tree farming territory. Over yonder is nothin' but loblolly pines," Virgil points out. Just past the clearing, stands never-ending symmetrical rows of towering, 90-110 feet high, carefully planted forestry. "Your daddy owned about an acre in. The next forty acres belong to a gent named Skeeter Wiles. Enjoy it while you can. Come next Fall, every last timber will be harvested and hauled over to the lumber yard. Oh, and listen up, wild turkey and deer huntin' season may be over, but that doesn't slow some of these local fellas down one iota. You'll probably hear the four-wheelers and dirt bikes out here tearing it up from time to time too. Skeeter turns a blind eye to any tomfoolery when it comes to his kinfolk playing in his dirt, and I kid you not, he's related to every simpleton this side of Atlanta. You girls be careful not to venture too far away from home now, ya hear."

"Yes, sir," reassures Darbie, envisioning her new neighbor's family resembling the cast from *Deliverance*. She shoos a fly away.

"I have an extra fly zapper I can loan ya. I'll try to remember to drop it off tomorrow. But I might forget, so remind me if I do."

"Yes sir."

"I'm serious, now. Remind me if I forget. I'm at that point in life where I could hide my own Easter eggs, if ya catch my drift."

The girls laugh. "Yes sir. Thank you."

"Alright then, I'm gonna leave ya to it." He closes his tailgate, climbs in his truck, and with a wave backs out of the dirt driveway. Lark puts the kickstand down on Darbie's bike. It sinks a little, but the bicycle maintains its upright position thanks to the buggy.

Side by side, Darbie and Lark stare stone-faced in disbelief at their new humble abode, a neglected 1970s Winnebago RV. A rusty boat trailer cradles a grimy old fishing boat still attached to the RV's trailer hitch. It sits almost hidden behind two feet high overgrown grass and even higher invasive weeds, nearly twenty yards from the edge of the so-called lake with a large metal utility shed out back.

"Can you believe this?" asks Darbie horrified as she reaches into the bag of dehydrated meat.

"I know! A Winnebago! It's even better than I imagined!" exclaims Lark delighted.

Darbie takes a bite of the jerky.

"I never would've figured you for a venison jerky kinda girl," says Lark.

"When in Rome," Darbie sasses. "I guess this was Daddy's little estrogen-free zone."

"It's a dream."

"A nightmare. Maybe if I slap you silly, we'll both wake up."

Lark chuckles. Darbie does not.

***

Unbeknownst to Darbie and Lark, the impeccably detailed black Lincoln tucks itself between some tall pine trees and brush near the dirt driveway. Cigarette smoke snakes out of the cracked, barely legal tinted window on the driver's side door. On the passenger seat sits a brand new camo tarp in its plastic wrapping.

***

Carrying a cardboard box of belongings, Lark pushes her way through the tall grass towards the camper. Trudging along, Darbie cautiously falls in step behind her. Pausing, she looks down at something on her black high-waisted skinny pants in horror and starts to strip them off feverishly. "What are those? Get them off of me!"

Darbie stands in her coral-colored boyshort panties that read *When pigs fly* on the booty. Lark looks down and pulls a small green fuzzy triangle off herself. "Simmer down. They're just hitchhikers," reassures Lark.

A puzzled look registers on Darbie's face.

"Seeds!" clarifies Lark, placing the seed in the palm of her hand; she holds it out for Darbie to examine.

Elated and feeling a bit silly for overreacting, Darbie giggles at herself, hands Lark the keys, and starts to pull her pants back on. One leg is in when Lark opens the door. A raccoon leaps off the kitchen cabinets. Lark ducks out of the way in the nick of time. It lands rampant on Darbie's chest and knocks her off balance. Darbie screams as she falls in the swampy grass; hitchhikers cover her auburn hair. The critter scampers off towards the shed, vanishing in the dense vegetation.

Lark offers Darbie her hand and helps her up. The pig cartoon on the back of Darbie's panties is literally covered in mud. "Well, at least he's happy. He finally got to fly," Lark giggles as she enters the RV. It's musty, with torn linens and an empty Lucky Charms cereal box on the floor, which Lark picks up and shakes. The residence has maintained all of its 1970s charms. "This place is so amazing!"

"This is what rock bottom looks like." Darbie plants herself on the bottom step, looking out over the provincial property.

"I think that was Rocket we met earlier. Let me know if you see Groot walk by," chuckles Lark over her shoulder.

"Hardy har har," says Darbie shaking the hitchhikers out of her hair.

Darbie takes in her surroundings. Cypress trees with swollen bases permeate the dank water's edge. Green algae skims the shaded stagnate water skirting the shoreline of the cove. A copperhead snake creates a rippling effect as he swims across the surface of the murky lake. Quickly she pulls her feet up, examining the earth for any slithering reptiles in her vicinity. She doubts she'll ever be able to acclimate to this countrified environment. "We're in hillbilly hell."

"So what if it's a little off the beaten path."

"A little off the beaten path?" repeats Darbie. "This here is the armpit of the South," Darbie snaps back, shooing a horse-fly.

"Oh, Come on! Check it out, lustrous burnt-orange shag carpeting, hippie floral upholstery, and wood paneling that goes on for days!" chimes Lark attempting to keep the atmosphere light.

"I guess I oughta be counting my blessings; it could all be a gaudy, avocado green."

Lark is only half listening. "Avocado green throw pillows would look amazing in here. Maybe we should ask your mom to make us some."

"No," barks Darbie as she reluctantly comes aboard. "What is that smell?" she asks, pinching her nose and starting to look a little avocado green herself. Opening a window, she grabs a dish-towel and waves it back and forth towards the opening. "Don't just stand there! Do something."

"Like what?" asks Lark.

"I don't know. Wave your arms around like a propeller. Circulate the air."

Lark halfheartedly does as she's told.

"Faster! I said propeller, as in a helicopter, not a windmill," the pitch of Darbie's voice says she means business. Lark flinches involuntarily. Usually, Darbie's personality is calm and soft-spoken, but Lark has worn her down to a nub.

Lark returns to the door, opening and almost closing it repeatedly. Well aware she's in hot water, Lark knows not to test Darbie.

With little to no improvement, Darbie gives up and returns to hanging her head out the window as she gasps for fresh air.

Lark walks around, sniffing the premises. "I think it's coming from this door over here," she suggests reaching for the handle on an accordion-style interior door.

"Don't open that! I think there is something dead in there," orders Darbie.

Disobediently, Lark swiftly opens the bathroom door and then closes it even faster. The stench burns her nose. "Jeez, Mr. Harrington. If it's brown, flush it down." Bending over, Lark picks up a dirty x-rated magazine lying on the floor by the door and hands it to Darbie. "Estrogen free, eh?"

"Yuck. We don't belong here." Darbie drops the periodical and seizes a dangling hand sanitizer bottle attached to her purse strap. She uncaps the lid and generously squirts the liquid in the palm of her hand — vigorously slathering and rubbing every circumference of flesh on both her hands. She makes a mental note to buy a larger bottle later and wonders if they sell the stuff by the gallon.

Lark reaches over to the nearby light switch and flips it 'on' and 'off' to no avail.

Queasy, Darbie hangs her head out the window. "There's a circuit breaker over by the shed."

Lark darts over to the window. "Did you say shed?" She nudges Darbie over so she can get a view. "Best day ever! I've always wanted a she-shed."

"Oh, brother. Must you try to spin every negative into a positive?" asks Darbie, rolling her eyes. "First of all, she-sheds are for married women escaping their husbands and children. Second, we are in the middle of the boonies. That ghastly old structure looks nothing like a she-shed. If the big bad wolf were here, he'd blow that thing down. And thirdly, this isn't HGTV. We aren't gonna be able to remodel that thing on a zero dollar budget." Gagging, she leans back in and turns on the sink; nothing comes out.

"Easy fix," Lark dismisses.

Lark takes a load off, plopping down on a built-in bench. A cloud of dust fills the air. "A Winnebago of our very own. I say we call her Winnie for short." She props her feet up on the bench in front of her.

Darbie sneezes fiercely, at an eardrum bursting octave, into her upper arm. "Great! You named her. Now she's ours forever," sneers Darbie, sniffling from the dust, invading her sinus passages.

Virgil had been kind enough to make a detour and follow them over to the apartment for a quick pit stop on their way to the lake house. There was no real cargo to speak of left to haul away. Thanks to the scavengers, virtually everything was already gone.

Darbie and Lark both cried on Virgil's shoulders, feeling like they'd been hit by a Mack truck and left to die on the side of the road. Shell shocked that it took no time at all for the vultures to descend and pick them clean of anything useful or worth any real value. They'd left only personal, nonprofitable type items behind.

Darbie pulls a faux silver plated picture frame of Rufus out of a cardboard box and stands it up on the fold-out table in front of Lark. "Momma's right. We've gotta get our acts together."

Lark picks up the frame, studying the photograph. "We're gonna get you back, boy." She runs her fingers across the glass like she's petting him and kisses the image. Changing her demeanor, she straightens her posture, putting her game face on. "Alright, We've only got two hours before dark to get this place livable. You tackle the inside. I'll cut the grass."

Darbie shakes her head 'no' and leans back out the window.

"Okay. Then I'll clean the inside, and you can take your chances with the varmints outside."

Darbie's eyes widen. Altering her apprehensive countenance, she gets on board with the operation. She sheds her blazer, wraps her daddy's scarf around her face, and rolls up her sleeves. Locating the cleaning supplies in a bottom cabinet, she rummages through them until she finds a bottle of disinfectant. Perking up, she spins like a ballerina while simultaneously spraying the container in the air like its air-freshener.

"Atta girl!" Lark smiles, picking up a coffee can resting on the counter and peeking inside. "Fifty bucks," she gleefully flashes the cash at Darbie. "How much money do you have?"

Darbie pulls two crisp twenty-dollar bills out of her wallet. "I've got forty dollars to last me until payday on Friday. How about you?"

Lark snatches the two twenties and adds them to the fifty dollars. "I've got ninety bucks," she beams, "I'll hitch a ride into town tomorrow, run some errands, and pick us up some basics."

"Pick yourself up a job while you're at it."

Lark gives a half nod, puts a pair of heart-shaped sunglasses on, and heads to the door.

Darbie pulls on a pair of yellow elbow-length rubber gloves. "There's no shower. How are we supposed to get cleaned up?"

Lark motions towards the lake and then towards a pump. "Take your pick."

"Lovely." Darbie picks up a mop and bucket and hands Lark the bucket bequeathing her with the task of filling it up. She contemplates getting permission to use the campus recreation department's showers or sneaking into a girls' dormitory, doubting anyone would notice if she got there early enough. College kids sleep in, and when they wake up, they're pretty much walking zombies. It's not until they get some food in their bellies that they finally join the land of the living.

While cleaning, Darbie reflects on her and Lark's unlikely friendship. There is, after all, undoubtedly no single solitary soul in the cosmos who drives Darbie Harrington more nuts than Lark Kingsley. Trying to talk sense into her is like trying to talk to a concrete wall, but she loves her just the same.

Darbie and her family rallied Lark when she was a youngster. Lark's mother abandoned her and her father when she was eight years old. Her father, sweet as he was, hadn't handled it very well and pretty much checked out emotionally for a couple of years. He focused more on providing financial stability by throwing himself into his work. In doing so, he quickly rose in the ranks, becoming one of Savannah's top high stakes litigators. Kingsley and Associates billboards were plastered up and down I-95 to Jacksonville and I-16 to Macon. In high demand, clients flocked to their doors for their ruthless and unbeatable services in civil defense, personal injury, wrongful death, and class action lawsuits. With their killer reputation preceeding them, a position at Kingsley and Associates was highly coveted and sought after by inexperienced budding new lawyers and established defense attorneys alike. Securing a status as junior or senior associate at the booming law firm equated to tremendous success. As vast and brilliant as her father's skills shined in the courtroom, they remained lackluster on the domestic home front. This pattern of behavior inadvertently generated an unhealthy living situation for Lark.

It was entirely discernible that the man by no means possessed any inkling of a skillset whatsoever for how to raise a little girl on his own. Even as a kid, Darbie often wondered if he even knew where Lark was half the time. Mind you, she could be a handful. She gave all her teachers a run for their money. The little rascal was always getting into trouble. Only minor infractions, thankfully. But she served her fair share of time sitting out during recess, and detention was a second home for her in high school. Darbie's house being her first. It was her happy place, her refuge.

The coin flips both ways, as Lark has consistently been there for Darbie too. Darbie recalls her first encounter with Lark when they were six years old and waiting at the bus stop. Much to Darbie's dismay, her momma who decided to invoke her barbaric, amateur cosmetologist skills on her poor innocent, unsuspecting daughter had just inflicted a hideous bowl cut hairdo on her. Her proud momma, who thought Darbie looked like a doll, sent her baby girl off to school with a pretty little pink bow, a lamb to the slaughter.

That wretched day, Gina Peevey, a local bully who could put any sadistic comic book villain to shame, was taunting Darbie about her new hairdo something awful. Gina made it a habit to hone in on the weaknesses and insecurities of others. She somehow felt feeding on their misfortunes and publicly belittling them, made her self-worth grow exponentially. Lark, tired of Gina's reign of terror, was standing behind her while the hurtful girl heckled sweet defenseless Darbie. Lark blew a gargantuan bubble with her grape bubblegum and casually hocked it into Gina's perfect, waist-length, spun from gold hair as she lackadaisically strolled past her. Darbie was the only witness to Lark's crime. That night Gina's mom, ignorant of the simple technique which involves rubbing a spoonful of peanut butter on gum ridden hair to dissolve the sticky substance, gave her a long feathered mullet hair cut instead. It was a monstrously loathsome sight to behold and categorically the most delicious and glorious revenge Darbie had ever seen served up with a side of humble pie. She made sure to sit next to Lark that day on the bus and every day after that. They've been inseparable bosom buddies ever since.

***

In dense woods, Dante, dressed to kill in all black, climbs a wooden ladder. At forty-five, hard-living has made him a little rough around the edges causing him to look about ten years older than what he is in reality. Once Dante reaches the top of a platform, he drops a heavy black duffel bag to the floor. The thud startles a broad-winged hawk perched close by who springs into flight, releasing a high-pitched whistle as he soars off into the distance over the treetops warning other woodland animals of the strange man's presence. The vast sky erupts in every direction of the deer stand with once dormant birds. The staggering number of ear piercing squawking flying creatures is enough to startle even the most loathsome beings.

***

Enjoying the fresh outdoors, Lark basks in the fruits of her labor, welcoming the smell of fresh-cut grass and honeysuckle. Physical work has never been something that she's shied away from doing. She's not wired for shuffling paperwork or sitting in a cubical all day. Which is probably why, as a youngster, she always rebelled against the institutionalized setting a classroom provides. She never minded helping Mr. Harrington out with yard work at Darbie's grandmother's house. Lark always thought of his riding lawnmower as her personal ATV. She and Darbie would take turns driving it when Mrs. Harrington wasn't around.

She abruptly ceases weed-whacking when she spots a disconnected hose that runs to a septic tank. Rainwater pushed the property's sediment towards the lake, burying the bottom half of the tube in the dirt, causing it to collect and build up against the detached tubing over time. Freeing the hose with a couple of swift yanks, she drops to her knees and shakes the excess grit off. She studies the connector at the end of the tubing and closely examines the sewage exit valve on the RV.

Inside, Darbie finishes mopping. Virtually every surface shines and sparkles like a diamond as the RV is almost entirely spotless. Almost being the keyword, she's been saving the worst for last. Dreading the elephant in the next room, she approaches the threshold of the contaminated bathroom, which stinks to high heaven. Her stomach churns as she hesitates with her hand hovering over the door handle. Trying to work up the nerve to do what she knows needs to be done, she counts, "One, two, three." Holding her breath, at lightning speed, she opens the accordion door, empties the bucket of filthy mop water into the rancid clogged toilet flushing it out. She steps out and slams the door shut against its frame. Proud of herself, she discards her daddy's scarf and breathes a sigh of relief.

Meanwhile, just outside, at the same time Darbie's putrid water hits the toilet, the valve unexpectedly opens as Lark's face is sheer inches away. Its nasty contents pelt her smack dab between the eyes, spewing all over her stupefied face.

Repulsed, she presently sits with brown excrement and muck dripping from her chin. Lark carefully removes her heart-shaped sunglasses revealing contrasting white hearts around her eyes.

***

Dante, wearing black leather gloves, reaches inside the duffel bag and methodically unloads a parabolic microphone. Spying, he listens to Darbie as she unremittingly scrubs every inch of the bathroom with a toothbrush ad nauseam until it's so immaculate she could eat off the floor. Through the transmitter, he hears her laughing and rambling about Lark's misfortune, "That's karma for ya. Rufus and I wouldn't be in this mess if it weren't for you." Once more, he reaches into the bag and extracts a tripod with a telescopic lens. Like clockwork, he systematically assembles it and adds it to his espionage style set up.

***

Nightfall descends on the RV with only the lights from the small windows illuminating the property. Inside, the girls lay shoulder to shoulder in bed, snug as a bug in a rug. Darbie's worried sick about Rufus. The thought of him being locked up in some cage surrounded by strange aggressive animals plagues her as she ponders how loud the kennel is at night with other dogs barking and howling. She realizes the animal control folks are just looking out for the best interest of the animals and Savannah's fine citizens. But Darbie imagines that no matter how tight a ship the shelter runs with all the unkempt and untrained animals they rescue, the smell of feces and urine is undoubtedly almost as bad as the RV had been. She's certain the poor thing must be petrified, held in a cage like a prisoner, punished for a crime he didn't commit.

Darbie about lost her mind when she found out where Rufus was held captive. She called Animal Control the second Lark explained the whole song and dance to her. Unfortunately, she got an after-hours answering service. They already closed for the evening and don't open again until 11:00 a.m. Lark mentioned that the Animal Control Officer had given her a business card, but true to her nature, she'd dropped it somewhere on the way to meet her at her mom's house.

Darbie intends to employ her lunch break tomorrow to bail him out. Surely they're reasonable folks she surmises. Crossing her fingers, she's hopeful that once they fully comprehend the situation, they'll release Rufus back into her eminent custody. If not, she'll pay the five-hundred-dollar fine off in installments. Come hell or high water, she's doing whatever it takes to bust Rufus out of there because she's not leaving that place without her baby.

Missing him something awful, she tosses and turns, struggling to fall asleep. She thought country life was quiet and tranquil, but the insects and nocturnal creatures are proving way noisier than South Georgia city life. The harder she tries to relax, the antsier she becomes. A million thoughts race through her restless mind. Lark, on the other hand, has only one thing on hers, and that's the painful price she is currently paying for her most recent poor decision.

"What's it all about, Lark?"

"Huh?"

"Life. What if our entire lives are already predetermined? Do you think things that happen to us are meant to be? Do you believe in destiny — soulmates? If it's all part of some grand plan, then what's the point to any of this? Or do we have free will? Is life all about the choices we make? How do we know if we've made the right ones? Is the key to success about taking risks, having gumption, or is it just dumb luck?"

There's a long silent pause. Lark farts. "I ate a can of expired Vienna sausage."

"Spectacular!"

Lark moans. "Every internal organ wrecked." She farts again, flapping the sheets.

Darbie folds her hands in prayer. "Heavenly Father, save me."

Lark rolls over in agony, stealing all of the sheets. Darbie lays there, chilly, staring up at the ceiling. A poster of a half-naked woman is taped up there. Lark starts snoring.

CHAPTER 5

Thunder clouds roll overhead as Darbie exits her BMW Isetta into the art gallery parking lot. Her product-less, air-dried hair has a beach babe wave vibe going on. Wearing clothes she borrowed from Lark, she wobbles in open-toed ankle boots with 3-inch heels as she crosses the parking lot tugging down on a short gray mini skirt. Her way too snug fitted top is ill paired with the same black blazer from yesterday. She whispers to herself, "Stupid 2B, I can't believe I have to go commando today — of all days."

To make matters worse, she has a giant zit the size of Texas parked on her forehead. Her face is now the collateral damage of not being able to properly perform her usual nightly beauty regimen without possessing her entourage of cleansers and moisturizers. She'd tried to pop the volcanic blemish this morning but wasn't able to extract the brain. All she really accomplished was angering the little devil, increasing its sheer girth twofold.

The same idiosyncratic patron from the gallery yesterday meets her halfway. More than his illustrious British endowment, Darbie is struck by the fact that the guy is sporting the exact same

"The Clash" t-shirt from yesterday. She finds the band quite favorable herself, an oldie but a goodie. Without meaning to do so, she starts humming "Should I Stay or Should I Go" in her head. She notices the paint splatters on his clothing and figures he must be an artist. Whenever she and Lark are ignorant of someone's name, they nickname the individual after a distinguishing characteristic until they commit their actual name to memory. Darbie decides this guy's temporary epithet is definitely going to be Clash.

"Hello. How do you do?" Clash greets her as he hands her a peach bubble tea.

"Um, thanks, but my momma taught me never to take any kind of fluid with bubbles floating in it from strangers."

"Apologies. That was quite cheeky of me. Never mind then, I'm not too keen on the stuff myself. Tastes like rubbish, and it does look rather suspicious," Clash agrees, staring down at his own. "I have a proposition for you. Yesterday, I couldn't help but overhear that you're in a bit of a pickle. I think we could come to an arrangement, a trade if you will, that would please both of us." He retrieves his wallet and pulls out a wad of bills.

"What?" gasps Darbie.

"You have something that I want, and I have something that you need. No one will ever have to know, Darbie."

Offended by his repulsive, ungentlemanly demeanor, Darbie pops the lid on the tea. "How dare you, sir! Just because I'm dressed like this doesn't mean I'm a prostitute! You and your pickle need to get away from me." She tosses the cold refreshment on his crotch.

Shocked at how chilling the dousing feels, he releases a grunt while Darbie storms off towards the gallery. Mainly he's extremely relieved and grateful he opted for one of the cold choices on the menu over the hot beverages. Tiny bubbles roll about the asphalt bursting colored goo in their wake. He gazes down at the wad of Banksy graffiti art bills in his hand. He's miffed at himself when it suddenly dawns on him how his words and actions were misconstrued. He curses, "Bollocks!"

Darbie walks with purpose, feeling quite liberated after defending herself. Not just herself, she thinks, but all women for that matter who choose to dress in this fashion. How dare he? She's no harlot! Terribly pleased with her exemplary conduct under pressure, she adds a little pep to her step and gives herself a pat on the back.

Anticipating her arrival, Walker is strategically positioned in the reception area when Darbie approaches the gallery. He spots her, and true to his good ol' boy nature, he chivalrously holds the door open for her. Impressed by his consistent benevolent manner, she loses her train of thought. He greets her with a surprised but approving glare. "Mornin', Ms. Harrington."

Following the direction of Walker's gaze, Darbie glances down at her abundance of cleavage, the only plus side of putting on more than a few extra pounds since her dad passed away. Her breasts are definitely on full display in this top. Altogether, half the weight she gained went directly to her boobs and butt, giving her curves for the first time in her life. She has an hourglass figure now, opposed to the stick straight one she's donned most of her adulthood. As a matter of fact, she was so flat-chested in high school, Lark once threw a spaghetti noodle at her chest because the directions on the box stated that the pasta was fully cooked when it clung to a flat surface. Not since the time. Darbie padded her bra to fill out a sequin prom dress has she noticed guys staring at her cleavage instead of her mouth when she speaks. She's gone up two full cup sizes, or as Lark likes to tease her, she went from "pebbles to boulders" overnight. On second thought, Darbie guesses, in this top, it's not the pimple on her forehead she should be worried about people staring at today. Blushing, Darbie pulls her blazer closed as best she can, and steps inside. "Walker."

"Call me Ja-"

"Darbie? I'm not liking this new look of yours," interrupts Bernice.

"Sorry, I can expl-"

"The Board of Trustees will be here this afternoon for our annual review and to see the completed Banksy installation. We have a lot of work to do to get the rest of the gallery in tip-top condition. Let's start with folk art — Howard Finster's piece."

***

The dimly lit motel room has its curtains drawn. There's a small crack between the curtain panels. The gap enables the light from the flashing vacancy sign to enter the meager space. Fluorescent light eerily reflects and bounces about the quarters. It's a time machine, decorated with a "Mad Men" vibe. Smoke from a cigarette left to burn permeates the stale air. The TV blares to an empty audience as steam from a shower escapes the ajar bathroom door. Pinned to a wall is a montage of pictures of Darbie, Lark, Mrs. Harrington, Rufus, Walker, Bernice, the museum, and the Banksy art crate coming off the delivery truck. A cumbersome, bulky black duffel bag sits on the disheveled bed.

***

Darbie observes Walker putting his cell phone to his ear. She listens intently in an attempt to discern if he's talking to his little lady. There's no wedding band on his ring finger, so Darbie's holding out hope that he's not in a serious relationship. From this distance, she can barely decipher the conversation. It's something pertaining to the Banksy's security protocol. Darbie suppresses a grin, relieved the verbal exchange centers around mundane work-related subject matter. Walker busts her eavesdropping on him, winks, and steps out the back door for some privacy.

Embarrassed he caught her, Darbie mentally kicks herself for being so obtuse. One simple dip of the eyelid from that good-looking man makes her weak in the knees. She's dated over the years, but no one noteworthy enough to bring home to meet the folks or her momma anyways. At least, not since Clay and that was ages ago. She can't recall ever drooling over a guy like this before. When Walker is in her vicinity, she can barely put one foot in front of the other. She knows she's ridiculous, behaving in such a manner. It's not as if dating him is even a remote possibility. The mere fact that he is a work colleague crosses a line of professionalism she's not comfortable violating.

Pleased he left, she focuses on her work. Finished up with the folk art pieces, she presently readjusts a series of permanent collection paintings as Bernice directs her. Bernice's mannerisms are stiff, lacking even the smallest hint of joy. She's wearing mismatched, uneven, orthopedic shoes. Darbie lifts a large painting to the wall with athletic grace and hangs the masterpiece perfectly straight in one fluid motion.

Bernice scratches the sleeve of her seasonally challenged wool suit and squints. "Nope. Not straight. Hurry up, Darbie. My hip is killing me today."

Darbie puts her hands back to each side of the painting and looks back at Bernice for guidance. Bernice continues to squint, then gives Darbie an unhelpful shake of the head. Darbie turns the picture of an idealistic family a couple of degrees counterclockwise. It isn't straight anymore.

"Bernice, your shoes don't match."

"A bit more, Darbie. Focus. Honestly, I don't think you should be doling out fashion advice today," clips Bernice.

Darbie takes it one more degree counter-clockwise. It's even less straight. Bernice shifts her weight a bit from her orthopedic wedge to her loafer, squeaking it on the concrete.

"No, it's just throwing off your balan-"

"More!" demands Bernice.

Darbie rotates the piece a few more degrees. It's obviously not straight.

Bernice circulates the room, accessing the artwork from various perspectives — moving at a pace that would bore a turtle to death. "I guess that will do," she finally decides, slapping her hands against her thighs.

"Okie Dokie," Darbie mumbles under her breath. She looks back at the row of paintings on the wall, all crooked by the same amount. Collaborating with Bernice ranks high amongst Darbie's least favorite things to do. The everyday grind of working for Bernice is a pride swallowing, conflict avoiding, test of her patience, and quite frankly, her sanity. Darbie's officially running on empty and too fatigued to care about the poorly hung art.

Yawning, it dawns on her that the reason she's running on autopilot is that she didn't get a wink of sleep last night. On the other hand, Lark slept like a baby, minus the whole soiled diaper bit. Darbie hasn't stayed up until the wee hours since her days of all-night cram sessions during finals week her last semester in graduate school. Once Lark mercifully stopped snoring, it was the quiet and pitch-black night that kept her awake. Darbie's gotten used to the sounds of people and the city lights that come with urban living. She's unaccustomed to the complete darkness of rural life and listening to the constant caterwauling of a nocturnal screech owl outside her window for hours on end. Residing in the country feels terribly lonely and isolating. If she or Lark were to scream, no one would hear them. No one would call 911. Exposed to the elements, they are entirely on their own with only a can of mace, a Swiss army knife, and their wits to protect them. None of which give Darbie any peace of mind.

To top it off, she has a crick in her neck; Lark stuck her with the flimsy decorative pillow. The pillow sham's corduroy fabric left prominent vertical lines on her cheek and forehead. She runs her fingers along her flesh, feeling the residual faint imprint. Darbie inhales exasperated.

Bernice fiddles with her ancient slider style cell phone, aggressively pushing buttons on the keypad. The gallery's phone rings. "Grab that, Darbie. I'm off to lunch," instructs Bernice.

"Yes, ma'am." Darbie gallantly steps behind the reception desk. She pulls back one of the balls on her Newton's cradle — *Clank. — Clank. — Clank.* Perpetually the professional, she clears her throat and answers the phone, "Hello. Savannah Seaside Art Institute Gallery. Darbie Harrington speaking. How may I direct your call?"

"Darbie, are you alone?" asks the caller using a voice disguising device.

Just for giggles, about once a month, Lark prank calls the gallery. Often with the aid of her adolescent co-workers or infantile friends and always utilizing their voices and cellular devices. The speakerphone feature is her M.O. as this childish ritual's intention is for everyone else's entertainment. Even though Darbie naturally loathes being the butt of the joke, she's a fairly good sport on slow days when Bernice isn't in earshot but not so much today.

"Ha, Ha," Darbie fake laughs, unamused. "Hilarious, Lark. Are you gonna ask me what I'm wearing next?"

"You're dressed like a two-dollar hooker today."

"Seriously, Lark! I'm in no mood. Bernice has gotten so frigid; black ice is forming on her glasses."

Darbie doodles devil ears on the back of a gallery brochure, featuring Bernice's picture as the gallery's chief administrative officer.

"Might want to add a pitchfork," suggests the creepy masculine sounding disguised voice.

Darbie drops the pen. Her eyes dart around the room.

"I'm always watching, Darbie."

Darbie reaches for her stress ball.

"I want the Banksy."

Darbie's altogether perplexed. "Okay, it's two million dollars. Will that be cash, check, or credit card?"

"No, Darbie. You're just going to give it to me."

A dog barks into the phone. "Do you hear that?" he asks in a condescending tone.

"Rufus?"

"Stealing an animal from a shelter is alarmingly easy, unlike that gallery of yours. I need someone on the inside, Darbie."

"You're nuts. You seriously think I'm gonna steal a two million dollar painting in broad daylight in exchange for my dog? I'm calling the cops!"

"No, Darbie. You won't be calling the cops or anybody for that matter because your precious fleabag is just the start... Lark... your mom. Look out the window at my associate."

The Associate, an insanely tall man, with a face only a mother could love, leans against a pecan tree a few feet away from a wall of floor-to-ceiling glass. He makes eyes at Darbie, picks up a pecan, and cracks it with his bare hand. His sinister grin reveals disgusting brown teeth. Darbie gulps and rapidly commences squeezing her stress ball.

"What do you say if I sweeten the pot a little? I'm a reasonable man. I know all about your financial woes. I'll give you one million dollars when we do the drop to keep your mouth shut. We'll do the Banksy exchange this Friday, at midnight, Bonaventure Cemetery. Don't breathe a word of this to anybody, or I'll take them out."

The phone clicks. Darbie grabs her crossbody bag and throws the purse over her shoulder as she bolts out the back exit, nearly hitting Walker with the door. Her tunnel vision fixes on her automobile as she speedwalks towards its whereabouts. The blue skies and dry pavement show no trace of this morning's pop-up thunderstorm as her heels clamor across the asphalt.

She quickly dials her mother. The call goes straight to voicemail. "Hey, y'all! This is widow Sue Ellen Harrington. Or is it widower Sue Ellen Harrington? Anywho, I can't come to the phone right now. Please leave me a message after the beep. Hmm, Which one do I push? Heavens to Betsy, these buttons are no bigger than a minnow in a fishing pond. Darn cataracts. I wish Hank were here. He was my eyes and ears. I reckon I best get my glasses." *Clank!* "Oh, Oh, okay. I see it now." She giggles. "This is it." *Beep.* A voicemail robotic voice comes on. "I'm sorry the mailbox you have reached is full. Goodbye." *Click.*

She's bewildered not only by the outgoing message but that her mother is so stuck in her ways that she insists on using a pre-historic landline. Her momma's had the same answering machine for twenty years. How is it possible that she still hasn't figured it out yet? Darbie bought her an inexpensive cell phone last Fall for emergencies. Her mother has yet to use it, and she doubts she even bothered to remove the device from its box. Darbie shakes her head and phones Lark. Instantly, a high pitched noise sounds which reverberates in her ear; another robotic voice follows it. "We're sorry. You have reached a number that is disconnected, or that is no longer in service." The same heinous high pitched noise sounds again. Darbie releases an audible, "Ugh!" as she starts up Isetta.

CHAPTER 6

The ramshackle shed's door sits wide open with a bike pump leaning up against its exterior wall's flaking paint. Lark lays reclined on a giant inflatable duck in cut off shorts, a pink bra, and Darbie's daddy's Ray-Ban sunglasses. An old boombox blasts music. A glass of Darbie's daddy's scotch with a buoyant umbrella in it rests gingerly on her stomach. Darbie races up the driveway to her, cuts the wheel, hits the brakes, and sends Georgia red clay dust all over Lark's oiled up skin. Powder orange, Lark sits up, spills her drink, and spits dust. Darbie hops out of the car.

"You've gotta get the H out of here, Lark!"

"Jeez. I can explain. I was just taking a break from filling out job appl-"

"Shh. They are watching us. Probably listening too."

"Oh, is this like a *Stranger Things* kind of scenario, because I saw the lights flicker last night too." Lark's eyes dart all around, scanning for signs of movement.

"No, some guy with his voice disguised just called the gallery and said he kidnapped Rufus, and he told me that I had to steal the Banksy and not to tell anybody or he'd kill them."

"So let me get this straight. A psycho holding Rufus hostage demanded you steal some piece of art?"

"Exactly! This is the anonymous street artist I was telling you about. You know the one who's a political activist. Loves social commentary."

"Ah-hmm — Bansky."

"Close. It's Banksy. Back in October, one of his most iconic works was being auctioned off at Sotheby's in London, and a hidden shredder built into the frame cut half the piece into ribbons the instant the sale finalized. The story made world news."

"Yeah, Yeah, Yeah," recalls Lark nodding along, "The little girl with the red heart-shaped balloon. I remember when that story made headlines. I'm vaguely familiar with his work. I dig his dark humor, and you know how I feel about an English man," she gushes.

"Yes," Darbie confirms, rolling her eyes. "So, we're on the same page?"

"Yeah, yeah. I'm picking up what you're putting down; I'm catching your drift. I got it already. So anyway, this guy, the one on the phone, he's threatening to kill anyone you tell?"

"Yes."

Lark recoils, flabbergasted, "So you rushed right over here to tell me?"

"Uh... Yes," repeats Darbie.

"Even though he said he'd kill me?" asks Lark mortified.

Darbie squirms, "Oh... Um... Yeah."

Lark's face softens, and her cheeks flush. "Awe. You really do love me! BFFs!" They do a top-secret finger-snapping, booty slapping, handshake. "Somebody needs a huggle!" squeals Lark. She throws herself at Darbie, smothering her with a giant huggle. Huggle is a term the girls came up with one frightful night spent together along with two other munchkins in a tent during a torrential downpour on a youth trip when they were kids. One of the other younger girls in their six-man tent wet her sleeping bag, making an already damp night absolutely miserable. Every time the thunder would roll, Darbie would hug Lark. Lark, equally terrified, would snuggle her in return. The term, huggle, is a combination of the words hug and snuggle. Cackling like a child, Lark squeezes her. Darbie chuckles and relaxes for the first time since the unsettling phone call. There is something about Lark's innocent laugh that reminds Darbie not to take life too seriously.

"Oh, and the creep said he'd give me one million dollars," Darbie elaborates.

"Hold the phone. He will give you one million dollars and Rufus for some graffiti art?" asks Lark excitedly.

"Well yeah. The piece is worth two million dollars. Why are you smiling?"

Lark's eyes flicker briefly before she eagerly bounds through the RV's doorway. Darbie warily follows her inside, knowing full well this look often leads to trouble. Lark starts in immediately, "This is a perfect crime. Banksy never makes a dime off of his work. Nobody even knows for sure who he is. Or she. Or they. It's a manhole cover for crying out loud. We paid for that with our tax dollars, and someone thinks they can just take it and make millions off it. It's just as much ours as it is theirs. It sure as heck doesn't belong up at that fraudulent school. I say we do this."

Lark shuffles through a stack of mail and hands Darbie a bill. "I thought it was one of mine, so I opened it. It's the bill from when you got your tonsils out last March. The school's crummy health insurance has a five thousand dollar deductible!"

Darbie rubs her forehead, preparing herself to see what she already knows is coming. She unfolds the bill, studying the fine print. "Okay. There is a payment plan." Darbie heedlessly sets the paper on the table.

Thwarted, Lark sweeps the invoice aside. "Give me a break. You've been paying those student loans off for your master's degree for years, and what do you still owe? And now this. We will forever be shackled to that freakin' school."

Darbie ignores her, shoves some nuts in her mouth, and downs a tall glass of water.

"I owe fifty thousand dollars for a degree in Culinary Arts," shares Lark.

"We've been through this, Lark. The school didn't loan you the money."

"No, but my adviser, Dr. Hicks, lied to me. He said top restaurants would be knocking down my door to hire me — total bologna. I'm a cook, not a chef. Any idiot with two brain cells could put together a dish at Angelo's. Some of them involve a microwave. That school owes us. We could finally get out from under all this debt and take that trip I planned."

"This is in no way feasible. It's not a vase; it's a manhole cover. You're talking about moving cast iron. It took two guys, who incidentally were built like action heroes, to move the thing in this morning. You can barely lift a bag of dog food."

"Why couldn't he just paint on a wall like he usually does?"

"You think moving a concrete wall would be easier? Or how about a phone booth? A cinch, right?" Lark retorts.

Determined to overcome any obstacle, "We'll find a way. I really think we could pull this off."

Dismissing her, Darbie glances at her watch. "Oh, jeez! I'm late. My lunch break is only a half-hour. And I need to fix the paintings before the board arrives."

"Oh yeah. Good thinking. Act normal. Act casual."

Darbie begins to nod in agreement but stops short, shaking her head side-to-side instead. "We aren't doing this! I'm gonna tell the board. They'll know what to do." states Darbie, taking a much more pragmatic view of the situation. "Besides, is money all you can think about? What about Rufus? I can't live without him! Do you even give a rip that he's been abducted and is being held for ransom?"

"You know I love that dog! We'll get him back. That guy is just bluffing. Nobody could hurt that big lovable bear. Won't you even consider taking care of this ourselves?" Lark stares pleadingly at Darbie, whose expression is unwavering.

"No," answers Darbie.

"Why must you always be a living monument of goodness and virtue?"

"Drop it."

"You're such a buzzkill," Lark pouts, folding her arms. "Hmmm."

"Be careful, that bottom lip is hanging so low you might trip over it," scoffs Darbie scurrying out the door.

Alone, Lark repeats back Darbie's last snarky statement. "Be careful, that bottom lip is hanging so low you might trip over it," she mutters to herself, using an exaggerated mousey voice and following it up with a mock laugh. Disgruntled, she picks up a dart, hurls it at the dartboard, and nails the center bulls-eye.

*****

Addressing several board members and the Dean, Bernice stands before a long table in a dark conference room. One by one, She flips through slides of Banksy Graffiti bills. "Just this morning, the New York Banksy Art Museum graciously agreed to loan us ten Banksy Graffiti bills for the duration of the Banksy exhibit. Their value is 1,500 dollars apiece. We will be showcasing them in this LED glass display case."

In a mad dash, Darbie absentmindedly speed walks through the gallery forgetting both to wear her blazer and to check herself for hitchhikers. She's riddled ankle-deep with them. Taking long strides, she enters the dark conference room and passes the board members. As she moves towards Bernice, she clumsily trips over the projector's cord, causing it and herself to crash to the ground creating a loud, chaotic ruckus. She drops her purse in the topsy-turvy process. Her car keys with her lucky rabbit's foot key chain, a keepsake she brought back from a trip to Gatlinburg when she was twelve, spill out onto the floor. Worst of all, her skirt splits up the seam exposing her bare hiney for all of tarnation to behold.

Board Member #1, a prudish female, dressed in modest clothing, gasps, and looks away.

Board Member #2, a male, wipes sweat from his brow and chugs a glass of water.

Board Member #3, a male, moves his hand under the table and bites his lip.

Board Member #4, a female, laughs and snaps a photo with her phone.

Board Member #5, a male, in a yellow sweater vest and baby blue gingham bowtie, shrieks and distorts his body as if something genuinely grotesque is attacking him.

Darbie gets up, unaware she split her skirt. She expeditiously places the projector back on the table. The Dean stands, scanning the floor. "Thank you. You needn't get up I've got it, sir," graciously insists Darbie.

"No, I need to retrieve my pen," he points out.

"Oh, allow me to assist you with that," offers Darbie, spinning on her heel.

"No! Please don't," he insists.

Locating it right away, Darbie bends over and fetches the luxury handcrafted pen off the carpet. Everyone flinches at the repeat peepshow. The Dean, who is close enough to see every nook and cranny north and south of the Chattahoochee, retreats to his chair as fast as his feet will carry him. Darbie hands his ballpoint pen back to him. Hunched over the table, he sinks into his swivel chair; his hands cup the sides of his face blocking his peripheral view of Darbie; his eyes fixed on a notepad before him.

"Sorry about that, sir," apologizes Darbie.

"No problem," he mutters in barely a whisper. Without making eye contact or turning his head in her direction, he shoos a wave with the tips of his fingers, continuing to shield his view defensively.

In a rushed speech, Darbie apologizes, "Sorry about that. I'm so glad to see you're all here. I have something deeply concerning I need to discuss with y-"

Bernice interrupts, "The board members are all very important and busy people, Darbie. I can assure you they aren't interested in anything you have to say." Setting her cue cards down, she turns to address the board utilizing an almost ceremonious voice. Pacing herself, she speaks slowly, making sure to enunciate every word correctly. "I apologize for the interruption. I can assure you it won't happen again. This concludes today's meeting. Thank you all so much for joining us." The board nods and exits the conference room. On their way out of the gallery, they all glance at the wall of crooked general exhibition paintings, scratch their heads and whisper snide remarks amongst themselves.

Darbie stands in the corridor, pleading, "No, wait. This is important." She catches Walker's arm as he approaches from the Banksy exhibit room. "This concerns you, too, Walker." She can feel his bulging bicep clinch beneath her grip. Looking down intensely at her hand, clasping his arm, he nods with a fire in his eyes she can't read. Sometimes with Walker, she's unable to deduce if she wants to hug him or run away from him. He has such a tough guy persona, but she can sense his soft side towards her. When she realizes she's physically touching him, she releases him.

No one else stops or even looks back. Bernice is huddled up with the Dean having an intimate conversation; she pauses long enough to scold, "Darbie, you're late! In my office now."

***

On the other side of campus, Gator, not the sharpest tool in the shed, prowls in his signature look consisting of a fraternity t-shirt, frayed khaki shorts, and flip flops. He's scavenging the quad, hitting on unsuspecting female students. Throwing his arm over the top of a bench, he hunkers down beside a girl who's entirely absorbed in a gripping, page-turning novel. Clearing his throat, he tries out a classic, "Hey, I lost my number. Can I borrow yours?" Floored, she slams her thick, hardcover book closed and walks off.

Unfazed, Gator clears his throat and approaches another girl reclining against a column, staring at her cell phone. "Well, hello there! I just bought a new strobe light. You wanna come back to my place and check it out?"

"Get lost," demands the girl, furrowing her brow.

***

Hanging her head, Darbie enters Bernice's sub-zero, arctic office. It's as dark, colorless, and lifeless as the vile woman herself. Darbie imagines if Bernice has an online dating profile, it reads that her ideal first date consists of a quiet moonlit evening spent creating gravestone rubbings.

As Darbie takes a seat in front of her mahogany executive desk, she runs her hands down the back of her skirt and feels the ripped fabric and her visibly bare butt. Horrified, she moves the slit to her side. She scans Bernice's desk for a, dare to dream, sewing kit. She'd settle for a safety pin, bulldog clip, anything that might help her out of her quandary. Darbie hardly ever visits Bernice's workspace as she actively avoids one-on-one time with Bernice like the plague whenever possible.

Until now, she never noticed that picture frames litter her desk. Not once has she ever heard Bernice mention anything regarding family or friends. Intrigued, she grabs one, flips it around, and studies it. Oddly enough, it's a picture of Bernice holding a Persian cat, which Darbie thinks is veritably kinda sweet. She flips a second one over, and it's a picture of Bernice with a Siamese cat. Quickly, Darbie flips the next one over, and again, the photo is of Bernice with a cat, a Russian blue this time. Sensing a pattern, she jumps up and leans over the desk so she can see the front of the other frames. Every last one of them is a photo of Bernice holding a different cat. The icing on the cake is an eight by ten group shot of her surrounded by felines. "Freaky," Darbie mumbles to herself, quivering.

Mystified Darbie flops back down on the icy vinyl chair. In doing so, she remembers the split in her skirt. She pinpoints the stapler, immediately grabs it, and staples the slit closed. "Ugh. 2B!"

Walker strolls down the corridor. He stops when he hears Darbie. "To be? Shakespeare? To be or not to be: That is the question-"

Crossing her legs, Darbie rises to the occasion and spouts, "Whether 'tis nobler in mind to suffer,-"

Walker steps inside the door frame filling it with his solid size. Towering over her he grins, enjoying the banter, he continues, "The slings and arrows of outrageous misfortune-"

Bernice pushes past Walker. "Please excuse us, Walker."

"Yes, ma'am," he respectfully agrees, leaving Darbie alone with Bernice but not before sending her an incredibly sweet and encouraging, hang in there look that makes her almost melt right out of her seat. That face. She adores that clean-shaven face. His masculine features are so strong and pronounced from his broad nose to his full lips and pronounced jawline. He's so yummy her heart skips a beat. Darbie fantasizes that if Walker were a cupcake, he'd be a sinfully rich chocolate lovers delight with a tantalizingly creamy center. Instantaneously, she's feeling famished.

All the excitement vacates the room. Bernice takes a seat at her oversized, too big for the space, desk. The leather on her chair makes a fart noise as she does so. Darbie fights a smile.

Bernice grows increasingly unhinged. "What is going on with you today? That horrid spectacle in front of the board. You're totally incompetent. You took an hour-long lunch break, dressed unprofessionally, and you still can't hang a picture straight."

"Me? You-"

"I'm terminating you, Darbie."

"What? You're firing me?"

"Effective immediately. It makes the Institute look bad for an alumnus to hold this job for so long. It's for students, Darbie. Administration overlooked your enrollment status because your dad served on the board, and he was ill for so long. I wanted to wait until this installation wrapped to train the new guy, but the Dean just insisted I do it now."

Darbie gasps. "You've already hired my replacement?"

Bernice lays the name badge for the new hire on her desk. "He's a sophomore, photography major. Oh, and I found this on the reception desk." She slides the brochure of herself drawn as Satan across her desk.

"Bernice, I-"

"This is the first time I've ever fired someone, and I'm rather enjoying it. Hand over your key-card, Darbie." She empties the last paper ream inside a packaging box. "You have five minutes to put your belongings in this box and clear out."

Biting her lip, Darbie closes her eyes and inhales. She's done for. Her innate people-pleasing skills aren't going to do her any favors with Bernice. It's time to wave the white flag of surrender and see if she can, despite being given the heave-ho, manage to part ways on amicable terms. In as level and even of a professional tone as she can muster, she utters, "I appreciate your candor, and I apologize for earlier." Swallowing what's left of her pride, she then humbly asks, "May I use you as a reference?"

"I think that would be ill-advised. Now, if you'll excuse me, I have work to do — yours and mine." Without further ado, Bernice vacates her office completely indifferent, wearing a cold and calculating blank facial expression.

Darbie's so mad her blood is boiling; her nails dig into the armrests on her chair, making permanent crescent-shaped claw mark indents in the vinyl. How is she supposed to pay her bills now? Darbie has played by the rules her whole life. Look at where that's gotten her. She can't comprehend the audacity of that cold-blooded woman. This defining event is clearly the straw that broke the camel's back. Darbie is normally quiet, introspective, and non-confrontational, whereas Lark is the boisterous, outspoken, witty one who carries a pocket full of zingers around with her everywhere she goes. But desperate times call for desperate actions, so she channels her inner Lark Kingsley. All at once, an ingenious idea occurs to her, and a devious smirk crosses her angelic face. She picks up the new hire's key-card, flips it over, and pulls off the bar code on the back. Embittered, she grabs a permanent marker, turns the cardboard box over, and draws something on the side.

Storming out of Bernice's office with the box in tow, she heads for the reception desk. Walker stands close by with an empathetic expression.

"Darbie, I'm so sorry. Did you have something to tell me?" he inquires.

"Nope. Here." Darbie relinquishes her key-card to him. She grabs a picture of her and her daddy flying a compound kite on Tybee Island beach, a cherished pastime of theirs. Then, she hastily drags her arm across the desk and knocks almost everything into a small metal wastebasket.

Walker picks up a few items that missed their intended target. His grand plan to slowly woo her has gone out the window. He touches her hand as she reaches for her purse under the desk. Walker sends Darbie another sympathetic glance, but this time it's up close and personal. Darbie freezes. The caress of his hand on hers accompanied by the warmth and the softness in his eyes paralyzes her. "You're overqualified for this job, Darbie. You'll find something way better. I'm sure of it." Swept up in his touch, she feels an electrical current flowing from his fingertips to the palm of her hand. Walker's irises are hypnotizing, majestic even. Mesmerized, they lock eyes. His captivating eyes burn deep into hers. Darbie can't look away; she doesn't want to. She could get lost in them forever, drowning herself in those ocean blue pools. She nearly forgets to breathe.

Blinking, she finally responds, "I-I appreciate that."

Running out of time, he goes for it. "I realize this is an inopportune time, but I was wondering if you'd like to go out on a date with me sometime?" he asks with his smooth Southern drawl, seizing the moment. He continues to look Darbie directly and intensely in the eyes. Mouth agape, Darbie's speechless. This was the last thing she was expecting Walker to say. She's having trouble believing that he's actually interested in her too.

"Y-you're asking me out?"

Walker nods.

"Oh, um... uh, maybe," she manages to answer him. Darbie's voice trails off as she snaps out of the trance, catching sight of Bernice in her peripheral vision.

Walker whispers to himself, "Maybe." He looks down at Darbie's smiling picture on her key-card. With an expression like he's been sucker-punched, he slides it into his chest pocket.

Darbie regains her focus and beelines it for Bernice. Seeing red, she places the box upside-down on Bernice's head, revealing the smiley face she sketched on its side. "Here ya go, Bernice. I've been waiting for years to give you a makeover. Perhaps now your cattywampus ass will finally get laid!"

In a tizzy, Darbie flees the gallery fuming. She heads towards the Admissions Building and plops down at a picnic table out front, huffing, and puffing; she plays back every belittling word Bernice said to her in her mind. A sliver of sunlight bursts through the willow tree's branches and reflects off a small brass plaque screwed to the edge of the tabletop. She rubs her thumb across the etching, which reads *IN LOVING MEMORY OF HANK HARRINGTON, 1961-2018*. At Hank Harrington's request, Darbie's momma dedicated the table to the college the month after he passed away.

Hank Harrington was, by all accounts, a remarkable and successful man; he made the bulk of his money as a commercial real estate investor. He went into early retirement at the ripe young age of fifty. Although Hank continued serving on the board for the college, he enjoyed his life of leisure, tinkering with old cars and creating utilitarian junk art sculptures from used car parts. He was never more in his element than when he was working with his hands — a talented craftsman who'd built this picnic table from the parts of an old school bus. Darbie adored watching his eyes light up when he was near the finishing line on a piece. Not a proud man by any means, but he did enjoy privately marveling at what he'd managed to accomplish with hard work and determination.

Darbie lays her head down on the table, extending her arms, and gives it a big bear hug. She can feel tears swelling beneath her eyelids; one escapes and trickles down her right temple, pooling where her cheek sticks to the smooth tabletop. Darbie misses everything about him. There is no one she'd rather talk to in her current traumatized state than him. Without a doubt, he would've known precisely what to say to ease her mind. Like Lark, Darbie is an only child; unlike Lark, she's a self-proclaimed daddy's girl. Her momma and her butted heads often, especially during those trying teenage years. She often escaped the house and sought refuge with her easygoing daddy.

She'd hunker down in his workshop for hours drawing and watercolor painting while he diligently worked on his projects. He'd offer her advice, often pointing out how Darbie's momma, difficult as she may be, had Darbie's best interest at heart. They'd spend hours out there, losing track of time, until her momma would ring an old cowbell to call them in for mealtimes. Her daddy enjoyed their alone time together as much as she did. She'd been blessed to have a father who encouraged her every step of the way with her artistic endeavors. In his office, he proudly showcased numerous works of art she'd created. He had no problem boasting about them to anyone who entered his domain.

After Mr. Harrington retired, he'd meet Darbie twice a week for a daddy-daughter lunch date. They'd spread out a patchwork quilt and picnic in the grass on this very spot. Darbie's grandmother, Nanna, who lived with Darbie's parents the last fifteen years of her life, packed them a yummy homemade lunch. Sadly, Nanna passed away in her sleep six months before her son's death. Darbie has fond memories of sitting on the front porch swing, sipping lemonade, eating raisin cookies, and listening to Nanna tell stories about her life. She could tear it up in a kitchen too, whipping up some of the best Southern recipes around. A creature of habit, every Thursday like clockwork, she'd make salmon croquettes, mash potatoes with gravy, fried okra, and apple fritters for dessert. Darbie's mouth watered just thinking about it. Darbie and Lark never missed a Thursday night supper. They were there with bells on and a fork in hand.

On the days Darbie and her daddy met up for lunch, Nanna would make sure to always include their favorites, chicken salad and deviled eggs. If they were lucky, she'd pack some sweet rolls and a small jar of her strawberry-rhubarb preserves. Her daddy always insisted there should be a picnic table here where they happily dined on the fescue and clover turf. They'd initially picked this particular location because there's a magnificent willow tree that sits on it, which provides full shade. Any local worth their salt will tell you full shade is the single most critical element to the survival of any picnic in South Georgia's merciless blazing sun.

Feeling pretty low, Darbie kisses the table and drags herself into a standing position. Needing a pick me up and to blow off some serious steam, she considers going for a jog when she recalls how she unknowingly sold her running shoes at a five-finger discount yard sale this week. She's smoothing her shirt and giving her mini skirt a tug when Gator scopes her out. He admires her outfit, checks his breath, and makes his move. "Hi, I'm Gator. And I really like your style. Wanna get a drink?"

"Sure," spontaneously responds Darbie, surprising herself.

"Really? I mean right this way, madam. Your chariot awaits."

They hop inside Gator's convertible International Scout. Victorious, he honks his insanely loud train horn and lays rubber.

***

Embracing and adapting to her new environment, Lark has strung twinkle lights up on the RV's extended awning. Folding chairs and a table are set up on the lawn. A makeshift shower has been made using a tarp, garden hose, and wooden posts. Proving that no matter what new surprises come her way with her perseverant attitude, she's always capable of bounding over any of life's hurdles, even the ones she creates. She diligently works away at the grill, flipping fish, listening to music.

An Uber pulls into the rustic driveway. Darbie stumbles out, drunk as a skunk. Lark's mouth falls open, stupefied. Tipsy, Darbie waves a bar code stuck to her middle finger around in the general direction of the school. Reeking of booze, she could kill a horse with her stanky breath. "Let's smake sem pay! Sit's our Banksy!" she says, slurring her speech.

"Hell yeah!" squeals Lark.

Darbie falls face-first onto the inflatable duck.

CHAPTER 7

Boom, boom, boom. Hungover, Darbie shoots straight up from a deep sleep and whacks her noggin on the bunk bed above her. She's disorientated and has a terrible case of bedhead hair. She yanks her silk eye mask off. Sunlight floods the RV burning her eyes and drilling a spike through her skull. "Ooooh," she moans. "Never — drinking — again," she vows to herself, squinting as the sun's rays violently sting her eyeballs, constricting her pupils.

Boom, boom, boom. The noise is coming from the roof of the RV. Darbie jumps up and studies the new makeshift bunk beds constructed from the old bed frame with the mattress sawed in half. The top bunk sits empty, sheets disheveled. She stumbles outside perplexed, dragging a blanket behind her.

Georgia's unfiltered and unsympathetic scorching rays instantly blind Darbie, making her worse off than before. Squinting, she rubs her throbbing head and looks around. She blindly calls out, "Lark!" Her dry mouth tastes rancid. Woozy, a hot flash hits Darbie, and her skin turns clammy. She's never experienced a hangover worse than this one. An intense, crippling pain radiates from her stomach. She hates herself for drinking so much last night. Her entire abdomen cramps and aches as though someone kicked her in the gut.

Boom, boom, boom. Darbie covers her ears, feeling as if her skull might split in two. Lark belays down from the top of the camper. "Don't you look ravishing this morning."

"Too loud. What in the H are you doing?"

"Training for the big day."

Woozy, Darbie curls up in the doorway of the camper, rubs her eyes, and yawns. "I've got a bar-code, Lark. This is a no brainer. I know the security procedures, everyone's schedule, and the location of all the cameras."

"Don't you think they changed some of that when they fired you?"

"Doubtful."

"Always expect the unexpected, Darbie. Let me show you something."

Lark unfastens her harness, dropping to the ground. She nimbly lands on her feet. Pulling a chair over to Darbie, she takes a load off. Retrieving her phone, she opens an app and scrolls through the web, clicks a link, and shows Darbie the screen.

"YouTube?"

"This is important research. What not to do."

Lark plays a viral video of two guys trying to break into a bank. Both guys carry bricks. The first guy pelts his brick at a glass door. Without waiting, he steps directly in front of his part-ner as he tosses his brick. The brick pummels the first guy in the head instead of the glass door, knocking him out cold, and leav-ing his be befuddled partner with the extraordinary task of trying to figure out how to carry his limp body off. Darbie grabs her mouth and groans. Lark turns her phone off and crams it in her back pocket. "These two idiots obviously had no plan. I have a plan."

Lark lays out a rudimentary hand-drawn map of campus and various sectors of Savannah. She runs her fingers over her child-like drawing. "Here is the fine arts building, gallery, McGuire dormitory, hiking trail, the banquet hall, and Bonaventure Cemetery," delineates Lark.

"Why is the banquet hall on here? It's on the opposite side of campus?"

"Spring homecoming is this weekend. Hurricane Michael canceled October's festivities," Lark reminds her.

"I think we'll be a little too busy committing a felony to attend."

"Darbie, you just got fired."

"All the more reason not to go," says Darbie, shrugging her shoulders and throwing her hands up.

"You just got canned. The jealous ex-boyfriend is who they always suspect. You'll need an alibi."

"Right. What will we tell people?"

"People? You mean those two asshats, Clay and Clementine?" asks Lark, revealing her biased opinion.

The mere mention of their names rips the lid off Darbie's psychologically impaired memory box. Clay still happily occupies the pedestal she long ago placed him on, and Clementine remains perched up there beside him, as painfully beautiful as ever. "I can't face them. Look at me," states Darbie, ludicrously perceiving herself inadequate.

"Well, for one," Lark holds out her index finger, "you're about to be a millionaire. And two," Lark gestures a peace sign, holding up two fingers, "who cares what those phony, two-faced, backstabbers think?"

"It's my fault it happened," confesses Darbie, dropping her shoulders.

"Your fault? Honestly, Darbie, sometimes you're too sweet for your own good. Heck, you apologize to furniture when you bump into it. You know, some girls would've scratched her eyes out and taken a sledgehammer to that shiny jeep of his, is all I'm saying." Gripping the handle on an invisible hammer, Lark takes a swing in the air. "And if you ask me, which I know you didn't, you let them off way too easily." insists Lark, getting riled up.

"Well, I was never around," confesses Darbie, strumming her fingers on the map.

"You were taking care of your dad, and she was our roommate."

Darbie gestures to Lark sarcastically. "Yeah, I guess I really know how to pick them." They laugh.

"I always knew she was a tramp," mumbles Lark.

She gives Lark the evil eye. "I reckon I have a type," she wisecracks.

They laugh again.

"I haven't thought about her in a long time. She was hands down the most annoying roommate we ever had. Do you remember how she would narrate her life?"

"Yes, but only the mundane stuff nobody cares about. She'd declare when she was finished with a meal." Darbie speaks in a whiny voice, "Clementine is finished with her lunch."

"Clementine ate all her mash potatoes... Clementine doesn't like asparagus," adds Lark doing her best Clementine impression.

"I mean, honestly, who gives a rip!"

"Nobody!" agrees Lark.

"I almost feel sorry for Clay now that I really think about it," Darbie admits, grinning. Her face drops, "I just hate showing up by myself and empty-handed, is all."

"You won't be by yourself. I'll be there," encourages Lark.

"Thanks," Darbie smiles, but then it falls flat.

"Look, if you're that worried about it, take notes from your mom — make stuff up."

Darbie releases a laugh so hard her already tender sides hurt. "Ain't that the truth." Calming down, Darbie states, "You know, Daddy used to tell me never to compare myself to others. And never conform to what people expect because the minute you do that, you're dead in the water."

"Yup. You can't control what other people think about you; You can only control what you think about you, but for what it's worth, I think you're pretty spectacular."

"Awe. Thanks. Ditto. Alright, I'm in," she submits, high-fiving her. "They probably won't even be there. What's the plan?"

Lark circles the Banquet Hall with her finger. "Before and after the heist, we'll show up at the banquet and pose in as many pictures as possible."

"The banquet hall isn't a hop, skip, and a jump away. It's clear over on the other end of campus. How are we supposed to pull that off? There are cameras in all of the campus parking lots. The gallery's golf cart is being used for the parade this weekend and won't be returned until sometime Monday morning. We can't just drive around in Isetta all night. We'll stick out like a sore thumb."

"Oh, she won't make a single film debut," reassures Lark.

Lark steps behind her, grabs her by the shoulders, and guides her to the side of the camper. She spins her around to the grand reveal of an elaborate obstacle course. "Ta-da!"

Darbie blinks her eyes a few times, unable to wrap her mind around what she's seeing. Spread out before her is a maze of orange caution cones, a zip line, hay barrels, planks, a water-slide, a golf bag, paintball guns with bulls-eye targets, a pulley system, a couple of climbing ropes hanging from trees, Darbie's new bike-buggy, Isetta, and a yarn course inside the shed. Wandering around, Darbie touches the yarn. "Let me guess. Lasers? The gallery doesn't have lasers, Lark," she informs.

"Hey, they could be installing them right now as we speak. Always expect the unexpected, Darbie," she repeats.

"You really did all this before, 10:00 a.m.?"

Lark dangles Darbie's car keys in front of her. "No rest for the wicked," she responds, feeling particularly cheerful.

"Wow," says Darbie, amazed.

"Honestly, I just pulled every bit of this out of the shed and set it all up. Your dad had a lot of toys."

"Yeah, he did. Thanks for getting Isetta back."

"Don't thank me. Thank that tall glass of Johnnie... Jack Walker. He said he found your keys in the conference room."

"Oh. That's right. How did Walker know where to find me?"

"Mother Dearest. He said he enjoyed the ride, but I think he'd like to take someone else out for a spin."

"Okay." smarts Darbie, hiding her embarrassment and insecurities with a grin.

Lark tilts her head, studying the absurdity of Darbie's expression. "Don't you look at me like I have a thousand eyeballs, Darbie Harrington. I know Walker asked you out."

"He probably just felt sorry for me," responds Darbie, skeptically rolling her eyes.

"You can't seriously be that dumb."

"It doesn't matter because hello! He's a security guard. I literally had the security strip stuck to the back of my finger."

"Okay, so he needs to work on his timing. I'm guessing time was of the essence since you were getting canned," reassures Lark.

"That's true," whispers Darbie.

Lark chuckles.

"What's so funny?" Darbie asks, certain she doesn't want to know.

"Oh, nothing. Just imagining how it went down. You're in the middle of getting sacked, and he lets you know he wants to sack you." She laughs again, louder.

Darbie cuts her eyes at Lark and sends her a crooked smile. "Aren't you clever?" she smarts. "Nice play on words. So funny, I forgot to laugh." Darbie rolls her eyes.

"He had a smile plastered on his face about a mile wide." This is a natural reaction to riding in Isetta that Darbie herself is quite familiar with. Isetta's just so adorably cute and fun. Everywhere Darbie goes, people are happy to see her. Total strangers will roll down their windows at an intersection to ask what kind of car Isetta is or inquire about what decade she originates. So unique, most have never seen anything like her. Folks will rev their engines challenging her to a race. Isetta's gas tank only holds two and a half gallons; a simple pit stop at a gas station which should take no time at all, instead takes thirty to forty minutes because everyone there wants to take a closer peek and gab about her.

"The three keys threw him for a loop. He said he had to search online for how to get a BMW Isetta started," continues Lark.

Driving Darbie's car is pretty straight forward, but getting her going isn't as simple as turning a key. There are three keys, one to unlock the door, one for the starter, and one that looks more like a screwdriver for the engine compartment, which incidentally is on the rear side panel of the car and must be turned several rotations to unlock. The gas switch, which, if you can believe it, located behind the seat, of all places, must be moved to 'on,' and there is a rather tricky throttle to fiddle with before the car will actually function properly. Built with a one-cylinder, 247cc motorcycle engine with 13 hp, the top speed Darbie's ever driven Isetta is around fifty miles-per-hour which works just fine when scooting around town but is hardly ideal for a racetrack.

Baiting Darbie, Lark jingles the car keys again. "Who's drivin'?"

Darbie snatches the keys and slides inside, claiming the driver's side of the small bench seat. Lark squeezes in next to her on the bench's passenger side. "Buckle up, buttercup. You're in for a rough ride and remember there's no 'oh, shoot handle,'" smirks Darbie.

"What's the 'oh, sh-" Lickety-split, Darbie gets the car started and takes reign on the steering wheel. She hits the gas like a race-car driver. The BMW Isetta rumbles to life picking up speed as it tears through the tight little obstacle course like wildfire doing donuts around orange caution cones. Georgia red clay dust sprays everywhere. "-hhhhoot'?"

***

Later that day, the RV's hood is propped open with Lark hidden below wielding a wrench. *Ring.* The buzzer on a wind-up kitchen timer resting on a primitive step stool goes off. Lark pulls her head out from under the hood and yells. "Time's up!"

Darbie swings from one rope to the next, struggling to secure enough momentum to reach the shed's summit. "This is impossible! I'm not Tarzan."

Lark wipes her grimy hands on an oily rag. "You almost had it that time, Jane." She resets the timer. "Try again."

***

The following day, Darbie takes a ten-minute break; she wanders off alone into the woods to hunt stray golf balls. Once a competitive high school golfer who won state championships two consecutive years, she's just been blowing the dust off her swing and discovering that she's still a natural on the greens. Scouring the forest floor for balls, she stumbles upon a brand new camouflage tarp neatly folded on the ground next to some fresh tire tracks that lead back out towards the road. Darbie bends down and touches the soft soil. She's no detective, but the tracks appear fresh to her. Curious, she scours the area looking for any signs of disturbance. She can see a faint compressed path in the pine needles fleecing the woodland terrain. Hidden in the tightly packed trees, Darbie finds a twenty-foot tall deer stand. She climbs the weathered ladder to a small six-foot by six-foot platform and discovers a cooler with an icy cold six-pack of beer and a tripod with a telescopic lens. She looks through the eyepiece and spies Lark. Appalled, she leans back, shaking her head. The thought that all this time they've been under the watchful eye of some weirdo lurking about royally creeps her out. Especially considering Lark had gone skinny dipping prior to rigging up the shower. Squinting, she peeks through the lens once more, seeing Lark, solidifying her suspicions. "Pervert," she mumbles to herself, snagging the beer and tripod. "Finders keepers."

***

Putting safety first, Lark pulls on a welding helmet and insulated gloves. She grasps a blow torch; looking fierce, she moves with purpose towards the rear of the camper.

Darbie opens Isetta's door and places the tripod, beer, and tarp inside on the parcel shelf. She traipses over to the shed and fetches a saw and a tackle box. In the act of vigilantism, she starts heading back in the direction of the dense woodlands to retrace her steps to the deer stand.

"Watcha doin'?" casually inquires Lark.

"Gettin' even," Darbie responds, gleefully swinging the tackle box as she ventures past her.

"That's what I'm talkin' about!" Lark flips the eye protection down and ignites the torch. "Yeehaw." She hits the back of the camper with the flame producing a shower of hypnotizing incandescent sparks.

***

The following evening, the girls are utilizing Darbie's daddy's two-seater fishing boat. Casting a line is second nature to Lark. Fishing is one of the few activities her father participated in with her growing up. Although, never on a boat. The two of them were no strangers to the local fishing enthusiasts. At least once a month, coinciding with her father celebrating a big win, you'd find them perched on the end of Tybee Island pier fishing for flounder, sea bass, and spotted sea trout. Baked flounder was a dinner time staple in their household. She'll never forget the day she caught a hammerhead shark. An immense crowd of onlookers gathered to watch that dramatic event. It was too heavy and cumbersome to reel in. In the end, her father resolved to cut the line. Besides, a cop was also in attendance waiting to issue a ticket the instant the shark left the water.

Disrupting Lark's stream of consciousness, Darbie whispers, "Would you look at that," admiring a magnificently horned buck, beautiful doe, and their sweet little fawns.

"What?" Lark follows Darbie's gaze and answers her own question. "Awe. Wow. Three deer."

"Four."

"Where? I only see three."

"Look closer. There is one laying in the grass."

Lark scans the surrounding area, catches the slightest movement in the thick grass, and locates him. "Ohhh. Yeah. Another fawn." The white spots on the fawn's brown fur make him blend right in with the surrounding flickers of cascading light permeating through the tree branches overhead onto the grass.

"Sweet, aren't they?"

"The buck is just sticking around long enough to mate. Bucks leave the does to birth the fawns and raise them on their own."

"Well, that just put a different spin on things. Thanks for raining on my parade."

"Just keeping it real. What are they chowing down on?"

"A salt lick. Daddy must have put one over there," ascertains Darbie. Something in the forest spooks the herd, and they all take off running like a bolt of lightning.

"I hardly miss cable TV. Living off the grid is like existing inside the Nat Geo Wild channel," states Lark.

"This is about as backwoods as you can get; I'll give you that. I don't know what network it comes on, but if we were contestants on that show *Survivor*, I would just graciously bow out and head home to my Wi-Fi and hot water," insists Darbie.

They've been unsuccessfully fishing for about an hour. Darbie is plum tuckered out from today's training session. She's so sore even her teeth hurt. Mosquitos and sand gnats are starting to come out, making matters worse; she knows they will soon eat them alive. "It's getting dark. Let's head back."

Losing steam herself, Lark submits. "Sounds good."

While they commence reeling in their fishing lines and packing up their gear, Lark reminisces. "I'm kind of excited about being back on campus — my old stomping ground. Maybe I'll get to finish my bucket list."

"Bucket list?"

"Fifty Things To Do Before Graduation."

"Oh, right. You carried that piece of paper around with you everywhere."

"I still have it in my wallet. I have three left to do."

"Three things or three people? Because I don't think Professor still works there anymore," kids Darbie, making a gagging face.

"Ah, yes. Professor Pervy, as we called him. Number thirty-four, lock lips in the photo lab's dark room. Check, check."

"Glad that's all you locked with him. Yuck! That old geezer was a praying mantis. He had kids our age."

"Yeah. He caught me on an off day. My self-esteem was kinda low. The Giants had just defeated the Patriots at the Super Bowl. I thought he was someone else. A student. He smelled like burritos." She shutters at the thought.

"Gosh, I was just kidding. I mean, I'd heard the rumors about him, but I had no idea they were true. I'm so sorry. How come you never told me?"

"Embarrassed, I guess. For the record, he kissed me. As a teenager, that wasn't exactly what I had in mind when I came up with number thirty-four. Some brave girl finally turned him in."

"Good." Lark watches the moonlight dance across the water. "Professor Pervy, indeed," she whispers.

Lark pulls the starter. Nothing happens. She tries again. Nothing happens. Darbie leans forward on the seat well. "No, you have to push the throt-"

Lark fails to notice Darbie leaning in and rigorously turns the throttle handle too hard. She simultaneously pulls back on the starter with her whole body and unwittingly elbows Darbie in the boob. The boat takes off at full speed with the throttle stuck. Cupping her breast, Darbie silently screams. She staggers around, the small vessel shakes helter-skelter, the fishing net rolls, and she lands on the net. The net's pole swings up with sudden force and unintentionally creams Lark in the crotch. They both moan in pain. The boat heads straight for the dock. Darbie's heart nearly leaps right out of her chest. "Watch it!"

Lark makes a sharp turn to the right. Before they even know what's happening, both girls plunge overboard, and the boat continues driving off out of the cove. Darbie scurries up the dock's ladder almost as fast as she hit the murky water. Panicking, she urgently checks herself for leeches. Lark, on the other hand, floats serenely on her back, gazing up at the stars without a care in the world.

CHAPTER 8

Sensing a perpetrator's following him, Dante swiftly rounds a corner down a dark and ominous back alley. Ornery, he curses as he fiddles with his days of the week pill container. He's peeved that his new neurological condition requires a daily medication regiment to manage his dizzy spells. Snapping open the lid, he tosses his head back, pours several tablets directly into his mouth, and swallows them dry.

Disoriented, Dante trips over his own two feet and stumbles. Catching himself, he wearily skirts past a dumpster. It reeks of rotting food and it's infested with crawling cockroaches. He leans up against a damp brick wall and gets his bearings while hoping that the timing of his medication kicks in and coincides with the upcoming hostile event. Dante grabs a discarded split two by four. Sweating, he wipes his brow with a handkerchief and waits.

Rapid, heavy footsteps clamor down the alley and splash in a dirty puddle. In a well-calculated attack, just as Dante's predator passes the dumpster's threshold, he swings the two by four out and clotheslines him right across the chest. The guy's feet fly

up from under him, causing his back to slam into the cracked asphalt. Stunned from the force of having the wind knocked out of
him, his would-be assailant doesn't make a peep. Without missing a beat, he places the guy in an armlock and pivots his upper
body, shoving him up against the dumpster making an audible
echoing thud against the metal. Fleeing the scene, a startled rat
scurries out of the foul-smelling dumpster. One of Dante's hands
pins the guy's shoulder while the other holds a switchblade to his
carotid artery. "Whoa, Whoa, Whoa. Dante, relax. It's me...
Tony," he rasps with a New York-Italian accent.

"What are you doin' here?" Dante scans the alley for ac-
complices. "Why are you tailing me?"

"I've been on you since yesterday, man. You're slippin'.
Simmons sent me. He's worried you've become a liability. You go
down; we all go down."

"What are you going on about? I could do this gig with my
eyes closed, kid." He releases Tony and slips his knife back into
his pocket.

"That whack you got on our last job really did a number on
you. You can't even walk in a straight line anymore."

"I wouldn't have gotten that concussion in the first place if I
hadn't been babysitting your worthless tail. I told Simmons that
I'm fine, you little snitch."

Tony releases an audible moan and rubs his lower back.
"Hey, I'm only here 'til tomorrow. This is what they call a working
vacation," Tony explains, tugging on his shirt. In contrast to
Dante, Tony is wearing a brightly colored tropical shirt, shorts,
and sandals. He's looking every bit the tourist he is. "I've got an-

other job lined up. From what I've gathered, it's time you tap out on this one, my friend."

At forty-five years old, Dante lacks any inclination to tap out on this job or any other. He's a ruthless career criminal, through and through. This is all Dante's ever known, and all he's ever gonna know. He'd grown up poor, dirt poor, and he's got no intention of returning to that provincial lifestyle.

However, no amount of funds has ever proved enough for him; he's acquired a rather nasty habit of gambling much of his earnings away, rendering himself nearly destitute within weeks of each payday. In a vicious cycle of his own making, he once again finds himself too poor to paint and too proud to whitewash. Dante isn't about to let some still wet behind the ears, twenty-two-year-old, pretty boy he trained, tell him what to do. Livid, his blood pressure spikes. "Tap out?"

"Yeah. Tap out. It means ri-'tī(-ə)r," Tony annunciates.

"I know what it means! And I'm not doin' it. What I am doin' is finishing this job."

"No, you're not. That bump messed you up, old-timer. You're not thinking so good," persists Tony, tapping his index finger to his temple for emphasis.

Half-crazed, Dante head butts him in the nose, causing a sickening crunch and crimson red blood to freely flow from Tony's nostrils, pooling on his lips. "Yeah, well, maybe you're not lookin' so good anymore." Tony covers his nose, cursing. Dante grabs him by the shoulders and callously shoves him backward, smacking his skull on the unforgiving brick wall. Tony's eyes roll back in his head. "And maybe it's you that don't think so good." He picks up the broken two by four and maliciously nails him in the shin with the board. Tony withers and wails. Dante clutches a fist full of Tony's shirt, spins him around, and kicks him in the backside, propelling him forward. "Uh-oh. You're not walking so good anymore either. Maybe you can report that back to Simmons."

Tony drags himself down the alley using the wall as leverage. Dante watches him go. As he edges the corner, Tony glances back. Dante is standing in the center of the alley, perfectly content, sporting a mincing grin painted across his wilted face. With a vacant stare, he disingenuously holds his hand up and flutters his fingers in a 'tootles' style wave.

CHAPTER 9

The heat index this morning is hotter than a jalapeños butt crack. Worn slap out, Lark peddles the bike-buggy to campus with Darbie hitching a ride in the shopping cart, sitting pretty she casually pushes her cuticles back on each of her fingernails. Lark, on the other hand, is sweating like a pig and mad as a hornet that she lost the coin toss. For the first time in her life, she loathes Darbie's car, Isetta. "Stupid, clown car!"

"Don't be a sore loser. It's not Isetta's fault you called tails," reminds Darbie.

Lark mocks her as she motions toward the bike-buggy. "This is so much more inconspicuous."

"Everyone knows I drive that car. While this rig of yours may draw in the same amount of attention as Isetta, I doubt anyone we know would be able to identify us at this rate of speed. They're all zipping right past us."

"Except for those two upstanding citizens in that ratty old pickup truck who slowed down."

"What did they yell? I couldn't make it out?"

Lark releases a series of giggles. "The toothless driver asked me to marry him. And his passenger said something about wanting you to have his baby."

"Charming."

"I thought so," pants Lark with a smile.

"Does it ever get old?"

"What?"

"Guys hitting on you all the time," clarifies Darbie.

"Occasionally," answers Lark, shrugging her shoulders. "I can't go any further," she states, breathless. Beads of sweat swim on her beautiful tomato red face.

"Great job, by the way, I think the lady pushing the double stroller only lapped us twice," jabs Darbie, grinning from ear to ear.

"Hey, it was once, thank you very much. And in my defense, she was wearing a triathlon t-shirt," Lark defends. "Why couldn't we just call a Lyft like normal people."

"You have to pay for a Lyft. And that would've emptied all of our reserves."

"Ugh," exasperates Lark. She'd rigged up this bike buggy as a one time only emergency moving apparatus, never intending for it to become their new alternate form of transportation. "I'm stashing this monstrosity behind Willy's Cafe. They don't open until noon." Without allowing Darbie to put her two cents in, Lark cuts through the empty parking lot to the rear of the restaurant, assertively parking the bike-buggy out of sight. Still straddling the bike, she pleads, "Hand me my bag, would ya?"

Darbie is seated with her legs in a pretzel formation. The book bag is wedged between her thighs and torso. She lifts her booty to unlock her legs from their knot positioning — freeing the bag and handing it to Lark.

Lark unzips the front pocket and removes a makeup blotter, tapping it to her face.

"Unreal! You've been holding out on me. You had those this whole time. There wasn't any room to save my makeup bag, razor, or even a stick of deodorant, but you have blotters. Seriously?"

"Seriously. These are a necessity," Lark flatly defends.

"My toothbrush is a necessity."

"You know how my face breaks out like a pepperoni pizza without them."

"Yes, I'm fully aware and empathic to your plight," Darbie says, pointing out the crater on her forehead.

"I'm sorry, okay?" Lark replies, plain and simple. "You can have one — here. And you're welcome to use my concealer anytime."

"You have concealer!"

"Err... Yeah." She reaches back inside her bag and retrieves the aforementioned concealer. "Keep it," she insists, handing it to her, "And you can have the rest of the blotters," she says, holding them out, causing a ceasefire to their bickering.

"Thank you," mummers Darbie, removing only one and handing the pack back to her. "We can share," she says, sticking the concealer in her pocket.

Lark dismounts the bike and arduously helps Darbie out of the cart. "If it makes you feel any better — I'm soaked. Even the backs of my knees are sweaty," Lark points out, wiping the sweat running down her calves. Then, she dries the palms of her hands by patting them on her shorts. Lark's long hair is swept up into a ponytail. She swings the book bag over her shoulder, covering the dark ring of perspiration on the back of her Savannah Seaside Art Institute t-shirt. Darbie's sporting athletic gear and an SSAI campus hat. They inconspicuously blend in as college students.

Lark tugs at various bricks on the back wall of the cafe. While Darbie double knots the laces on Lark's borrowed tennis shoes she's sporting. "What in the tarnation are you doing?" asks Darbie.

"There's supposed be a geostash back here — somewhere." Lark locates and dislodges a loose brick. She inserts her hand into the rectangular hole in the wall and extracts a small metal canister containing a joint. "Number twenty-five."

"Smoking cannabis is number twenty-five on your bucket list?"

"Not me. You. Get Darbie to loosen up is number twenty-five."

Darbie snatches the canister and brick and inserts them back into open space in the wall. "Very funny. I feel like I'm stuck in a bad after-school special. Did that DARE pledge we took in the fifth grade mean nothing to you? Focus, Lark. I'm gonna jog our route and stake-out all the cameras while you surveil the gallery and make sure there aren't any discrepancies in the security procedures. We'll rendezvous back here in one hour."

"Roger that."

"Oh, and try to be discrete," instructs Darbie.

"Not to worry, I brought my invisibility cloak," jokes Lark, referencing her second favorite novel. *Pride and Prejudice* takes the number one slot.

The girls head out determined in opposite directions. Darbie's first steps are hunched over from the cramped ride. Straightening herself, she finds a nice steady rhythm and loosens her muscles before channeling her spirit animal, a gazelle.

Lark makes her way to the art gallery. Fit as a fiddle; Darbie jogs around campus scouting cameras on buildings and in packed parking lots.

Blowing the seeds off a dandelion she plucked from a sidewalk crack, Lark traipses by an apartment-style housing complex. Before she can make a wish, a small group of beatnik students send an ill-kicked hacky sack in her direction. Showing off some fancy footwork, Lark juggles the footbag and kicks it back to them. Astounded, they enthusiastically cheer and whistle. She gives a twirl with a flirtatious curtsy and saunters off. So much for not bringing any attention to herself.

***

Darbie finished her ten-mile mission in seventy-eight minutes flat. Certainly, not her best time, but she had to do some serious backtracking and tediously log the location of each and every camera. Killing time, she'd decided to significantly increase her cardiovascular benefits by tacking on ten stadium bleacher intervals. Darbie had initially celebrated the fact that she was able to turn her covert operative assignment into her daily exercise regimen, thus killing two birds with one stone.

Nonetheless, this secret agent is now kicking herself for not quitting while she was ahead. The heat increased drastically over the course of an hour. Perspiration glistens on her sun-kissed skin. Overexerting herself has caused her calf to atrophy. She moans at the painful spasm. With both hands pressed against the rear wall of Willy's Cafe, she leans forward in a long stride, breathless, stretching out her cramping leg muscle.

Lark strolls up, licking an ice cream cone. Darbie notices the bandaid on her arm. "What happened to you?"

"The blood drive is giving out free ice cream in exchange for a few pints. Win. Win," Lark cheers, licking a creamy drip of sweet butter pecan off her wrist.

"Oh, right. I saw them setting up. I should've doubled back and done that instead of running the bleachers."

"You're a machine."

"Hardly. So, how did it go?" inquires Darbie.

"Good. The guy told me I have beautiful veins."

"Of course he did. I meant, how did it go with the gallery? Did Bernice remember you?" asks Darbie.

"No, I don't think she woulda noticed me if I'd been wearing a cowbell. But Walker sure did and right away too. Here." She hands Darbie a tape dispenser. "Not to worry, I made up some bogus story about how you left behind your favorite tape dispenser."

"And he fell for that."

"Hook, line, and sinker. Just like he's fallen for you."

"Whatever," dismisses Darbie. "That's just great," she sarcastically says, fidgeting with the tape dispenser. "He probably thinks I'm a total weirdo now."

"Oh, he knows you're a total weirdo. He doesn't care; he's so into you. It's so glaringly obvious; it's ridiculous."

"No way."

"I'm telling you, the man thinks you fart rainbows."

"Psh," Darbie says, waving her hand dismissingly.

"Trust me, Walker finds your idiosyncrasies endearing," persists Lark, sticking her index finger in her mouth, fake gagging, like a seven-year-old.

"Really?"

"He asked about you," sings Lark, beaming.

"Walker asked about me? "Okay. We're gonna stick a pin in this for the time being, but I wanna hear every word later," Darbie insists, smiling. Trying to stay on topic, she shifts gears, "How did your surveillance go?"

"Two-step procedure like you said."

"See, it's a no-brainer." She takes a long swig out of her water bottle, emptying half of the contents and then holds the container out, offering some to Lark.

Lark declines, knowing full well that if she accepted her generosity and partook in a swig, Darbie wouldn't drink the rest due to the cootie factor. Harnessing this knowledge, she holds out her ice cream cone, offering a lick to Darbie. To which Darbie declines the gesture just as Lark predicted she would. "Yep. Swipe the key-card. Do the thumbprint scan," confirms Lark.

"What?" Darbie tosses her head back and polishes off the remaining water by dousing her face with it; she wipes her eyes on her sleeve.

Lark reenacts a card swipe and thumb scan with her hand. "Card. Thumb."

"Are you sure?" Darbie asks, rubbing her forehead.

"Well, I'm not very tech-savvy, but I know what a card and thumb scan look like," maintains Lark.

"Oh, no! No, No, No, No, No. Uh, they changed it! I can't believe it!" Storming over to a recycle bin, Darbie chucks her bottle.

"You said it'd been the same for ten years!"

Darbie's baffled. "Yes. No. It's swipe the key-card. Do the code. A thumbprint — Walker must've tightened security protocol for the Banksy exhibit."

"We're doomed," asserts Lark.

Frustrated their plan has gone awry, Darbie kicks the wall and heads off with the bike-buggy. The unsecured geostash brick falls off the wall. Lark looks around to make sure no one is looking, reaches in, and snags the metal canister. She serendipitously stashes it in her bag before heading off after Darbie and climbing in the basket.

"They are interchangeable, ya know," Darbie informs.

"What?"

"The thumb and the key-card. We talked about getting the same Aegistratican 290 system last year. I personally looked into it, but it was expensive, and our budget was pretty maxed out at the time. I figured there wouldn't be funds for it anytime soon. Anyways, it only records the key-card code, not the thumb; any combination of key-card and thumbprint will open it."

***

At the Harrington House, Ada Mae descends the front step and strolls down the walkway holding a pie. "Thanks, Sue Ellen."

"You're welcome, doll."

"Be sure and lock that door up behind you."

"Psh. I'm already trained to do that. Hank, God rest his soul, was worthless in that department. Nothing chapped my hide more than having to go behind him and lock up at night."

"Mm-hmm. That there falls under man duties."

"Same as taking out the trash and washing the car."

"Amen, sister!"

"I'm preaching to the choir now. I won't keep ya. Goodnight, Ada Mae."

"You too, Sue Ellen.

Mrs. Harrington stands on the porch in her apron waving. "Be good."

"And if you can't be good, be good at it," finishes Ada Mae.

***

Dusk descends, and an unusually cool breeze blows in from the north whistling through the pine trees surrounding the deer stand, sending tiny goosebumps up Dante's arm. Unsuspecting Darbie's boobytrap, he climbs the ladder just as he's done before. He nearly reaches the top when the sawed in half step snaps off in his hand. Losing his footing, he grabs madly at the side rail with his free hand saving himself or so he thinks until he hears the popping sound of the section of split wood breaking. His heart stops as he eyes both pieces of broken wood in his clasped hands. Plummeting to the earth, he lands in the patch of Christmas ferns. Darbie previously ornamented them with fishing hooks.

Five minutes later, he hunches at the edge of the dense woods. His left arm hangs from his throbbing dislocated shoulder. Mentally bracing himself while standing face to face with the trunk of a substantial pine tree, he holds the wrist on the arm of his injured shoulder. Cursing, he pulls his hand up enough so he can grab a thigh-high tree knot. Then, he sinks to his knees in agony until his arm is extended at the same height as his shoulder. The joint pops back into place.

Ready for round two, Dante takes a sharp breath and steadies himself, rips a piece of bark off a tree, shoves it in his mouth and bites down. He putters several short, shallow breaths as he painstakingly pulls fishing lures out of his neck and face, one by one. When Dante sees a small piece of his flesh stuck to the end of the second hook, he nearly blacks out. Squeamish, his hand slightly trembles as he wipes his bloody fingertips on his black jeans. Dante doesn't mind the sight of blood as long as it's somebody else's. Standing, he feels around on his butt cheek and howls. Bending over, he pulls the last lure out from where the sun don't shine. Passing out, he crumples to the soft pine needle covered forest floor.

Moments later, Ada Mae is cruising along, rocking out to the oldies on Q96.8. When the song ends her much anticipated, Clint and Marie show begins; she turns up the volume and sits up a little taller in her seat. "Stay tuned because up next we are going to play a little round of 'Have You Ever'," enthusiastically pipes Clint. Ada Mae listens intently as she picks up her big gulp slushy and inhales a long, drawn-out slurp.

"That's right, and our topic is..." (*drum roll sound effect*) "... blind dates," quips Marie.

"Ewww. Those are the worst," shares Clint.

"Absolutely! We want to know, 'Have You Ever' had to sneak out of a blind date?" asks Marie. Ada Mae lets go of the wheel and raises her hand. "Call in and share your horror story and let us know how you pulled off your Houdini act," beckons Marie. A possum strolls out in front of the van, alarmed Ada Mae stomps the brakes mid-slurp. Cherry slushy drips all down her chin and onto her white cover-up as she squeezes the steering wheel with her free hand.

"Ohhh. Ditching your date, that's just all kinds of wrong right there. You have to face the music the next day with the friend who instigated the disastrous pairing." judges Clint. Ada Mae slams her big gulp into the center console. The lid pops loose, and it erupts like a volcano all over her right sleeve and pants leg as she simultaneously grabs the wheel and swerves to miss the possum.

"Our phones are ringing off the hook, let's go to our first caller," eagerly states Marie. Shaken up, Ada Mae turns the radio off and accelerates. She watches in the rearview as the possum takes his sweet time crossing the street. Most are relatively skittish, so she decides this one has a death wish.

"Oh Man," says Ada Mae looking at her ruined cover-up doused with a red slushy. She wipes her chin on her collar because she figures it can't get any worse at this point. The van slows as it approaches Darbie and Lark's driveway. She notices Dante's mangled appearance as he lumbers out of the woods, gripping a tactical flashlight. He sluggishly places something in the trunk of his car. The van idles as she turns down the radio and leans out the window. "You're plumb tore up. Everything alright?"

Dante, who's never woken up on the right side of the bed, gives her the bird with his middle finger.

"Alright, then. No need to be ugly about it."

Ada Mae observes the arsenal of guns in his trunk, and the one holstered on his waist. She speeds up, drives past the driveway, and turns off just a little ways down from it onto the circular dirt driveway of a vacant double-wide trailer. She covertly cuts her headlights and waits. He pulls out onto the rural road, passing her. She shadows him.

***

Music flows from a boombox outside as Darbie and Lark prepare dinner. A refreshing, gentle breeze circulates through the RV's open doors and windows. The delightful aroma of marinated garlic and rosemary pork chops coming from the grill awakens Darbie's nasal passages and causes her mouth to water. She pauses long enough to pull on one of her daddy's flannel shirts. She sniffs the collar, bummed it doesn't smell like him, she swiftly cuffs the sleeves just below her elbows and returns to dinner time chores.

In her element, Lark dances and sings as she moves in and out from the kitchen to the grill. Darbie thoughtfully arranges slices of a cantaloupe in a fan shape on each of their plates. Mindfully slicing and dicing with a dull paring knife. While humming to the music, Darbie's extra careful not to cut herself when applying a little more pressure than she's accustom to while chopping a fresh lemon for the ice tea. A little bit of juice squeezes into a hangnail she didn't realize she has. She flinches and sucks on her index finger.

Chef Lark whips up a tasty fig, arugula, and goat cheese salad. "I bet you're counting your blessings that you got canned."

"Why do you say that?" asks Darbie.

"I think you oughta be grateful, is all. You don't have to work in that horrid environment with that insipid woman ever again."

"Was Bernice in rare form today?" inquires Darbie.

"The new kid was so scared he was shakin' in his boots." Lark crinkles her forehead, distorting her eyebrows and sucking in her chin, reenacting the terrified expression on the new hire's face as he trembled in fear.

"Bless his heart. She can be pretty terrifying."

"She could haunt a house... Oh, oh, oh! And the sound of that viper's voice as she tirelessly yammers on is like fingernails on a chalkboard!"

Darbie bursts out laughing. "No need to sugar coat it; tell me what you really think."

"She's the kind of woman people fantasize about hitting over the head with a baseball bat, wrapping her up in a shower curtain, and burying her in their back yards because ain't nobody, and I do mean nobody, gonna miss her."

"Her cats would miss her. She's got a house full."

"Shocker," Lark flippantly whispers. "I wouldn't have made it one day with her. I would've been heading for the hills," finishes Lark.

"Yeah, I guess I just didn't know if the grass was greener on the other side of that hill."

"Darbie, the grass isn't just greener on the other side; it's neon electric green."

Darbie sets down a memo style report, takes a seat at the table, and stares at the map. "The marshmallows represent cameras. I swung by Momma's earlier and took the liberty of typing up our itinerary."

Lark nods and eats a few marshmallows out of the bag. "I say we cut off Bernice's thumb."

"Lark!"

"Okay. The new kid then. He kinda looks like a lizard. Maybe it will grow back."

"He's a photography major. I'm pretty sure he needs all his digits."

"Let's get him drunk and take him along," suggests Lark.

"Be serious."

Lark tosses the empty bag down and walks outside. A bonfire's lit and the twinkle lights are on creating a camp like ambiance. She opens the grill, checking the pork chops with a thermometer; the temperature reads *145 degrees Fahrenheit.*

Inside, Darbie picks up the empty marshmallow bag and discerns by the weightlessness of the wrapper that it lacks any contents. "So I guess that's a hard no on s'mores for dessert," she injects disappointed. Joining Lark outside, she holds the plates she prepared with the side dishes. Lark transfers the pork chops from the grill to their plates.

Famished, Darbie initially digs in but then gradually tapers off her pace so she can savor the flavors in each morsel. It's hands down the best pork chop she's ever eaten, and the homemade dressing on the salad is to die for. "Mmm... ooh... wow... oooooh."

"Ugh! You and your plate oughta get a room already. Do you mind? I'm trying to eat over here."

A deep blood-curdling noise comes from the woods, sending a shiver up Darbie's spine. "Did you hear that yowl?"

"Sounded less like a yowl and more like a howl to me."

"A coyote?"

"Probably," dismisses Lark, poking her fork into a beet. She moves her salad around on the plate, slathering each bite with dressing dippings that missed their intended mark.

Just to be on the safe side, Darbie scoots her chair closer to the RV's door. A small patch of soft clouds slowly drifts apart, revealing the crescent moon. Darbie stares off into the distance. Right around eye level, a handful of fireflies blink and float about the flat scenery. Mingling amongst the far-off tree line, they dissolve into the unknown blackness of the forest. For a fleeting second, she questions if her boobytrap had been triggered but dismisses the idea because the eerie noise didn't sound human.

"Ya know, all we need to get is a mold of one of their thumbs," Darbie pipes up.

"Alright. Now you're talkin'. Sculpture 101 is finally paying off."

"We'll just get them to stick their thumb in a bowl of plaster."

Lark's face lights up. "Piece of cake." Suddenly, her expression darkens. "How do we that?"

Darbie tilts her head and rubs the back of her neck, watching the glowing hot embers flutter off the fire. "No idea," she finally responds.

Struck by what she considers a genius idea, Lark blurts, "Seduce Walker. He's dying to butter your biscuit."

"The new security officer? I barely know him. I — I can't. I'm not you!"

"Gee, thanks." Lark knocks the salt shaker over as she sets her plate down on the table. Salt spills all over the table.

"I'm not brave like you. You're not afraid of anything. Well, except for bees, maybe," reminds Darbie.

Lark fixes the salt shaker. "And mannequins... draw-bridges... and spiders." Lark shudders. "Hell is just a room full of spiders."

They laugh.

"Anyway, I'd look utterly ridiculous," shares Darbie, staring down at her shoes.

"It's better than being utterly boring." Lark picks some salt up off the table and tosses it over her left shoulder. "Besides, being brave is just like being happy. It's a choice. You always say I'm the happiest, most carefree person you know. But it's a choice; I wake up every day and choose to be that way. "

***

Ada Mae cruises down industrious Habersham Street. The van slows as the Lincoln enters the Dolphin Landing Motel parking lot. A pretty, little, pink Volkswagen Beetle hijacks Dante's usual parking spot. The motel must be booked at full capacity because all the surrounding spaces are taken. A group of girls in bikinis and flip-flops pile out of the Beetle and head towards the pool and hot tub area. They're discussing whether the government should increase environmental regulations to prevent climate change. Just kidding, they're talking about who's playing at the Bonnaroo Music and Arts Festival this year. Dante parks further down than he'd like and exits his car. As he crosses paths with the Beetle, he vindictively flicks his still-lit cigarette onto the cloth seat, singeing a hole in the mint upholstery.

Ada Mae pulls off onto the shoulder of the road just beyond the motel. She hops out and removes the "Animal Control" magnet from the van and takes off her cover-up, tossing it willy-nilly on the passenger seat. Then, Ada Mae climbs back in the vehicle, does a U-turn, and pulls into the motel entrance. She circles the parking lot before snuggling up beside the black Lincoln. Ada Mae shuts off the van's engine.

CHAPTER 10

Awestruck, Darbie leisurely drives Isetta down the grand Avery Plantation's pebble driveway with the sunroof open. Darbie and Lark gaze up at the magnificent Greek revival architecture illuminated in strategically placed spotlights. It stands proud, encompassing 547 acres of gorgeous Southern grounds, adorned with mature pecan groves and peacefully situated massive oaks dripping with Spanish moss. Lark shifts uncomfortably in her seat while Darbie sits spellbound. Completely and incandescently enamored by the picturesque property which is alive with fireflies tonight, she leans forward over the steering wheel.

"Now, this is an example of beauty, grace, and distinction," swoons Darbie as she places the car in park.

"Are you describing a house or a Miss America contestant?" asks Lark.

"I've always adored this estate. I go to go in it once with momma when I was in high school on one of those historical Pembroke home tours. All the crown molding and Venetian plaster, just gorgeous. Can you smell the tea olives and camellias?" The girls disembark Isetta together through the front end door onto the pristine property's driveway.

"I can smell the eucalyptus," states Lark turning her nose up. "This old place gives me the heebie-jebbies. Are you sure that tour y'all took wasn't a haunted house tour? I mean, can you imagine how many people have died in there? We're probably standing on one right now." Lark glances down at the ground and does a series of side steps.

"Generations of Averys have lived there, lovingly tending to it, and handing it down to their children, and their children's children," responds Darbie.

"And their children's children, and their children's children," finishes Lark.

"Over the years, I'm certain they've had their fair share of loved ones pass away in those walls, but I'm also certain a fair share have been born in there."

"Born and bred — double yuck!" Lark shivers at the thought. "One ill-lit candle and the whole thing will go up in smoke," she continues. "I was really rooting for Walker, but he's losing some major brownie points for residing in a house straight out of *Interview with a Vampire*," states Lark. Her eyes dart from window to window, searching for signs of the living dead.

"Come on, smarty britches. If I recall correctly, the carriage house is tucked somewhere around back. Follow me," Darbie says, leading the way.

They take the pathway under the wisteria-covered pergola. Darbie, all dolled up, holds a pie pan wrapped with an embroidered tea towel. Lark tries to apply red lip gloss on Darbie's pinched lips. "Lips without lipstick are like cakes without icing," coaches Lark.

"You sound like my momma." Darbie pushes her hand away. "Enough already. We only have ten minutes."

Lark turns the lip gloss over reading the label. "It's called *Man Bait*."

"Okay. Yeah. Give me some of that," agrees Darbie, decidedly changing her mind. She pooches out her full lips, a willing and eager participant.

Lark applies the lip gloss and looks her over. She steps back, gazing at her masterpiece. "Damn! You're hotter than a worm on asphalt." She hands Darbie a tote bag.

"What's this?"

"I whipped you up a little 'hoe on the go' bag."

Appalled, Darbie hands it back. "Thoughtful, but I'm just gonna be in there long enough to get him to stick his finger in the pie."

Lark nods and shakes the tote at her. "Hey, whatever you kids are calling it these days."

"No, really. In and out."

Lark smirks and starts to say something quite sarcastic. Darbie puts her finger over Lark's lips stopping her. "Don't say it."

Lark snickers. "Alright. You got this."

With perfect posture, Darbie takes a seat on the grass crisscross applesauce.

"What are you doing?"

"Relaxation technique. You oughta try it sometime," suggests Darbie.

Lark rolls her eyes and impatiently taps her foot, "I'm good. Thanks."

Practicing the breathing techniques she learned in yoga class, Darbie attempts to calm herself slowly. In doing so, her nervous jitters begin to dissipate.

Lark losing patience, picks up the pace, rapidly tapping her foot, breaking Darbie's concentration; her eyes spring open.

"Knock it off. I can't meditate."

Lark stops tapping. "Sorry. I didn't realize I was doing it."

Darbie starts reciting *Mary Had a Little Lamb*.

"Are you okay?" inquires Lark.

"Shhh. Yes. It distracts me. I usually do it in my head." Darbie closes her eyes and starts over.

Lark looks at her like she's a stark raving lunatic and mouthes the word, 'whoa.' "Ya know, most people simply combat negative thoughts with positive ones."

"Shhh," repeats Darbie without opening her eyes or moving a muscle.

Sixty seconds later, Darbie finishes, and then stands up nonchalantly feeling relaxed and confident.

"Ready," declares Lark with an air of concern she tries to mask. She spins Darbie around, pinches her booty, and thrusts her towards the five-bay carriage house. "Be cool. Be caszh," encourages Lark. Lark ducks down between two bushes holding a second pie.

Darbie thought she was feeling relatively self-assured until Lark left her side. She's become so dependent on her in the same way a child is with their security blanket. Darbie feels like the cowardly lion from the *Wizard of Oz* attempting to muster up the courage. Nervous energy accompanies her on the last ten steps of her walk.

She is entirely out of her element here. The art of seduction is not something she's familiar with; this is more Lark's territory. Darbie's the kind of girl guys want to take home to meet their mothers, whereas Lark is more the kind of girl that guys just want to take home. She approaches the wooden steps and grabs hold of the railing. "Be cool. Be caszh," whispers Darbie to herself. Darbie lifts her foot to make the first step.

A sharp pang of guilt rushes over her and instead of placing her foot on that first step, she sets it back down. Using Walker like this weighs heavily on her conscience. She's disgusted with herself. Toying with his emotions so she can get what she wants is just so conniving, deceitful, and manipulative. She's already lost her job; jeopardizing his for personal gain is unforgivably selfish. Darbie gazes back up the stairs to Walker's place, feeling inept and downright evil, she chickens out and does an abrupt about-face.

Flustered, Lark, ready to object, opens her mouth when a burly German Shepherd, Gus, starts ferociously barking and charges Darbie.

A floodlight turns on, the front door to the carriage house flings open, and out steps a ripped, shirtless Walker. He's barefoot, in jeans, and pulling on a t-shirt. "Gus, hush! Get!" Gus releases a whimper and heads off out of sight. Walker climbs down the steps.

Growling, Gus turns his full attention to Lark. She sticks the real pie in the thick of some branches, kicks off her flip-flops, and climbs a mature magnolia tree in the shadows. She settles herself in and throws some pie crust down, which Gus gobbles up.

"Sorry, neighbor's dog. Darbie?"

Darbie, still reeling from the sight of his chiseled body, is so distracted she can't think straight. *People* magazine's "Sexiest Man Alive" has got nothing on Walker. Caught in a trance, she bites down on her lip.

"Darbie?" he repeats, snapping his fingers at her catatonic face.

Now that the moment has arrived for her to deliver her well-rehearsed opening line, she's at a loss for words and puzzled about her purpose. Darbie struggles to form a complete sentence in her mind. "Huh? W-Walker?" she stutters, royally tripping over her once memorized speech, "err... Hey, Walker. I was in the neighborhood and thought I'd do you — bring you one of my momma's blackberry pies." What a nightmare. She'd like to dive into the bushes and hide with Lark or off a cliff. Either sound like a better option than this humiliation.

Walker's lips curl at the edges. Trying not to gloat that his physique is causing Darbie to short circuit, he responds, "Is that right? Blackberry pie. Well. Well. Thank you kindly. That there is my favorite."

"Sorry to impose on you like this. I just wanted to thank you for bringing me my car, is all," Darbie explains, practically drooling. She intentionally plays with the beads on her bracelet, a self-soothing mechanism for slowing her heart rate.

"Oh, no problem. Happy to oblige. Your roommate gave me a lift back. She insisted we go down Ghost Road so she could flash her headlights six times at some old oak tree with a knot in it that kinda looked like a face."

"Were you scared?"

Closing the space between them, Walker leans into the conversation. "Terrified. She was already screaming by the second flash. The way she high-tailed it out of there, I thought we were gonna be goners, for sure," laughs Walker, touching Darbie's arm.

Lark totters on a branch when her worst nightmare comes true. She spots a huge web holding a rather menacing looking yellow garden spider just above her head. Shifting away, Lark contorts her body. Desperate, she too attempts to soothe herself with one of Darbie's relaxation techniques. Inhaling deeply, she begins whispering to herself, "Ten Mississippi, nine Mississippi, eight Mississippi, seven Mississippi..." The eight-legged creature descends. Just when Lark thought things couldn't get worse, as she starts to slide away, she hears buzzing. Alarmed, she glances down at her foot. It's dangling next to an active beehive. In her present state, Lark's finding it enormously difficult not to scream like a banshee. As a last resort, she begins reciting *Mary Had a Little Lamb*.

Walker rubs his chin as an intriguing thought occurs to him. The corners of his mouth curl again, revealing his perfectly straight teeth. "How did you know where I live? Are you — stalking me?"

The wonderment of Walker's dazzling smile causes Darbie's heart to flutter in a way she'd long forgotten possible. She can't help but return his smile as his warms her from the tip of her nose to the ends of her toes. Her cheeks flush with a rosy glow.

An expression of mischievous contemplation crosses her face; she bashfully replies, "Maybe," topping off her response with a nervous giggle.

"Maybe," he repeats, eagerly raising his eyebrows.

"Momma said you'd mentioned when you called that you were renting the carriage house at the Avery plantation."

"Your momma certainly did her due-diligence before handing over your address."

"Yeah, she's pretty nosy."

"Protective, actually. I thought it was sweet," Walker clarifies.

Darbie sarcastically snickers. Self-conscience, she catches the negative tone in her laugh and nips it in the bud, ending abruptly with a rather humiliating snort.

"Would you like to come in?" Walker reaches for the pie pan.

"It's such a nice night for stargazing. I thought maybe we could sit over on the chaise lounge." Darbie gestures to the large enough for two chaise lounge, seductively nestled amid the adjacent lush formal garden. It's surrounded by a cypress and boxwood formed privacy wall, which makes it feel alluringly secretive. She sets the pie pan down on a wrought iron table beside the chaise lounge.

"Tastes better if you let it cool a little bit." Darbie reclines on the mattress like cushion and gives Walker a come-hither look, patting the spot next to her. Bewitched, he obliges. He sits close, real close; they're almost touching. Darbie scooches over a smidge, so his rippling biceps graze her arm. His body heat makes her feel warm all over. Walker smells good, amazing actually. He smells clean, irresistibly so. She decides he must've just gotten out of the shower. Darbie steals a glance. His hair appears to be slightly damp. That would explain the no shirt, no shoes look. She can't believe how hot he looked in a pair of jeans and nothing else. Salivating, she swallows hard, too hard; it's more of a gulp. They gaze up at the starry night's sky together before she breaks the silence.

"Sorry about Monday," she apologizes.

Walker chuckles. "That was quite an entertaining show."

Darbie nervously giggles a tad too long.

"The gallery is dull without you. Nothing pretty to look at."

"Nice," whispers Lark to herself, snooping. The bloodsucker descends closer anchored to his classic circular formed web. Lark gasps and closes her eyes tight. She slowly opens them one at a time as the eight-legged creature is about to land on her nose. Twisting her face, Lark releases a silent scream. In a tizzy, she flails her arms, swats at it, kicks the hive with her foot, loses her balance, and falls out of the magnolia tree. She lands on a bed of early blooming Black-eyed Susans, coneflowers, and Shasta daisies, squashing them flat. Sticky, gooey honey covers her bare-skinned foot. Vindictive bees swarm her. *Buzz!*

Alert to some sort of commotion, presumably involving Gus, Walker starts to rotate his head in Lark's direction. Thinking fast, Darbie grabs his face and feverishly kisses him in a way that makes him forget anything exists other than her. He tastes yum-my — minty fresh.

Coming up for air, she releases him, looking a little windswept. She's never dared to seize the moment by attempted to dominate a man like this before. No doubt about it, Darbie's more of a wait for the guy to make the first move kind of a girl. "Sorry, I — I hope that wasn't too forward of me."

"You're apologizing. Are you kidding?" Aroused, he stares at her mouth, longingly.

Buzz! Giving the bees a run for their money, Lark sprints barefoot in zigzag patterns out in the open. She loses the bees. That's when Gus goes in for the kill. Chasing her like she's a doggy treat on roller skates. Darbie watches in horror over Walker's unsuspecting shoulder.

Cornered by boxwoods, Gus charges Lark. Bracing herself for impact, she flinches and sticks her hands out in defense. Gus tramples her, knocking her over onto the grass, and doing a one-eighty, he zeros in on her foot. Going to town, he aggressively licks her arch. Slathering the balls of her feet and digging into the space between her toes with his large wet slithering tongue, Gus licks her clean. Hysteria courses through Lark's body as she spasms and convulses under the tickle torturer. Dying to release a cackle, she covers her mouth to muffle the frenzy of laughter building within her.

Walker breaks his gaze and yet again begins to turn in Lark's direction. Suddenly, Darbie pushes him backward on the chaise lounge and straddles him. Acting impulsively, she kisses him hard, and he pulls her close. She feels his lips moving against hers, moving with hers — in perfect rhythm. He runs his hands down her back onto the exposed skin between the bottom of her shirt and the top of her pants. Darbie relaxes into him. Her fingers are woven in his thick hair as he eagerly kisses her neck. Any trepidation she felt earlier melts away in his strong arms. Walker kisses her softly on the lips a couple of times, teasing her. He pauses long enough to see the wanting in her eyes. Taking charge, he kisses her with unmitigated passion.

Her willpower and focus are rapidly diminishing. Consumed with a fury of raw sensual desires, she yearns to get even closer to him. She's seen the delicious body beneath that t-shirt. All she wants to do is rip it off.

Instead, she forcibly snaps out of her lustful state when something sure to leave a mark pinches her right leg. Regaining her wits, she glides her hand onto his and tries to direct it towards the table, but he rolls her over. His hands are everywhere. Although his eyes are closed tight, hers are wide open. She looks frantic when she discovers the real pie sitting on the table instead of the towel-wrapped decoy. Then, Lark's hands magically appear from under the chaise lounge, holding it close to Darbie and Walker. Knowing the plaster is about to set, Darbie shoves his thumb into the decoy. Completing the bait and switch, Lark disappears into the dark with the thumb mold. Walker's eyes fly open, and he studies his hand. "What was that?"

"You accidentally stuck your thumb in the pie." Before he can get a good look at it, Darbie instantaneously sucks on his thumb titillating him further. His eyes widen with excitement. Then she abruptly jumps up, planting both feet firmly on the ground, and backs away. "Uh, I — I gotta go. Early morning with the — job hunt and all. Thanks again. Bye, Walker."

Darbie straightens her top and saunters off into the night. Walker sits up, dazed and confused. "Sure, anytime. Call me Ja-" Scanning the general direction of her last words, he realizes he's alone. Throwing his arms up, he cups the back of his head with his interlaced fingers and leans back, sprawling out on the chaise lounge. Crossing his ankles, he gazes up at the crystal clear night sky. A shooting star soars past him. "Best night ever!"

Propelling herself forward with each step, Darbie uses every ounce of her willpower as she rushes to catch up with Lark. She aches to stay here with Walker. Her only desire is to scrap her and Lark's plan, do an about-face and return to Walker's eager arms.

Darbie knows she should feel downright terrible, just awful, for tricking Walker in the scandalous way she did. She used him appallingly and in doing so, flushed her ethics right down the toilet along with the last of her self respect and dignity. It's just that the blissful happiness of their moment under the stars is presently clouding her mind with a frenzy of unladylike thoughts. Currently, it's making it awfully difficult to tap into those feelings of guilt. Instead, a super huge smile stretches across her fiercely ecstatic face.

Picking up the pace of her strides, she finds Lark running in circles around the outer perimeter of the driveway like a crazy woman trying to get a flip-flop out of Gus's mouth.

Darbie giggles, and then her face suddenly turns sour. She spits and licks her shirt. "Ew. Yuck!"

"Bad kisser, eh?" asks Lark, yanking her mauled flip-flop free.

"I have plaster in my mouth."

"Kinky."

***

Bolt cutters slice through the motel's door chain like butter. A brute force kick slams Dante's motel door into a door stopper, sending it rebounding back on Tony's already broken nose with severe force making a sickening crunch. He whimpers in pain while accidentally swinging the bolt cutter into the knee of Simmon's monstrously huge goon. The beastly behemoth crumbles in torment. Dante grabs his 9mm pistol off the nightstand, ready to put an end to any trouble headed his way.

"Incompetent ingrates," belittles Simmons, a waif of a man in his sixties, as he raps his goon and Tony on the back of their heads with his cane. "Lower your weapon, Dante," he orders.

"Sorry, boss. Didn't know it was you," apologizes Dante, nervously setting his gun back down.

"Look who's about to get the last laugh this time. It's on now, Dante. No more Mr. Nice guy. You're gonna pay for what you did!" vows Tony, smugly sitting down in a chair like he owns the place. He twists the end of a tissue and shoves it up his left nasal passage stopping the blood flow.

"You think I'm afraid of you, kid? I've seen bunny rabbits scarier than you." taunts Dante.

"I brought reinforcements this time," Tony states, tapping on his forehead, indicating that he's a genius for using his thinker. "What should we do first, Uncle? Shall I cut off his big toe?"

"Shut up, Tony. I ain't your uncle. I thought you said it wasn't a fair fight. Look what you did to Dante."

"Huh? My pa is your brother. And I didn't-"

"I said, shut up! You think just 'cause my imbecile of a brother married your dim wit, bimbo ma five years ago that makes us kin? We ain't blood. I'm not even Italian." He wipes the sweat from his brow with a folded handkerchief. "You dragged me all the way down here for this; I ought to beat you myself. I've known Dante here for thirty years. He's more like family to me than you'll ever be," shares Simmons. Sulking, Tony sinks into the chair, quiet as a mouse. Simmons's goon rests at the foot of the mattress on top of a folded down bedspread nursing his sore knee like an overgrown man child.

"I explained in layman's terms to Tony that I'm fine. I'm sorry he wasted your valuable time."

"Me too. If that is indeed true, a lot is riding on this one, Dante. I needed to see for myself if you're capable of performing your duties," explains Simmons, picking up a pill container that reads *Calcium*. Never wanting to reveal his weaknesses, Dante always disguises his prescription medications in vitamin containers. Pulling the wrapper off a plastic cup, Simmons asks, "Mind if I take one of these? Osteoporosis runs in my family."

"Knock yourself out. With all due respect, sir, I've never let you down once in all these years. Rest assured, you'll have the Banksy by week's end. You have my word."

Simmons removes the plastic cover to a flimsy complementary motel cup, fills it with tap water, and swallows a pill. Pausing before the mirror, he picks up Dante's comb, runs water on it, and combs it through his own hair, styling it. Glancing around, Simmons strolls over to the photo collage wall and reviews its imagery. He peeks inside Dante's duffle bag with a satisfied look. "Everything seems to be in order — good enough for me. Wish I'd gotten here earlier. I would've liked to have seen you wipe the floor with Tony." Simmon's faith in Dante seems renewed. He shakes hands with him and departs with his goon nipping at his tail like a well-trained lap dog.

Tony follows closely behind them. Dante grabs his arm, preventing him from escaping. While maintaining his composure, his cheek muscle twitches ever so slightly as he makes a faint deep snarl sound when he exhales. He's so angry he could spit nails. "I don't appreciate you trying to sabotage my whole plan. You don't seem to play by the rules. What you did is an act of treason that I will not soon forget. You're not capable of running with the big boys. I suggest you find a new line of work and leave well enough alone," he indicates, squeezing Tony's arm tighter. "Or it will be you who will end up missing a lot more than just your big toe," he threatens in a low voice, drawing a line on his neck with his finger.

Tony shudders and swallows hard, catching the full meaning of his words. Dante releases his arm and Tony slips out the door looking like he might pee in his pants.

CHAPTER 11

L ark flings back a tattered, moth-eaten dressing room curtain and sashays out into the showroom of a thrift store which reeks like dirty socks and aged cheese. She parades in front of a full-length mirror wearing black fishnets, a short black leather skirt with matching halter top, elbow-length black satin gloves, black lipstick, and black stilettos. Darbie flings back the mangy curtain next to her and struts out wearing an oversized, frumpy black jogging suit, ski mask, and black combat boots. They turn and look at one another. Puckering their lips off-center, they scrutinize the appearance of each other. "No!" they forbid in unison. Both girls do an abrupt one-eighty and return to their designated dressing rooms.

This time they fling the curtains open simultaneously. Both are dressed in all black again. Lark has on jeans, a tank top with a leather jacket, a beanie, and Mary Janes. Darbie's wearing leggings, a fitted running jacket with thumb holes, canvas shoes, and her daddy's Ray-Ban sunglasses. They step out at the same time. Spinning on their heels, they turn to examine one another. "Perfect!" they harmoniously praise.

***

Lark drives the RV to the far back perimeter of the rear parking lot behind the Banquet Hall. The lot appears altogether deserted. She hops out and pulls a release lever. The back of the RV falls, forming a ramp. Darbie drives Isetta down the ramp onto the Bermuda grass and enters a hiking trail-head. Following the tree-lined path, she drives a little ways, pulls off in the woods, and throws the camouflage tarp she found by the deer stand over her car.

***

An army of volunteers gathers at the campus banquet. The preparations are in full swing with decorations and an assortment of catered food for the alumni homecoming party tonight. The Mardi Gras theme is glaringly evident with a kaleidoscope of green, yellow, and purple color schemes invading every nook and cranny. Darbie and Lark arrive and approach a group of women they recognize. "Hey, Ladies," greets Darbie. "We are at your full disposal. How can we help?" Everyone sports casual spirit apparel except for Chrystal, the leader of the minions, who's dressed in her Sunday best.

Lacey, who wears her heart on her sleeve, releases a high pitch squeal. "Darbie and Lark!" She squeezes them so tight their eyes bulge like Darbie's stress ball. "Aren't you a sight for sore eyes?" joyfully remarks Lacey, holding on a tad too long before finally turning them loose.

Natasha, smacking on gum, leers at them. "Look at you two. Y'all look exactly the same."

Chrystal eyes them with uppity condemnation. "I guess some people never change."

Lark returns a dig. "Congrats, Chrystal. When are you due?"

"I'm not pregnant!" protests Chrystal, sucking in her muffin top.

"My bad."

Bragging, Chrystal shows pics on her phone. "I do have two beautiful children, though. And Hudson just made partner," she raves.

Darbie reviews them. "Well, isn't that nice."

Lacey takes a quick peek. "Precious."

Natasha hardly glances in Chrystal's direction. "Thanks for sharing."

Lark, unimpressed, remembers the purpose of this cattle call. "Wanna take a selfie?"

"Always. Let's just turn my filter on," affirms Chrystal in her element. They all strike a pose. *Click.*

"Ladies, why don't you go hang these banners," orders Chrystal, tapping a pile of them stacked on the parquet floor with the tip of her strappy high heel sandal.

"Super," Lark responds.

Working as a team, the girls grab a ladder and a couple of banners. "We don't have time for this garbage," Lark sighs, exasperated.

Darbie nods and gestures to two women. "Heya, Ladies! We just got pulled to go see about a melting ice sculpture that got dropped off at the theater by mistake."

"Oh dear," respond the women simultaneously.

"Chrystal's gonna need y'all to take over hanging these banners," directs Darbie.

"Of course," oblige the two women in sync.

"Y'all are the best." Lark slides in between both ladies. "How about a quick photo op? Say, cheese." *Click.*

***

Darbie and Lark lay on top of the Anderson Fine Arts building's roof, munching on a bag of potato chips they snagged from the banquet hall. They observe the art gallery. Adjusting the tripod to its lowest setting, they take turns peering through the lens of the telescope that Darbie confiscated from the deer stand. They watch as Bernice and the new hire leave the gallery.

"Right on time. I wonder how the opening went," says Darbie in a curious tone.

"Who cares? Where's that tasty new beau of yours?" questions Lark, getting antsy.

"Walker?" Darbie asks, playing dumb. "He's always the last one out."

"Yes, of course, Walker." Lark gives Darbie a half-smile. "Mmm-mm. He is fine as wine. Say, how would you rate his kiss on a scale of one to ten? One being it was like kissing the tenant from 2B, ten being it made your panties blush," she shamelessly pries.

"Lark!"

"What? It's not healthy the way you keep everything all bundled up inside."

"No, I don't," denies Darbie, sitting up, folding her arms in objection.

"Darbie, you didn't cry at your dad's funeral."

"Everybody grieves differently," responds Darbie.

"You didn't go off on your fiancé when you caught him playing pin the tail on the donkey with our roommate."

"They broke my heart. Nothing I could say would've changed that."

"No, but it might've made you feel better."

"Eh." Darbie gives a dismissive shrug.

"You never even got mad at me for losing the apartment and all of our stuff."

"I laid awake that first night thinking of ten different ways to murder you."

"For real? What were they?" pleads Lark, laughing.

Darbie shakes her head 'no.'

"Come on. Just tell me one," begs Lark, staring through the telescopic lens.

"I thought about ramming a can of Vienna sausages down your throat. Then beating you to death with one of your high-heels and dumping your body out on Ghost Road."

Lark gulps. "On second thought, it's probably best if I don't know. Seeing as how we sleep in the same quarters and all."

In her heart, Darbie knows Lark is right. She should speak her mind more. To her, it's not about taking the high road. Drama just isn't a genre she buys. She despises conflict and avoids confrontation at all costs. As for Lark's mistakes, Darbie takes more of the "it is what it is" approach. In Clay's case, her response had been to simply walk away. She knew enough from dating that if someone makes it clear they're into someone else or that they just aren't feeling it anymore, you should listen. She couldn't make someone love her back. They either did, or they didn't. No ifs, ands, or buts about it, she didn't want to be with someone who didn't want to be with her, and she certainly wasn't going to try to convince them they felt something they didn't, so why fight for it.

Unfortunately, with Clay, he went straight for the "show, don't tell" method. This tactic proved painful for Darbie. It also seared a visual image into her mind that even time hasn't extinguished. She had it all planned out for them, married by twenty-eight and pregnant by thirty. They were supposed to grow old together. The blurry mental picture of what their lives were pre-supposed to be lays torn and hidden deep inside a hollow chamber in her heart once reserved for him. She's yet to fill it with another.

"There he is, Mr. Easy-on-the-eyes." Lark abruptly interrupts Darbie's thoughts, pointing out Walker as he leaves the gallery. They watch him drive off in a white F-150 pickup truck. Darbie's heart does a somersault staring after him. In a jiffy, they both assume a ready position.

Lark catches sight of Darbie's cheeks flushing. "Man, you've got it bad. That must have been some good smooching."

"Alright, if you really must know-"

"Yeah." Lark smiles.

"I suppose in the spirit of full disclosure-"

"Uh-huh," nods Lark, rubbing her hands together.

"On a scale of one to ten-"

"Mm-hmm," encourages Lark.

"I'd give it a twelve," beams Darbie.

"I knew it!" Lark slaps her hands together.

"Enough gabbing. It's time to commence operation, 'Take Out the Video Cameras'," declares Darbie. Her face turns serious, and her eyes focus on her intended target, a camera fixed to a light pole.

Playing a caddie's role, Lark hands Darbie her golf club and sets a golf ball down on top of a tee. Darbie grips the driver using a conventional reverse-overlap style, takes the stance of a professional, and swings like Tiger Woods. The ball's velocity, launch angle, and spin rate align for perfect trajectory creating optimum impact. She eradicates a parking lot camera in one swift blow. Shards of glass rain down on the asphalt below. "Beautiful," cheers Lark.

Darbie points out precise coordinates in the distance. "The hiking trail picks up behind the dorm parking lot. That's where I left Isetta." With aerodynamic optimization, they repeat this process twice, taking out two additional cameras. "Are you ready to get this show on the road?" asks Darbie.

Lark rarin' to go, rubs her hands together. "Honey, I was born ready."

Facing one another, they go to bump tummies but bump boobs instead. Both grab their breasts. "Ow," they groan.

"I got them both this time. Maybe now they'll finally be the same size," teases Lark. They rappel down off the back of the building.

"You know, we really could've just taken the stairs back down," chimes Darbie, trying not to look at the ground below.

***

Pine bark mulch digs into the palms of Darbie and Lark's hands as they crawl behind a string of compact boxwood bushes over to the gallery's back door. Laying on their bellies, they wait. Pink and purple silk eye masks with ruffles and eye holes cut into them partially obscure their faces. Loudly beeping, a garbage truck backs up to angle itself ahead of a dumpster, obscuring the security camera's view of the gallery's door.

"Now!" commands Darbie.

In stealth mode, the girls readily make a break for the door as the garbage truck slowly lifts the dumpster. Darbie swipes the makeshift key-card while Lark pulls a silicone thumb created from the plaster mold out of her front pocket. She hoovers it in front of her pelvis. "Check it out. World's smallest ding-dong." She chuckles.

"Grow up! Only you would look at something like that and make it gross." Darbie holds the palm of her hand out like an impatient mother, and Lark relinquishes the thumb to her.

"Everyone thinks like that, Darbie. Everyone. Not to worry, God is a fair guy; for every itty bitty willy, there is an even teeny tinier flower looking for it. Just ask Hector."

Fighting a giggle, Darbie jovially swats Lark's shoulder as she scans the thumb. "The camera's view is only waist high on this one," reminds Darbie.

"Righto," confirms Lark, giving a thumbs up.

Mirroring her, Darbie holds the thumb mold up.

Darbie opens the door, and they surreptitiously drop to their knees as the dumpster lowers. Infiltrating the building, they crawl catlike down a hallway over to the sleek frosted glass top reception desk. With the sting of carpet burn fresh on their knees and their backs to the counter, they squat. Covertly pointing to her eyes and then over her shoulder, Darbie pinpoints a camera. Giving a reassuring nod, Lark withdraws a compact mirror and a paintball gun from her backpack. She precisely angles the mirror while Darbie examines its reflection and points the toy weapon backward over the desk's ledge. She aims and fires. Jittery, her angle is a little too low. She misses and hits the abstract action painting. Fortunately, the splatter mark blends in seamlessly with the painting's other vivid splashes of color. Exhaling slowly, she concentrates, tries again, and creams the camera's lens.

Accessing a janitor's closet, Darbie uproots a large trash can off its rolling base. They wheel the mobile platform to the entrance of the Banksy exhibit room. With their backs pressed to the wall just outside the passageway, Darbie clandestinely points to her eyes and then over her shoulder to the left. Lark positions the mirror, and Darbie skillfully shoots the camera with the paintball gun. Taking long strides like a ninja warrior into the room, Darbie inspects the perimeter. Deeming the area safe, she signals Lark with the 'all clear' cue. Receiving the green light, Lark nods and approaches before briefly hesitating at the threshold, staring at the spotlighted Banksy manhole cover display. The circular shape has been skillfully transformed into one large red drippy peace sign, including his trademark stenciled white rat wearing a parachute backpack. Upon closer inspection, she notices that the painted rodent is holding a spray can and thus is depicted as the culprit of the spray-painted peace sign. "It really is something."

Darbie pauses to examine the masterpiece. "Yes. Quite extraordinary," she agrees with enthusiasm.

"Still, two million dollars for a manhole cover."

"It's unorthodox. The imagery and stencil technique are consistent with Banksy's signature political activist style. He deviated from his normal mediums: walls, signs, money. Don't get me wrong, his portfolio is quite diverse. He does film and three-dimensional stuff too. But this piece is special. This piece is the first of its kind found after the shredding incident, increasing its value drastically."

"Wicked." Lark enthusiastically nods, grinning.

"Indeed. His style is so eccentric. Astonishing to think that folks paint over Banksy's art all the time. Vandalism in their eyes."

"Chumps." Lark approaches the Banksy and sets the rolling base down. "You grab one end. I'll get the other."

"No. Wait. It has a weighted alarm," warns Darbie. She pirouettes towards the alarm, slides the card, and scans the thumb. The girls grip each side of the manhole cover. "Ready. One, two, three. Lift," she instructs. Together the girls lift it a few inches and moan.

"Abort. Abort. Abort," shrieks Lark. They carefully lower it back down, panting. "I think my tampon just fell out," reveals Lark.

"Let's try again. Wide stance — good posture — lift slow — hold it close to your body — use your legs — and lower," instructs Darbie.

Darbie and Lark set it down on the base and roll it up towards the front entrance. Overcompensating a turn, they bump smack-dab into a pedestal causing the Venetian Vase on top to teeter-totter. Darbie steadies it. "That was close," she whispers, nearly having a heart attack. Sweating bullets, Darbie reaches in her jacket pocket, extracting the key-card and silicone thumb. She hands them both to Lark. "Stick these in your bag. I'm afraid I'll lose them." Darbie yanks a tablecloth off the entry table and cleverly drapes it over herself. Peering out the main entrance's glass door, she sees a cluster of onlookers in her direct line of vision and scraps her original getaway plan.

On the fly, she contrives a new course of action and wheels the Banksy over to an employee exit door. This particular exit previously served strictly as a fire exit door with a built-in alarm that would sound upon opening. Too many illiterate students unintentionally set off the fire alarm exiting the gallery that way. Fire trucks and ambulances became a regular fixture in the parking lot. Darbie got on a first-name basis with all the first responders who were dispatched there at least twice a week. The school finally had to disable the door's built-in alarm system. Thankful their departure won't alert fire and rescue, she opens the door and pushes the base out onto the concrete landing.

Lark makes sure to be vigilant while placing the key-card in the small side zipper compartment of her bag. However, her nervous excitement over being in the home stretch causes her to suffer a momentary case of butterfingers; she inadvertently drops the thumb. It thumps the ground and bounces. Scrambling, she almost catches it but misses, and it whops the floor again, sending it bouncing over and over again until alas it ceases. Chasing it the whole way, she breathes a sigh of relief as she bends, picks it up, and gingerly crams it in her bag. In her haste, she swings the backpack on a little too overzealously. Unbeknownst to her, the bag hits a pedestal causing it to wobble back and forth. She returns to Darbie, ducks under the tablecloth, and then vacates the premises.

Inside, the stand continues to rock. It falls into the pedestal next to it, generating a domino effect of pedestals and pieces of art crashing and clamoring onto the floor, leaving the place in complete shambles.

CHAPTER 12

A cluster of tourists gathers in front of a ghost tour guide gripping flashlights and cameras with their backs to the art gallery. Everyone appears fully engrossed in the ghoulish tale articulated by their guide except for an unquestionably bored four-year-old little boy, Billy. "They sometimes say late at night you can see the apparition of Jebediah Pucket's horse searching for his master," eerily informs the guide.

***

Cloaked by the tablecloth, Lark and Darbie sit on the manhole cover and rolling base. "Number seventeen, commit a felony," announces Lark proudly. They hastily push-off, roll down the wheelchair ramp and sidewalk like a bat out of hell or a horse searching for his master and zip across the crosswalk.

The tour guide continues to divulge every gory detail of the spooky ghost story to his captive audiences. Young Billy is the lone spectator to Darbie and Lark's white blur streaking through the night. Terrified, he endlessly tugs on his mother's maxi skirt to no avail crying, "Mommy, Mommy, Mommy."

"Stop that, Billy," she scolds, pushing his hand away.

"But, Mommy!"

"Shhhhh. Listen to the story. If you're a good little boy and you listen, you might see a ghost," informs his mother.

As they zoom along, Darbie peeks the paintball gun out from underneath their draped concealment. She takes out the lens of a camera located on the dorm. Their speed increases the closer they get to their destination. They're hopelessly barreling towards calamity. "How do we make it stop?" asks Lark, her eyes widening by the second.

"I didn't think that through. I'm kinda flying by the seat of my pants here," admits Darbie.

"You can say that again. Aim for the bushes."

"Those are holly bushes!" Darbie assumes the tornado drill position and protectively shields her head. Lark buries her face in Darbie's back, bracing herself for maximum impact. By the skin of their teeth, they hit a section of tactile pavers and come to a rest just shy of the dorm's side doors. In nothing flat, they remove the tablecloth revealing their static hair that's sticking up in every direction. This reminds the girls of the time they went to the science museum and touched a static electricity plasma ball lamp.

Lark elated to be unscathed, literally kisses the ground.

Darbie scouts out the call box. "Who do I call? What do I say?" asks Darbie.

Lark scans the numbers and points to one at random. "Amber Greene. Think like a college student."

Darbie dials Amber Greene's number. "Hello. Who is it?" asks Amber Greene.

"Willy's. Some hot guy ordered you a pizza."

Buzz. The door unlocks. Lark checks to see if the coast is clear. They duck inside, pulling the Banksy along with them. The back wheel gets caught on the lip of the door frame and snaps off along with a chunk of the base. The Banksy slides off clamoring on the gritty cement. The girls heave it inside onto the linoleum floor.

"Can you fix the base?" Darbie asks, trying to fit the impossibly broken pieces back together like a puzzle.

"Uh...No."

"Okay. This presents a challenge. Maybe we can find another trash can," suggests Darbie.

"Let's slide it into this corner."

They fold the linen tablecloth and discreetly cover the Banksy. Then, they carefully place the ficus tree that was in the corner on top of it. Both rigorously check unlocked doors and bathrooms on both sides of the hall.

Coming up empty, Darbie tosses her hands up in the air, "Nothing."

"Me either," states Lark, parroting Darbie's body language.

Darbie checks the time on her watch. "It's a quarter 'til nine o'clock."

"Plenty of time," reassures Lark.

Up ahead, they hear banging and a whimper. Curious, Darbie and Lark investigate the disturbance.

The girls discover a small communal area with ugly as sin, very basic, dated dorm couches and tables. Daisy, an irate girl in a wheelchair, deliberately rams her motorized chair into the furniture. While another girl, Caroline, lays her head on a round table and weeps.

"Girls? What's the major malfunction?" asks Lark.

"I'm losing my mind because my roommate is completely nuts," indignantly declares Daisy, the girl in the wheelchair. Her elbow-length, stick-straight blonde hair frames her supermodel face and body.

"Been there, my friend," sympathizes Darbie.

"I think she can hear you." Lark eyes the hysterical girl at the table.

"That's not her," clarifies Daisy.

"Okay. We'll get to her in a minute. What's the problem with your roommate?" asks Darbie.

"Everything!" Daisy swivels her chair around. "She uses my toothbrush! She walks around naked all the time. She sits bare butt on my bed to put her socks on!"

"That's not hygienic," replies Darbie, disgusted, and watching her toes as Daisy — plowing forward — misses them by a hair.

"Well, that's not even the right order. Socks are last. The skirt goes first," reasons Lark.

"Underwear goes first, Lark," Darbie corrects with a half-grin.

"She buried our silverware in the front flowerbed. She uses a jar to save all of her toenail clippings. She's in there right now snoring like a freight train. I haven't slept in a month," she bellows, wheeling her chair back around.

"She sounds awful." Darbie glances at Lark. "I can empathize."

Lark smirks and hands Caroline, the girl sniffling at the round table, a tissue box that was sitting on the coffee table. The poor kid has been wiping her nose on her sleeve, leaving snail trails up and down her arm. "And what about you, crocodile tears?"

"Thanks." Covering each nostril one at a time, Caroline blows her nose in a Kleenex. Minus the snot, she's attractive in a homely kind of way. "My name is Caroline, and my roommate's in the shower — naked — with my boyfriend."

"Yep, I think I caught a little sneak peek of Adam and Eve a minute ago," recalls Lark.

"It's my fault," explains Caroline, waving a fresh tissue about like a damsel in distress from some old picture-show.

Lark rolls her eyes and directs them at Darbie. "Oh brother. Why do women always blame themselves?" It's more of a rhetorical question, but Caroline half-answers back.

Caroline sniffles, "No. He wanted to have a three-way."

"And you said no. Good for you," praises Darbie, rubbing her on the back.

"No," whimpers Caroline, shrugging Darbie off and moving from the chair to a couch. Sitting sideways, Caroline folds her knees up to her chest and wraps her arms around them. "I said yes." Her voice rises into a hysteria level.

Darbie and Lark are aghast.

Darbie takes a step backward. "This is the problem with the youth of today," judges Darbie, shaking her head. She's glad she always wears flip-flops in a public shower.

"Ain't nobody got any sense," agrees Lark.

Troubled, Darby decides she's going to have a little "come to Jesus" session with Caroline. "Ya know, a shower is only big enough for one person," alludes Darbie.

"Two is pushing it and three, well..." elaborates Lark, shrugging.

"Never agree to a such a thing," lectures Darbie. Caroline blows her nose again.

Lark nods, agreeing, "Rookie mistake." She wraps a random blanket draped over the couch around Caroline.

Impossible to console, Caroline continues to cry. She stands up, allowing the fleece blanket to fall off her shoulders and back. Swept up in her emotions, the pitiful girl shuffles across the linoleum with her head hung low, dragging the blanket behind her like Linus from *Peanuts*. She returns to her chair at the table. Despite her current state, she is naturally lovely.

"Especially with someone who has bigger ta-tas than you," states Lark. Everyone shoots Lark a questioning look. "Sorry, but they were seriously ginormous."

Caroline ugly cries. "Noooo, that's not it." she sobs. Her voice is the lowest of low. She's reached her breaking point and is about to crack. It's up to the girls to help hold her together.

"Sorry. I thought maybe they kicked you out. What happened then?" pries Lark, feeling as though she's walking on eggshells. She takes a seat at the round table beside Caroline.

"I was on my way back from a Bible study when he called me up and asked if we could have a three-way with my roommate. I thought he meant a three-way phone call. He asked if I'd ever done one before, and I said no but that it sure sounded like fun. I had no idea it was — you know," she whispers, "sexual."

"No offenses, honey. But have you been living under a rock?" inquires Lark.

"I was homeschooled until college I'm saving myself for marriage."

Darbie breathes a sigh of relief. "That's wonderful! Bless your heart, though. Your parents didn't talk to you at all before they just sent you off to be a babe in the woods," empathizes Darbie.

"Huh?" asks Caroline, not following.

"It means you're just a kitten in a lion's den," explains Darbie.

"Uh, sorry. I'm from Ohio. I don't speak Southern," shares Caroline, shrugging her shoulders. "No offense."

"None taken," says Darbie.

"Like I was saying, I was supposed to live with my Great-Aunt Caroline, whom I'm named after, who's retired on Saint Simons Island, just down the coast. But last August, right before the start of the semester, she slipped and fell on the corner of an area rug and wound up breaking her hip and had to undergo total hip replacement surgery. She's got a long road to recovery, had to be placed in rehabilitation facility over in Brunswick," she pauses to catch her breath, "and once we came down here we realized the commute wasn't going to work, especially with all the construction traffic on I-95 so at the last minute, against their better judgment, my parents resolved to allow me to obtain campus residency with the understanding that I call them at least once a day," explains Caroline, stringing her words together at maximum velocity.

"Wow. There went 5 minutes of my life I'll never get back," quips Lark.

"Anyways, my boyfriend never called. Then I got this strange text that said to meet them in the dorm bathroom."

"That wasn't a red flag for you?" asks Darbie, utterly astonished.

"I thought maybe the acoustics were better in there. When I ran out screaming, Daisy here explained to me what three-way means." She adds another wadded up tissue to the pile before her on the table.

"This was obviously a trick," judges Darbie.

"What do you mean?" questions Caroline, confused.

"You were hopelessly clueless, and he used your naive state against you. He got you to agree to allow him to have sex with your roommate," points out Daisy.

"Yep. You gave her your blessing too," agrees Lark.

"It's the ultimate scheme," confirms Daisy, wheeling up to Caroline.

"A dirty trick," reiterates Darbie.

Lark talks dirty. "A dirty, dirty, dirty trick."

Caroline wails and throws her head back on the table, covering it with the blue blanket.

Darbie cuts her eyes at Lark. "Not helping!" she scolds.

"She's my roommate. I can't live with her anymore. I'm — I'm going to have to drop out of school. My life is over!"

"Oh, there, there... Sweet Caroline," sings Lark, patting her on the top of her draped head.

"I think we can help both you girls out." Caroline looks at her with big puppy eyes like she's a beacon in the dark, dismal void that is her life. "But we're gonna need one small favor," barters Lark.

"Two, actually," says Darbie, upping the ante.

***

In a somewhat evasive coup d'etat, Darbie and Lark sneak Daisy's slumbering roommate down the corridor on her bunk bed mattress to Caroline's room. Sleeping beauty snores in Lark's face as she's toting her. Lark winces, "Oh... her breath could kill an elephant." Tossing her and the mattress down, she frees a snack bag from under the girl's drooling face. "She needs to lay off the..." Lark reads the packaging, "...dried wild fish." Everybody shivers with disgust.

Just outside Daisy's room is another smaller manual wheelchair, which she quickly shifts into using her arms. Leaving her motorized chair in the corridor, she navigates inside her dorm room. Tickled pink, Daisy expeditiously performs a clean sweep of her room, collecting all of her roommate's bizarre para- phernalia and drops it off at her newfangled living quarters.

Crossing paths, Caroline gleefully totes her belongings, along with Darbie and Lark down the hall to Daisy's room. "Look at the size of this room!" she exclaims, spinning in circles with arms raised. The place is double the square footage as her last. It features separate twin beds, a double window, two long handicap accessible desks, and two full-size dressers. "And a walk-in clos- et!" shouts Caroline. She peeks in another adjoining room and flipping on the light switch. "And a private bathroom!" she squeals.

Daisy wheels into the room, catching Caroline's last enthusiastic statement. "One of the perks of being in the chair," shares Daisy, smiling.

"I've done died and gone to heaven," surmises Caroline.

"Listen to ya. You sound like a local yokel already!" encourages Daisy. "Mind if I put on 'The Avett Brothers' new album?"

"I love 'The Avett Brothers'!" pipes Caroline, pulling up her playlist on her laptop.

Perfectly matched, the girls boast identical Llama pillows and duvet covers. Daisy and Caroline, well suited, are blissfully happy and cozy in their new living arrangement, two peas in a pod.

"One more thing before we go," says Lark.

"What?" asks Darbie.

"We've got a little score to settle for one of our new friends," answers Lark.

With Daisy and Caroline preoccupied, Darbie and Lark sneak off down the hallway towards the communal bathroom. Lark cracks the swinging door just enough to check out the status of the two distracted occupants. There is a wall of toilet stalls on one side of the room and a section of shower stalls on the other. Lark can see the new couple's bare feet beneath the curtain's gap. And she catches a little bit of action as the fabric flutters about. "Ew. Cover your eyes." The vulgar noises coming from the stall would make a hooker blush. "No, make that your ears. Close your eyes and cover your ears."

Darbie gives Lark a one, two, three hand-gesture, and they bolt inside. Darbie snags the towels hanging on the hooks outside the stall, and she grabs the roommate's keys sitting on a bench. Lark scoops up both sets of clothing. Fast as their legs will carry them, they charge directly to Daisy and Caroline's ex-roommates' dorm room. They dump the contents they're carrying inside the room, lock the door, and hand the keys off to Daisy and Caroline.

Lark steals a glance at Darbie and whispers, "We oughta shove off."

CHAPTER 13

The Banksy rests on the seat of Daisy's motorized wheelchair in the dorm parking lot. Lark sits perched on top of the masterpiece, and Darbie stands astern, holding on tight. They once again fit right in as college students, wearing Caroline and Daisy's clothes. "The trailhead is back on the right. That's where I left Isetta," directs Darbie, extending her arm in the precise direction.

They reach the remote corner of the parking lot; it's a ghost town. Lark hands Darbie a walkie-talkie. "I knew these would come in handy. They're both set to the same channel."

Darbie rolls her eyes. "Hopefully, this will be the only time we get separated." She starts to take off.

"No, wait. We need code names," Lark insists with childlike enthusiasm.

Darbie stops abruptly and thinks. "Okay. I'm Anna and you're Elsa." She starts to set out again.

"Wait, I wanna be Anna," whines Lark.

Darbie freezes in place, releasing a long impatient sigh and yields, "Fine. I'm Elsa and you're Anna."

"Great. I'll wait here," responds Lark, satisfied.

Darbie turns on her flashlight, illuminating her path; she darts over to the trailhead. After briskly jogging a short distance down the winding dirt path, she locates her car. Once inside, Darbie tries to start the ignition, but nothing happens. Unfazed, she checks the gas switch, works the throttle, and turns the starter key once more, but again, nothing occurs. Perplexed, Darbie gets out to take a gander under the hood, which by design, is located on the rear side of the vehicle. She notices the engine compartment is already ajar. It's quiet. Eerily quiet. She notes the faint smell of cigarette smoke in the air and senses something is amiss as she opens the hood. There's a wire hanging loose from one of the components which Darbie knows absolutely zilch about how to fix. She desperately wishes she'd paid more attention to what her daddy did when he worked on Isetta. Leaves rustle on a nearby tree, breaking the silence, and she hears what sounds like a twig snapping underfoot. Her eyes dart around, but no one is there. A gust of wind whistling through the trees, blowing her hair about wildly. Racking her fingers through her tangled tendrils, she hurriedly moves the black elastic scrunchie from her wrist to her head, tucking loose strands of her baby-fine hair into a high ponytail. Upon closer inspection of her automobile, she observes that the rear end appears slightly lopsided. Shining the flashlight on the lower side, she discovers a hopelessly flat tire. Suddenly it dawns on her that the camouflage tarp is unaccounted for.

Panic-stricken, she holds down the push-to-talk button on her walkie-talkie and puts it to her mouth, "Man down, over!" She releases the button anticipating Lark's response, but there is nothing but static. Yet again, she holds the button down and reiterates, "I repeat, we have a man down! Over." Releasing the button, she hears indistinguishable static noise flowing through the handset. "Ugh." She bangs it on her the palm of her opposite hand. Venturing one last time, she holds the button down and asks, "Anna, do you copy, over?" Detecting the same relentless void static, she grows unnerved and resolves that something must be dreadfully awry. She sprints down the path and races out of the woods.

Horror-struck, Darbie skids to a halt when she beholds a black Lincoln with its trunk open, parked a few yards away from Lark. Dante, whose face and neck are swollen and infected, stands near his vehicle. He's pointing a 9MM pistol with a silencer at Lark. Her hands are raised above her head, and the walkie-talkie lays at her feet. Without hesitation, Darbie throws her hands up too. "Sir, I'll do whatever you want. Just don't hurt her," she pleads. Her voice quivers a tad in the midst of her shuddering involuntarily.

Dante's skin is all clammy and looking like he's running a fever. "You two amateurs are jeopardizing my entire operation." Staring at Darbie, he orders, "Get over there and help your partner put the Banksy in my car." He has a deep raspy voice, one that comes with decades of chain-smoking.

Darbie complies. "Yes, sir. You're the boss."

In vain, Darbie and Lark attempt to hoist the Banksy long enough to carry it to the second location. Grunting, they return it to the wheelchair, dropping it down on the seat. They both shake their strained wrists and knuckles in the air.

"Let's go, already," he barks, shaking his gun at them.

The girls try again but fail miserably. Dante curses and waves the firearm around in a hissy fit. Seizing the moment, Lark inconspicuously unzips her bag, which is hanging on the side of the seat.

"It's too heavy," whines Darbie.

"She has zero upper body strength," explains Lark. Darbie cuts her eyes at Lark. They both know who the weakest link is out of the two of them and it's not Darbie.

"Do I look like I was born yesterday?" hisses Dante with gilded eyes.

"No, sir. No, you do not," responds Lark, taking in the bags under his eyes accompanied by the weathered skin on his battered face.

"You got it out here. Stop messin' around and put it in my trunk."

The girls try yet again. In vain, they heave the manhole cover only to set it back down once more. Darbie catches sight of Lark as she clandestinely slips two darts out of the bag and into her back pocket.

"We didn't exactly carry it."

"How about I drive it to you?" suggests Darbie.

Dante yells, "Keep your hands where I can see them!"

Lark tentatively stares off into space, brainstorming. She perks up when an 'aha' thought occurs to her. "You could back your car up to us?"

"No," snaps Dante.

"How about you let Darbie hold the gun, and you can help me move it?" proposes Lark with her eyes steady and her voice calm.

Miffed they're undermining his intelligence, he steps closer to them and threatens, "Or maybe I kill one of you to let the other one know I'm serious."

A white van's headlights flip on, letting its presence be known, as the driver revs its engine and tears off straight for Dante. Dante instinctively turns his gun towards the oncoming vehicle. He fires a single shot at the windshield.

"Now!" orders Darbie.

Darbie instantaneously hops on the wheelchair and flees full speed ahead. Lark throws the first dart full tilt. It whizzes through the air and hits the back of Dante's hand, splitting a metacarpals bone and slicing a nerve. Crippled, he drops the gun and releases a deafening howl. The gun fires as it clammers to the ground; the bullet pops his tire. All the while, the out of control van crashes into the Lincoln, further distracting Dante. Darbie watches over her shoulder as the chaos unfolds in her wake. "Lark!" she screams, terrified for their safety and well being. "Let's get out of here!"

Lark rushes to catch up with Darbie and leaps on to the back of the wheelchair. She hurls the second dart, displaying excellent eye-hand coordination, and it hits Dante in the upper thigh. Ripping it out, he grunts as he stares down at both of his fresh wounds. Grateful to be alive, the girls flee the scene unscathed.

"Who was that guy? Is that our art thief?" asks Lark mystified.

"I don't think so. His voice sounded way different." Darbie checks her watch. "It's only 9:25 p.m. Our rendezvous isn't 'til midnight."

The wheelchair, losing momentum, slows to a crawl. "The 'low battery' light is on," observes Darbie.

"There's a bus stop up ahead."

"No! I-I can't do buses. Motion sickness," Darbie reminds.

"Relax. We aren't going far," dismisses Lark.

"Remember what happened in 4th grade — the Space Center field trip?"

Lark laughs. "Ronny Pinkard!"

"It's not funny. We didn't even make it two blocks from the school. I yacked all over that poor kid," recalls Darbie.

"Darbie, this is life or death. Take deep breaths. Focus on something up ahead. You'll be fine."

"Fine. The buses typically run in thirty-minute intervals," Darbie informs, creeping the dying wheelchair down the road.

"Perfect timing," chimes Lark, hopping off and walking faster than the motorized wheelchair; she easily beats Darbie there.

Lark and Darbie wait at the bus stop; every second feels like an eternity. Lark sits with her legs crossed. Her shaking foot vibrates the entire bench. Darbie snags a piece of grape gum from Lark's bag. Without warning, the bus stop's glass shatters into a million pieces. It rains down all around them. Shocked, they continuously scream and duck down. They take cover behind the bench.

Dante is in the distance, looking like something the cat dragged in. Hell-bent, he relentlessly limps towards them, holding his smoking gun with his uninjured hand. Fortunate for him, he is ambidextrous. Suffering the side-effects of yet another one of his spells, Dante sees double. He blinks hard and beats himself on the head with his own gun in a rather ludicrous attempt to get his eyes to focus.

The bus arrives and opens its doors. "Get on the bus!" orders Darbie. She's nervous they're an easy target, standing under the street light in the dark.

"Not without the Banksy!" insists Lark.

The handicap door opens, and the ramp starts to lower but gets stuck. The bus driver, older than dirt and slow as molasses, makes his way to the back of the bus. Disoriented, Dante fires another shot and hits the ramp. Darbie and Lark scream bloody murder and beat on the door. The oblivious bus driver smiles innocently at them and motions 'one minute.' They frantically pace. "You've gotta be kidding me with this," utters Darbie.

"We're sitting ducks," cries Lark. Dante discharges his firearm again, and the bullet clips the wheelchair. Lark's eyes widen with dismay. "Hurry up, you old geezer," she mumbles through clenched teeth. The ramp thumps the ground, and the front door opens.

Darbie blows a bubble with her gum and steps up onto the bus. She takes the bubblegum out of her mouth, reaches up, and sticks it on the bus camera's lens obscuring its view.

Dante pulls the trigger, but as luck would have it — his gun jams. Ballistic, he fiddles with his faulty weapon. At a snail's pace, the ramp lifts Lark and the wheelchair. The doors close, and they take off. In desperation, he fires once more and sinks a hole into the rear bumper.

Darbie looks around the bus, astonished that no one seems to have noticed the gunfire. An aloof girl stares at her iPad with headphones on. A hot and heavy couple make out in the backseat, and a stoner gazes off into space. One guy sleeps. Four drunk guys sing the college fight song, and two girls do sign language. "Only four stops, and we'll be there," says Darbie, reassuring herself. "Who was in the white van?" she asks, sliding into the seat ahead of Lark.

"It looked like Ada Mae," answers Lark.

"Who?" Already motion sick, Darbie breaks out in a cold sweat and clutches her side.

"The animal control woman."

"Huh? That doesn't make any sense. Do you think she's in on this?" Darbie asks as her stomach flip flops. Desperate to alleviate her misery, she attempts to focus on something up ahead. Sadly, her effort is in vain due to the lack of visibility. It's pitch black outside, and while the street lights aid the driver, all she can ascertain from this angle through the windshield are the tail lights of the car ahead of them. From her perspective, they are lucent red balls that bounce and move as the weak hydraulics jostle the bus with every imperfection in its path, exasperating her symptoms.

"You said the guy stated he had Rufus. Maybe they're partners. And one decided to cheat the other one and us," hypothesizes Lark.

Darbie turns around in her seat, so she's facing Lark. She rubs her stomach in unadulterated agony. "No, No. His partner is a tall guy with discolored icky brown teeth."

"Hey, are you alright? You're turning green," inquires Lark.

Nauseous, Darbie groans loudly and covers her mouth. Her alert eyes desperately search for something to get sick in. She clings to the back of the seat in front of her. In vain she searches for a nowhere to be found pocket, containing a nonexistent vomit bag. Unfortunately, this is a barebone campus bus and not an airplane or well-equipped charter bus. Out of luck and unable to hold it in any longer, her abdominal muscles contract. She projectile vomits out her window. Due to the momentum of the bus, it comes back in Lark's open window and directly sprays her.

"Jeez, Darbie!" Lark holds her soiled shirt away from her body. Ahhh. Nasty!" Repulsed, Lark strategically sheds her shirt careful not to get puke in her hair. She uses the dry end to wipe the Banksy off.

Darbie presents Lark with her red hoody. In haste, she puts it on and zips it up.

"I feel better," reveals Darbie leaning back in her seat with her eyes closed.

"Fantastic! If any more bodily fluids end up on me, I'm gonna straight lose my sh-." Lark stops short of saying the curse word.

"Interesting choice of words."

They laugh. The bus stops for no apparent reason. The compressed airbrake releases with a hiss. The doors open, and the ramp lowers.

"What's happening?" asks Darbie bewildered.

The driver approaches with a disgruntled look on his face and points to a *No Vomiting* sign.

"Oh, this you see," croaks Lark.

"Nah. I didn't see it," he reports, perturbed.

"You actually heard that?" asks Darbie, floored.

"Nope. No, ma'am — smelled it. Sure enough."

"Swell. The DMV issues bus licenses now for a keen sense of smell," Lark smarts off, rolling her eyes. Her and the wheelchair exit the bus onto the sidewalk. Darbie heads for the front door. The Associate enters the bus and smiles at Darbie. She backtracks and beelines it for the handicap door, leaps onto the ramp, and ducks out as the door closes. The bus takes off down the street, leaving a thick cloud of exhaust in its wake. The Associate glares at Darbie with the palm of his hand pressed up against the rear window as they depart.

Panting, Darbie maneuvers the wheelchair into the shadows of some cedar trees bordering the Alpha Omega Nu fraternity house. She has to really put her back into getting the chair to clear some exposed tree roots. "Remind me to schedule a chiropractor appointment first thing on Monday."

"We've gotta find something else to push this thing around on."

Loud country-rock music streams out of the lively frat house. A roaring party is in full swing. Lark and Darbie observe a man unloading a keg from a delivery truck, utilizing a dolly. The lanky fella wheels it into the bustling fraternity house. They follow him.

The girls enter the packed, up to its rafters in festivities, frat house. A scarcely dressed blonde circulates, holding a pizza pan full of jello shots. Lark starts to snag one when Darbie swats her hand away. In the next room, a lively round of beer pong is in full swing. Students cheer and root for their team. A song plays that Lark fancies. She commences dancing, commingling in with the mob. "Yes! This is my jam!"

Darbie, unable to keep Lark on a short leash, continues to follow the keg and enters the chaotic kitchen stocked with pizza, chips, and beer. Passing a line for body shots, she hopes the alcohol kills the germs spread from that bizarre party ritual.

Ecstatic, Gator zeros in on her. "Darbie!"

"Gator?" Darbie is amazed she can recall his name. Quite frankly, she'd gotten smashed so early on the evening they'd partied together that she's stunned she can remember anything. She masks her discomfort with a smile.

Stoked, he double high fives her. "You came!" he exclaims, lifting her feet off the floor as he embraces her.

Darbie scans the area, desperately searching for the keg. "Oh, uh, right."

Gator puts his arm around her. "Party animal. I like that."

"You know me," agrees Darbie, playing along.

Gator summons his frat brothers. "Hey, guys! Look who's here!"

Fired up, they begin chanting, "Darbie! Darbie! Darbie! Darbie..." Each of them is well built; they easily pick her up as if she weighs no more than a feather. At first, Darbie resists, but then she catches sight of the keg and points to the specific location. With gusto, they pass her overhead through the masses toward the barrel of brew. Lark, proud to know her and dying to find out what on earth happened the day she went off with Gator, meets her there.

Walker, wearing a frat t-shirt, stands on the balcony socializing when he hears Darbie's name unceasingly echoed below. He catches a glimpse of her gliding above the thoroughly inebriated attendants below and yells, "Darbie!"

Unable to hear him over the booming music and boisterous students singing along to "Chicken Fried" by the Zac Brown Band, Lark and Darbie fetch the dolly. Walker advances, shouting from the stairs, "Darbie!" He plows his way through the packed like sardines partygoers. The girls escape the prolific bash, head directly to the wheelchair with the dolly, and make a prompt transfer. Just as they return to the sidewalk, Walker steps out the backdoor onto the porch, looks around, and sighs.

The girls notice the wrecked black Lincoln with a flat tire parked on the other side of Greek Street. Spoiling their yet to be determined next move, the battered Dante steps out from behind the driver's side door with his pistol in hand. Darbie quickly steps in front of Lark, prepared to use herself as a human shield. Lark clings to Darbie's shoulders. Paralyzed with fear, they're both trembling defenselessly in horror. Unbeknownst to Dante, the white van from earlier sneaks up behind him with a long taser pole hanging out the window and electrocutes him on his already injured neck.

With no time to spare, the girls make a break for it. Bolting, they take a sharp turn at the end of the block. The Banksy tumbles from the dolly, jumps the sidewalk curb, rolls down the street several blocks into a taped off construction zone, and lands perfectly on an open manhole.

The white van does a wide U-turn hastily hitting the curb and starts heading their way. Lickety-split, they run and jump onto a waterslide lying in the grass, which is the length of two frat houses. Fearless, Lark slides face first, hitting an inflated bump that sends her flying like nobody's business. Darbie slides on her bottom, attempting to slow herself with the palms of her hands on the slick surface. When Darbie hits the bump, she goes airborne, and spins out of control. Water splashes in their eyes, blurring their vision. Darbie squeals and Lark cackles the whole slippery way down. Lark tumbles off the plastic tarp first, and Darbie awkwardly crash lands on top of her chest. They both lay in their current positions moaning.

Darbie finally stands up and offers Lark a hand. Their drenched clothing sticks like glue to their bodies.

Lark catches her breath. "What's the deal with those guys?"

"No clue. But we've gotta hustle. It's 10:05."

"We're three blocks to that manhole cover."

"We've gotta lose them. Just try to blend in."

Darbie peaks over at Lark and does a double-take. She's topless and kicking her shoes off. "What are you doing?" asks Darbie, shielding her eyes.

Lark points to a crowd of streakers huddled together like cattle. "Blending in," she retorts matter of factly.

Joining in, Darbie reluctantly discards her top and stands there in her black bra. A thin five-inch scar that only she'd pay attention to runs diagonally across the side of her torso. She removes her pants. "Okay, but I'm leaving my underwear on."

Lark stands before her unashamed and naked as the day she was born. "Not an option, remember."

Darbie gazes down at herself, surprised. "2B!"

Walker scans the scene trying to scout Darbie when he gets more than he bargained for; he gets an eye full of Darbie and Lark. "Have mercy!" he bellows, biting his fist, gawking at Darbie's nude body. Practically salivating, he leans out over the porch rail, cranes his neck, cups his hands on both sides of his mouth like he's about to yodel, and he yells, "Darbie!"

It's a lost cause as she still can't hear him. This time his voice is muffled by the wasted streakers chanting, "Streak! Streak! Streak!" Darbie and Lark mix in with the naked crowd as they tear off running behind the frat houses, crossing the street, and sprinting behind the active sorority houses.

CHAPTER 14

Drunk and disorderly, the rowdy streakers race into a murky man-made retention pond. Water splashes everywhere as the crowd wades, dives, and swims across. "Let's just go around," pleads Darbie, skittish.

"Too dark. We have moonlight this way."

"Right."

Free of inhibitions, Lark dashes into the stagnant water. She swims freestyle a few yards before she realizes Darbie's not beside her. Dillydallying, she's still cowardly planted on the shoreline. Mentally unable to continue, she crosses her legs and covers herself as best she can. "The clock is tickin'. Get a move on it, slowpoke!" bosses Lark.

Not budging, Darbie shakes her head 'no'.

"Don't be such a nervous Nellie!"

Caving to peer pressure, Darbie yells, "Hold your horses." Filled with trepidation, she tiptoes into the inky, mirror-like pond. "Mud is squishing between my toes!" she squeals.

Lark watches as the crowd of streakers disperses on the other end of the pond. "We're losing our cover. Come on, already! Poop or get off the pot."

"Something just touched my leg!" screams Darbie. Weaseling out, she promptly backs out of the tepid water.

"It was probably just a plant."

"I saw bubbles."

"A fish, then."

"No. I don't think so."

"A turtle?" guesses Lark.

Darbie shakes her head 'no'.

"Honestly, what do think is in here? It's a pond, for Pete's sake," declares Lark.

"Leeches, snakes, alligators..." exasperates Darbie.

"Alligators? Get real. This isn't the Okefenokee Swamp. The campus is surrounded by fences."

"Alligators can climb fences, ya know. I saw it on the news just last week. There was one in someone's backyard, over on Wilmington Island. He had climbed their chain link fence, sure enough, and was taking a dip in their swimming pool, right next to their kids' floaties. They came home from a long day at the office and went outside to let the dog out, and there he was. He gobbled up their sweet little Zuzu right before their very eyes like she was an apple fritter. True story!"

Knowing this is a lost cause, Lark notes two naked people on a yellow paddle boat. She gets out of the water and jogs over to a vacant paddle boat. "Don't just stand there, scaredy-cat. Help me push it in," pleads Lark. Darbie pulls on an orange life vest, assists Lark scooting the boat into the water, and starts paddling.

"I've always loved these things," shares Darbie, grinning.

"Me too. Who doesn't, really. They are so much fun."

With all the cycling they've been participating in lately, the girls' leg muscles are strong. They make some serious headway in no time at all.

Trudging along, they reach the halfway point, the deepest section of the pond, when the paddle boat starts filling up with water. Unexpectedly, Darbie and Lark aren't making any progress what-so-ever. Lark puts her feet down on the deck and feels them submerge ankle-deep in water. "We're sinking!" she shrieks.

"Now we know why this one was left behind," states Darbie. Panicking, she stops paddling and looks behind her to see if turning around would be the better bet. Nope, both choices are equally ill-fated.

"Paddle faster!" bosses Lark. Giving it their all, they vigorously paddle faster. "We aren't making any distance."

"I'll paddle. You scoop the water out," dictates Darbie.

Darbie's thighs burn as she pushes herself further than she thought feasible. Accelerating the movement of her legs, she rotates the peddles at supersonic speed. Lark grabs a sand bucket and scoops up water with it, but when she turns it over to dump it, nothing comes out. She examines the bucket's base and discovers a hole in the bottom of it. Rendering it utterly useless and dead weight, she tosses it overboard, cups her hands, and tries to scoop the water out by hand. Darbie turns the rudder to steer, and the handle breaks off. With only one person paddling, the boat spins aimlessly in circles. "This is hopeless," breathes Darbie. The capsizing vessel sinks deeper and then tips like the Titanic. Darbie ceases paddling.

"Get off the boat! Get off the boat!" commands Lark.

On the double, they jump off, splashing in the water, and float, Darbie in her life preserver and Lark on her back. Once the initial shock of hitting the water subsides, Darbie relaxes. The deep tranquil water feels surprisingly welcoming to Darbie's body as she acclimates to its temperature. Letting herself go, she enjoys herself for a moment. "Okay. This isn't so bad," she mumbles as she slowly glides her arms back and forth, relishing the way the liquid feels skimming her fingertips. "Is that Aquarius?" she asks, gazing up at the starry night's celestial sphere. Before Lark can respond, quite unexpectedly, something rather significant in size surfaces in the murky water. "What's that?"

"An alligator!" squeals Lark. The girls freak out, scream, and haphazardly splash about. The 800-pound alligator sinks back down underneath the surface. "Where did he go? Where did he go?" she echos, scanning the water.

"Get on the boat! Get on the boat!" screams Darbie. The girls scramble to get onto the tipped over, downing paddle boat. Darbie hangs on for dear life, bending her knees, ensuring that every square inch of her body, right down to her pink toenail polished tootsies get liberated from the omnisciently doomed water. Lark shifts slightly, trying to get a better grip and starts to slide off. They reach for each other, but only their fingertips graze for a split second. Lark sucks in filling her lungs with one last breath of air. They lock fearful eyes with one another as Lark helplessly descends out of sight, submerging deep into the water. Darbie screams, "Lark!" Without blinking, she scours the periphery for any trace of her. There's no sign of any movement from the water. Seconds feel like minutes. "Lark!" she cries, banging her hand on the side of the boat. Time crawls by wickedly slow. Unbridled hysteria consumes her. "Lark, where are you?" Out of the water, something powerful reaches up and clamps down, digging into the flesh on Darbie's leg. She shrieks and kicks herself loose. It drops back down under the surface only to pop back up and clamp down again.

"Get me out of here!" whoops Lark, her nails claw their way up Darbie's prickly calf. Elated she's alive, Darbie heaves her halfway out of the pond.

"Geez, when was the last time you shaved?" asks Lark.

"I would've if you'd bothered to grab my razor," chastises Darbie.

Lark scrambles to clear her legs. The paddle boat's glossy veneer finish proves too slick, and she only succeeds in creating perpetual squeaking noises with every failed slippery endeavor her naked body attempts.

Doing her darnedest not to let go, Darbie's lips quiver while she desperately clutches Lark's wet hand. "I can't hold on much longer," Darbie warns, losing her grip. The alligator rises, opening his gargantuan jaw wide enough to reveal all eighty of his carnivorous, sharp, pointy teeth. He is sheer inches from devouring Lark. The girls close their eyes tight, anticipating their painful demise. They both start reciting *Mary Had a Little Lamb*.

Out of nowhere, three tranquilizer darts rapidly fire and whiz past them, hitting the alligator. Its mouth snaps shut with immense, unnerving force, and he sinks back down into the turbid water. A canoe with Ada Mae holding a tranquilizer gun deliberately drifts towards them. Lark recognizes Ada Mae as the animal control officer. The girls' eyes expand into saucers as they fully take in the crimson red splatter marks on her stark white cover-up, luminescent in the moonlight. Darbie cries, "We're gonna die."

Lark recalls Ada Mae's name from her business card. "Please, don't kill us too, Ada Mae," pleads Lark. She attempts to hold her hands up, but the water is too deep, so she has no choice but to utilize them to doggy paddle; it's literally a sink or swim situation.

"Slow your roll. Why would I just save your arse if I was gonna kill ya? Besides, he ain't dead. I just immobilized the big lug. He's taking a little siesta is all, see," Ada Mae points over to the shoreline. An extremely sluggish full-grown, fifteen-foot, male alligator creates a path in the water's edge before parting cattails and waddling out onto the shore, collapsing in the marshy grass. "He won't cause any more fuss tonight. I'll come back in the morning before he sleeps it off with my crew and we'll relocate him."

"Uh. Oh. Okay. Um... Thank you. We really appreciate you saving us." Darbie insists.

"Which time?"

"Uhhh... All three, come to think of it. Say, are you alright?" Darbie points out the red stain on Ada Mae.

Ada Mae looks down at herself, and it dawns on her that she looks like either a butcher or someone gravely injured. "Oh yeah. Fountain drink got away from me, is all."

"Oh, good. Thanks, Ada Mae. We would've been goners for sure," Darbie praises.

"You're welcome. What are you waiting on — a formal invitation? Get in, already."

The girls haul themselves abroad from each side, rocking the boat moaning and groaning as they bump and knock each other, topsy-turvy. Full moons shining, boobs bouncing, and naughty bits flashing in every direction. Repulsed, Ada Mae turns her head to look away. "Hells Bells. Y'all ain't right."

Finally, they get themselves straightened out on the cold aluminum front bench, hunched over, cheek to cheek, twisting their arms and legs — covering themselves the best they can.

"Well, this is embarrassing," says Darbie.

"There's no unseeing that," complains Ada Mae, shaking her head.

"Ma'am, with all due respect, I'm just gonna cut to the chase. Do you have my dog, Rufus?" Darbie anxiously asks.

"Nah. A woman stole him."

"A woman?" Darbie and Lark ask in unison.

Ada Mae nods, confirming, "A woman."

Darbie exhales in a confused whisper, "A woman?"

"Yeah, a woman. Good gracious, you got water in your ears? I swung by the RV last night. I was fixin' to tell you about Rufus when I witnessed Dr. McEvil lurking around your place, lookin' like an ugly stick had hit him. I started tailing his shady arse."

"Thanks, but why would you do that for us?" questions Lark.

Ada Mae softens and lovingly nods towards Darbie. "I did it for her."

"Golly, I'm flattered, but I like men."

"No. I knew your daddy, Darbie."

"Ah-ha. That's how you knew where we live. I knew it! Darbie, brace yourself. The man wasn't who we thought he was," states Lark.

Darbie gasps. "That explains the dirty magazine and poster. He was living a double life!"

"You — and Mr. Harrington!" accuses Lark, glaring at Ada Mae.

"Ew. Was the lake house y'alls love shack?" inquires Darbie.

"Shame, Shame. I know your name," rhymes Lark.

"Shut your ignorant pie holes and lemme finish. He knew my son. And before you two nitwits ask — No, they weren't lovers either. And no, we weren't his second family neither. Land's sake! You girls would make a preacher cuss." Ada Mae continues to row, shaking her head.

"Sorry, Ada Mae. Please go on," apologizes Darbie.

"Your daddy and my son, Calvin, met at a cancer support group. My son was diagnosed with leukemia when he was eighteen."

Darbie's eyes well up. She gently rests her hand on Ada Mae's shoulder blade. "I'm real sorry to hear it, Ada Mae."

"He was only supposed to live six months. But your daddy made sure he received the best treatments. He bought Calvin three years he wasn't supposed to have. Cal always dreamt of having a place of his own. Your daddy let him stay out at the lake. He threw a lot of parties. Lord willing, on his good days, he lived like any other heathen his age. Scared all the fish off with his foolishness."

"Daddy never said anything to Momma or me."

"Well, that just wasn't his way. He encouraged me to get my real estate license, sure enough. Oh, he was real proud of you, ya know. Talked about ya all the time. You too, Lark. After meeting y'all, I have no earthly idea why," professes Ada Mae. They all laugh.

CHAPTER 15

S oaked through, Darbie and Lark shake like two wet kittens crouched behind a theater sign. Dripping wet hair clings to Lark's shoulders and back. She's wearing her birthday suit, and Darbie has on a life vest and nothing else. Ada Mae hands them both two branches. "Y'all best scurry in there and get some clothes on before you catch your deaths — or die of shame. I'll grab the van."

Darbie's so cold her teeth violently chatter. "Th-Th-Theater costumes. G-Good plan."

"Can you get my backpack?" asks Lark. "I left it by the waterslide."

"Good gravy. Is there anything else I can get for you? A juice box? Some Gummy Bears?" quips Ada Mae.

Ada Mae leaves as Walker's truck creeps along, puttering. With his eyes peeled, he canvasses the area searching for the girls.

Darbie grabs Lark's arm. "Walker," Darbie warns in a low voice.

The girls hide behind the theater sign in a bunch of lilac bushes; huddled together, they wait for him to pass. Shivering, they cover their naughty bits and faces with branches and tip-toe barefoot in front of the surveillance camera and into the theater hall's main entrance door.

***

Ten minutes later, Darbie and Lark escape the theater undetected with a new wardrobe intact. Darbie sports a 1960s men's golf outfit complete with a handlebar mustache, vest, and her hair discretely tucked up into a golf cap. Walking bow-legged, she gives off an overly masculine vibe, while hoping whatever polyester blend these hideously plaid bell-bottom trousers are contrived of doesn't induce intense chafing. Whereas Lark shines in her disguise. Lark parades about in a Roaring 20s black fringed flapper dress with a simple blunt cut wig and low heeled shoes. Lark is intentionally swinging her hips, so the fringe fans out from her legs. She's pushing an early 1900s baby carriage. Not exactly inconspicuous in their new incognito threads but more so than being stark-naked.

"Why do you get to wear the pants in this relationship?" jokes Lark.

"Hey, stop your bellyaching and hold my hand, woman."

Lark clasps her hand.

"It's 10:35 p.m. You're the worst mother ever," teases Darbie.

Ada Mae drives up, leans out the window, and tosses Lark her backpack. Born and raised in Savannah, she was taught right from wrong, to mind your Ps and Qs, and to help your neighbor and folks less fortunate than yourself. Accordingly, she has lived her life by this credo. When Ada Mae had attempted to give Dante aid last night, she was just minding her manners. Without hesitation, Ada Mae did what any good and decent Southerner would; she stopped to offer her assistance. Once she saw he was up to no good and that Darbie was in danger, Ada Mae knew she had to look out for her, especially after all Hank had done for Calvin. Even though Darbie is not her child, she willingly steps up and plays the part of the concerned parent; Ada Mae lectures, "I don't know what you girls are up to tonight, but I sure hope it's honest."

"It's all good, Ada Mae," reassures Lark.

"Do yourselves a favor and quit while you're ahead," reasons Ada Mae. The girls stare at her blankly. She counters their poker faces with one that indicates she's calling their bluff. "Alright then, I gotta go. I just got a call about a bunch of kittens trapped in a sewer."

"Thanks so much for everything!"

"We'll pay you back for the damages," adds Lark.

"Mmm-hm," mumbles Ada Mae. "Y'all be nice to somebody today."

"Daddy used to say that."

"Sure did." Ada Mae drives off. Her bumper sticker reads *I brake for possums.*

The girls walk over to the road construction in front of the Hearst Library, pick up the painted manhole cover, and load it into the baby carriage. The recklessness of tonight's events begins to weigh on Darbie. They've been using deductive reasoning to rationalize and justify their criminal activities. The mitigating circumstances surrounding their decisions to commit a felony are weak. She'd reacted out of spite when she'd stolen the security strip from Bernice. This has been a recipe for disaster right from the start; everybody knows two wrongs don't make a right.

Ada Mae had reminded her what a good, honest, and decent man her daddy was. Darbie wasn't raised to behave this way. A strong moral compass was instilled in her by her parents. If truth be told, her conscience has been nagging her this whole time. Justifying her criminal actions is foreign to her. Pinning this on Lark like she's the devil on her shoulder would be nonsense. Darbie pulled the trigger on the plan. After all, she'd been the one to steal the keycard. Instigation may not be hers to take responsibility for, but her knowledge and inside information is the glue holding this operation together, which is quickly unraveling. She's no Robin Hood; Darbie's not stealing from the rich to give to the poor. Somehow she's been condoning this selfish deed. Stealing is stealing, and she knew better from the get-go. She hates to surmise what her daddy thinks about this whole debacle if he's watching her now. "This was a huge mistake!" Darbie blurts out.

"Yeah, you're not very believable in that getup," Lark agrees, missing her meaning.

"I meant stealing the Banksy."

"I told you. It's not really stealing."

"No one knows we took it. We oughta just put it back." Darbie pushes the baby carriage in the direction of the gallery.

Lark steps in front of her, clearly miffed. "Over my dead body!"

"Exactly. That guy just tried to kill us over a manhole cover. A manhole cover, Lark!"

"But, he didn't."

"I swear, you're gonna be the death of me, Lark Kingsley," predicts Darbie. Once Lark gets something set in her mind, there's no stopping her. She's a force to be reckoned with. "This is more than we bargained for. The plan should've been null and void the moment that guy pulled a gun on us."

"Silver lining, we lived." Lark smiles.

"You're downright pigheaded; you know that? This isn't a joke. You don't get it. If we do this, it will end up in some rich person's private collection," Darbie heatedly declares.

"So!" yells Lark irked.

"So! Banksy wanted everyone to see it in its natural habitat. It has a message, a purpose. This is bigger than us."

Lark grits her teeth. "Get off your high horse. You're just scared. You're always scared."

"Nu-uh!"

"Uh-huh!"

Darbie goes ridged, standing straight-laced and fuming, curling her fingers into fists at her side ready to blow her top. "Lark, why don't you ever listen to reason? I mean, have you for one second even weighed the repercussions if we get caught? How about this? Let me spell it out for you; we could go to jail. Orange is not a color that will look good on you. The banquet will be over soon, and we've missed it — no alibi," Darbie fumes, standing her ground.

"Oh, hush. It's only a quarter 'til eleven. We can still make it."

"You're nuts!" spits Darbie.

"Oh, that's the pot calling the kettle black." Lark crosses her arms — holding her own.

"What's that supposed to mean?" sputters Darbie.

"Oh, nothin'. Just that you lost your marbles a long time ago, little Miss germaphobe, and you didn't have that many in the first place!"

Darbie scoffs and places her hands on her hips, jolting her shoulders as she speaks. "At least I'm not delusional enough to think every horrible thing that happens to me is bad luck instead of owning what I did to make it happen."

"Hey, it's true — I really do have bad luck. And I know I make mistakes but nobody's perfect — not even you. That's just part of life, ya know."

"Yeah. Well, if making mistakes is how you learn, then you outta be a freaking genius by now."

"Living with someone who is OCD is no walk in the park either," spits Lark.

"Living with someone who is a walking tsunami isn't exactly a piece of cake either!" jabs Darbie. "Did it ever occur to you that maybe I'm sick and tired of cleaning up your messes? I can't believe I let you talk me into this." Darbie's so mad her blood is boiling.

"Oh, that's rich, before you rally the villagers to stone me to death you might wanna own your part in this whole debacle, Darbie." Lark fires back, folding her arms smugly.

Caught up in the intensity of the verbal altercation, Darbie resists the urge to launch into a whole tirade about how dangerously ill-prepared they've been for all of tonight's hiccups. Knowing full well, she can't pin that on Lark. "Fine! You win, Aphrodite. You're the fairest of them all! I'm done."

"The heck you are!" says Lark tossing her hands up. "And I'm not finished talking about the onset of all the lovely little paranoias you've developed since your dad's death."

"Hey, you wanna stand here and wave a red rag at a bull — go ahead, but don't you dare talk about my daddy!" Darbie's eyes fill with tears as her mind reels with emotions. Releasing the baby carriage, she hurriedly walks away, fuming.

"Oh, I've kept my mouth shut for months," reveals Lark, stomping after her. "And I'm not talking about your dad's life. I'm talking about his death. Darbie, he'd hate to see how ridiculous you've become. Your dad died of the flu, and that sucks because he was the strongest person I've ever met. He was more than a survivor; he was a warrior. The man beat cancer and even thrived after y'alls' organ transplant. But he caught the flu, and it killed him. And Darbie, it's not your fault, dang it!"

A single tear sneaks down Darbie's cheek. She quickly swipes it away. "If only he hadn't brought me that jar of elderberry syrup."

"He didn't even come inside. Your dad could've picked it up anywhere. You completely quarantined yourself. I lived with you, and I didn't catch it from you. It was just his time, Darbie. God was calling him home," Lark expresses with a quivering voice.

"This fear of germs and death. It's no way to live. He wouldn't want this irrational, cumbersome lifestyle you've created for yourself," Lark points out, amid her spontaneous intervention.

Darbie stares off into space, processing Lark's words. The tension in her shoulders tightens. Tears freely stream from Darbie's eyes as her throat closes up. She smears the moisture on her face and chin with both hands. Forcing herself to swallow hard, she does her darnedest to hide her grief. "Maybe, so," she manages to choke out, fighting more tears. "But he wouldn't have wanted this either," she declares, motioning towards the Banksy. Emotionally drained, Darbie lacks the strength to argue anymore. "I'm out," she states, walking away.

"For someone so intelligent, you make your terrible decisions not based on what you know but off of your emotions. You can't quit. What about Rufus?" Lark hollers after her, bullheadedly.

Losing her tenacity, Darbie stops in her tracks and drops her shoulders; she's stuck between a rock and a hard place. Staring off into space, she mutters, "Rufus." Surrendering, Darbie waves her internal white flag on the warfare and holds her hands up in the air. She can't believe she forgot what should've been tonight's real motivation. It's not about revenge or money or that she's tired of living in squalor and smelling like a bonfire. It's about Rufus.

A wave of guilt crashes over her, stinging her eyes, causing her welt-up tears to once again pour freely down her cheeks and drip from her jawline as she reconciles with how poor Rufus is the one true innocent victim caught up in this mayhem. Although Darbie has only known Rufus for less than a year, he is family to her.

She'd never had a pet growing up. Her daddy's allergies caused his sinuses to react miserably to cats and dogs alike. He'd always felt guilty because Darbie adored animals and as an only child longed for a fur baby. As she got older, Darbie grew to understand that due to residing in a semi-metropolitan environment, the dream of even an outdoor dog was out of the question. Despite all this, after years of begging, her parents finally allowed her to feed a stray cat with the understanding that it would remain outdoors.

After Darbie's daddy took his last breath, she slipped into a deep depression. One that was far darker than the physical and emotional toll she'd experienced after losing Clay. Darbie hardly left the loft except to go to work. During her off time, she put absolutely no effort into her appearance, holing up inside her apartment in sweat pants and one of her daddy's old flannel shirts. Lark desperately attempted to cheer her up by luring her to the beach, a dance club, a concert, or even a comedy act. Nothing worked; she refused to budge, and on some days, refused to brush her hair. Without a doubt, Darbie was in the bell jar. Lark even threatened to cut off bringing food back from the restaurant, fearing she was enabling her.

Prior to her daddy's passing, he'd sworn to send her a sign from the promised land to assure her he was alright and that he was watching over her. Seven weeks after his funeral, Rufus greeted Darbie as she exited the gallery and escorted her to her car. Instantaneously, she was taken by him. His big brown eyes bore into her with a gentle understanding she couldn't shake. She went home that night, thinking about him.

The next morning, there he was, elated, patting his large paws back and forth the asphalt. Tail wagging, panting with his long tongue hanging out, he waited on her to get out of Isetta.

She found herself equally enthused to lay eyes on him. A loyal companion already, he ushered her to the gallery's front door and himself into her heart. While stooped over petting him, she'd noticed she could see and feel his prominent ribcage protruding through his smooth coat. Alarmed he was suffering from severe malnutrition, she opened her lunch box and supplied him with half of her leftover roast beef sandwich which he gobbled up. Upon finishing, she watched as he lapped up the water in a near-by rain puddle.

Doing her due diligence, Darbie snapped a quick photo of Rufus, and she devised and printed up a few flyers she planned on distributing. She also posted his pitifully sweet mug shot on several local online forums. Almost immediately, she received a message from a certified nursing assistant that worked at a nursing home located in close proximity to the campus. Rufus's owner was a long term resident. The elderly woman had been placed in the around the clock care facility last Spring when dementia took away her ability to care for herself. Rufus swung by the facility and visited her every day, sitting outside her window. While he was prohibited from entering the nursing home, they'd bring the woman out to see Rufus. Sadly, the woman overcome by her illness no longer recognized Rufus. The CNA explained that the resident had no family and that Rufus was indeed a stray. The animal shelter had worked tirelessly to place him multiple times with families, but inevitably he'd run away only to return to the frail woman he loved. What's more, the message from the CNA stated that if Rufus wanted to live with Darbie, he was free to do so but that in the end, it would be his choice as he is only loyal to the owner of his choosing.

Later that day, Darbie went to eat lunch by her and her daddy's willow tree. Rufus accompanied her there. She relinquished the other half of her sandwich to him, consuming only her chips and apple sauce. She poured some of her water into the empty apple sauce container for him. He accepted all of her generosity and showed his gratitude by repaying her with sloppy wet kisses that made her laugh hysterically for the first time since losing her daddy. Then, he gently laid his sweet head with floppy ears and a pleading expression in her lap. Darbie knew as she pet his short red shiny coat that he belonged to her, and she belonged to him. Like a shooting star, he'd been sent to her by her daddy. He was her sign.

Darbie didn't adopt Rufus; he adopted her. He rescued her. Rufus slept at the foot of her bed, ready to nuzzle her at the first sign of distress. Smart as a whip and completely in tune with her, he sensed emotions churning inside Darbie long before she did. She made sure to take him to the nursing home for regular visits, and she got to know several of the other residents.

Even though Rufus is technically Darbie's dog, Lark loves him like he's her own. He brought her best friend back to life, and for that, she'll forever be grateful and indebted to him.

CHAPTER 16

Interrupting Darbie's thoughts, she spots Dante sneaking down the staircase of the campus dining hall. She freezes like a deer in headlights. He's looking worse for wear but much to her surprise still kicking. A bloody limping mess of a man, however, he's highly dangerous with a lethal weapon. Dante's a threat she wants to avoid at all costs. "Whoa," she whispers, clotheslining Lark across the chest, stopping her in her tracks. She discreetly points him out to Lark with wide eyes and a head tilt in his direction.

"Does this guy ever give up?" asks Lark.

Darbie directs Lark straight ahead to a historically robust Regency style building. "Library."

"Think like a ninja."

Darbie gives her a reassuring nod. They attempt to be covert, all bent over, taking long strides on their tiptoes up the handicap ramp to the Hearst Library. However, the old baby carriage squeaks terribly under the weight of the Banksy. "Ugh, Faster!" breaths Lark. They dart up to the library rapidly squeaking all the way. Dante recognizes them, but he's moving slower than a Sunday afternoon. This is when he observes poor innocent Kenny sitting on the bottom step. Kenny is a sophomore who incidentally broke his right leg sliding into home plate on his intramural softball team last Saturday. With a heart of gold, he fractured the same bone twelve years earlier, climbing a tree in an ill attempt to rescue a cat. This evening, Kenny had a late-night hankering for waffles, but he'd misjudged how tedious the distance would be on crutches in his new handicap condition. He'd nearly forgotten just how trying the recovery process had been the first time. The skin on his armpits has been rubbed raw by his crutches. The cafeteria stopped serving at ten o'clock, adding insult to injury. He was out of luck. Famished and unable to go any further, he decided to sit for a spell. Moments earlier, Kenny sent out a massive SOS text message in the hopes of finding someone awake and sober to drive him to a twenty-four-hour diner. If not, the bus is his plan B. No one has yet to respond.

Holding on to the railing, Dante hobbles down the steps towards unsuspecting Kenny. As Kenny pulls himself up to make his pilgrimage to the bus stop, Dante reaches for Kenny's crutches. They're leaning on the staircase's railing. "Allow me," Dante insists.

"Oh, thanks," says Kenny, naively thinking Dante is behaving in a charitable manner. Kenny loses his smile when he takes a closer inspection of Dante's haggard appearance. "Dude, no offense, but you look like you could use a tetanus shot."

Before he can object, Dante swipes Kenny's crutches, using them to increase his speed drastically. Irate he's unable to chase after his mugger, Kenny's now completely stranded. He curses, helplessly watching as Dante makes a clean getaway.

***

In route to the art gallery, Clash idles his Dnepr MB-750 Russian military motorcycle with a sidecar at a stop sign. Up to no good, he looks around, surveying the area for onlookers. He removes his full-face helmet and begins to pull a ski mask down over his head when he notices Darbie sprinting. His eyes follower her. He catches the unusually curious sight of Lark shadowing her all glitzed up, a flashback to the 1920s. Lark's running like a maniac with a baby carriage. The Banksy lays lopsided poking out of the old-timey baby buggy. He steals a glimpse of the valuable piece as the tablecloth flutters up and down. Clash pulls the ski mask off and revs his engine. His bike rat-a-tat-tats as he slips the antique motorbike into a parallel parking space out front, and races on foot trying to catch up with them.

***

Inside the library, the woody scent of old decomposing books prickles Darbie and Lark's noses. Dust particles shimmer in the light cascading into the vast open space. They place the Banksy on a media cart and stack books on top.

"Quick, let's take the elevator," advises a breathless Lark, clutching her side. Despite her naturally small frame, athletics have never been Lark's forte. In contrast, Darbie lacks Lark's metabolism. As a result, her weight has to be maintained by rigorous exercise. She was once a pleasantly plump kid, a product of her sweet tooth and her momma's cooking. In high school, she hit a growth spurt, slimming her down some. That's when her gym teacher recruited her for the cross country team. Any extra pounds melted away in no time. The stress of this year has caused Darbie to overeat, and her weight has fluctuated, altering the size of her pants more than she'd prefer. As of late, Darbie's been combating her recent weight gain by intensifying her exercise routine.

Additionally, she's doing her best to be more mindful of what she eats in order to regain and maintain her figure. Although she does like some of her new curves, taking the stairs falls in line with her health goals. Besides there is a bigger issue at hand, whether Lark wants to hear it or not — the cootie factor.

"I don't do elevators," proclaims Darbie.

Lark pushes the 'up' button. "Not this again. Don't they make patches for motion sickness."

"Hey, elevators are just giant enclosed Petri dishes with no ventilation."

"Give me a break with this already."

"It's true! They're confined spaces that act as breeding grounds for germs and diseases. The tiny buttons alone have significantly higher levels of bacteria on them than a public toilet seat. They're coated in E.coli and Staphylococcus Aureus."

"Staphyloc- What?"

Darbie heads for the stairs. "Staphylococcus Aureus. Besides, there are twenty-seven deaths a year resulting from elevator accidents," informs Darbie. Momentarily she pauses, suddenly dropping her head in shame and acceptance. "Okay, maybe I do have some issues," she admits.

"Ya think?" The elevator door dings and swooshes open. "Meet me on the top floor, fruitcake."

Lark wheels the cart onto the empty elevator; the wheels bump over the gap and lip of the imperfectly aligned parallel surfaces. The doors are about three inches shy from closing when

Clash sticks his hand between them. They spring open, and he steps in broadening with tenacity. "Bollocks, that shut bloody fast," he declares. It's a tight squeeze with the cart. Ogling, he openly admires Lark's costume. "Blimey, aren't you a posh little thing."

Enchanted, Lark swoons when she detects his irresistible British accent. "Breeding ground, eh," she mumbles to herself, drinking him in. She's thankful the theater's dressing room was equipped with a shower, so she smells more like rosewater and less like pond water.

Everything sounds smarter, funnier, and a thousand times sexier with a British accent. Their manner of speaking has always moved her. She's never seen a British film she didn't relish. Over the years, she and Darbie have read and watched anything and everything Jane Austen based, devouring them like they were the last dinner roll. The BBC is a favorite amongst them. Lark is enraptured by Mr. Darcy and, therefore, by default, infatuated with the British actor who plays him, Matthew Macfadyen. So much so that Lark has seen every dark and gory episode of *Ripper Street* just to behold his smoldering self and hear that bewitching accent.

The unmitigated bliss of falling in love has always been an experience wholly lost on Lark Kingsley as she has at no time in her twenty-nine years of existence actually been in real love. She doesn't seek it. Furthermore, she guards her heart, never giving it away. Unlike most females, the dream of love does not dwell within her. If a cardiologist was capable of testing her heart for the desires of love, the medical diagnosis would read that Lark Kingsley suffers from severe love deficiency. Her laissez-faire lifestyle has opened the door to only fickle, light-hearted crushes and momentary flirtations.

Lacking any ambition to tether herself to a man, she chalks up the disbelief in true love to fantasy and fiction reserved for movies and novels like *Pride and Prejudice*. With nearly fifty percent of marriages ending in divorce, she earnestly feels the other half merely stay together out of fear of judgment, cowardliness, sheer stubbornness, or obligations, albeit family or financial. What's more, she ponders how many of those are void of infidelity. Every blue moon she'll meet a couple that seems blissfully happy, like the Morrisons or Barfields, and she skeptically wonders if they're just pretending, highly skilled actors masquerading around as common folk performing mundane tasks alongside the rest of us. Perhaps her parents' unraveled marriage has made her bitter about love after all. She only allows herself to occasionally contemplate on the matter for the tiniest fraction of a second.

Unlike Darbie, she wasn't fortunate enough to bear witness to the inner-workings of a devoted loving couple in her own broken household growing up. She's heard that the opposite of love is not hate but indifference. Forget love, for her mother to walk away from her father the way she did and never look back, she feels the woman never vehemently cared for him or her for that matter. Not for one second has Lark ever bestowed her mother with the extraordinary honor of hating her for her treacherous abandonment. Instead, she's chosen to harden herself to any pain by reflecting the same empty, unfaltering indifference towards her mother, sending it out into the abysmal cosmos. Lark sometimes wonders if her mother is even someone capable of embodying such a quality as deep as unwavering love. Lark didn't need or require any such validation from someone who didn't accept and value her in return. In the past, she'd questioned if her inability to experience romantic love was a defective gene that she, herself, could've inherited from her mother.

In her eyes, all wholehearted romantic love has ever done for her father is make him absolutely miserable. Not once has she ever desired to experience the unadulterated torment of love. She prefers to keep her romantic life light and breezy. Instead of waiting around for lightning to strike or a man on a white horse to rescue her, instead she chooses to love life itself with every fiber of her being.

"What floor, love?" Clash requests. Their hands touch as they both reach for the same button.

A sudden jolt zaps her and travels whimsically to her chest like magical pixie dust triggering a visceral response; her skin prickles, giving her goosebumps. She pulls back her hand as if she's touching a hot stove. "Top, thanks," she says. Squeezing her knuckles, she enjoys the sizzle his flesh left on hers.

"My pleasure," he graciously retorts in his British accent, causing Lark's eyes to sparkle.

"So glad I could pleasure you." Lark flirts, unable to resist the opportunity. Both steal sly peaks at one another until they simultaneously share in one. Their mischievous lips curl as they maintain mutual prolonged eye contact while the old elevator jostles about ever so slightly. Their shared gaze is intimate; there's a pull to it. The creaking cables continue to shift and shimmy, moving them up the elevator shaft.

***

Two minutes ago, Dante infiltrated the library, rhythmically swinging on his hijacked crutches. He observed Darbie heading up the stairs, but in his profoundly poor condition, he opted for the elevator instead. Dante watched without a prayer as the elevator door closed with the Banksy inside. He hit the up arrow button, but it was too late.

Dante watches the indicator gauge above the door. He waits for it to reveal which floor the elevator reaches. A tremendously annoying tic is causing his eye to twitch.

***

Lark pushes the wonky, unevenly balanced cart off the elevator. Clash studies the sway of her hips and departs behind her. Wearing her wig, he examines his reflection in the elevator doors as they close. "Bloody brilliant, I really should grow my hair out."

"Does the carpet match the drapes?" teases Lark. She casually rolls the cart between two isles.

"Why the disguise, love?" Clash tries to peek under the tablecloth. "Mind if I take a gander under here?"

Lark seductively moves his hand away. "It's a secret. It may be a teensy-weensy bit illegal."

"Nicked that, did you? Not to worry, I know a little somethin' about keeping naughty things secret."

Clash, being suave, leans in and caresses Lark's face with his index finger. He pulls away, flips his hand over, and reveals an eyelash. "Make a wish." He stands closely, invading her personal space, presenting the eyelash on his fingertip before her lips. He's so close she can smell the shea butter and sandalwood oil in his aftershave. Nearly palpating right out of her chest, her heart drums to a beat it has never played before. "Blow, love," he encourages. There it is again, that accent. They stare intensely at each other. It's no secret what she'll wish for. She closes her eyes and blows. And just like that, her whole belief system is shattered. She's heard of love at first sight before but wonders if there is such a notion as love at first sound. His voice penetrates any walls ever placed around her heart.

The elevator opens with a ding and out steps Dante. Lark presses her finger to her lips (implied shh). Keen to assist this fine damsel in distress, Clash grabs her waist. Wrapping his arms tightly around her, he pulls her to him and whispers in her ear, "Trust me." Lark can feel his warm breath on her neck.

"Oh my," she murmurs, swept off her feet. The instant their lips meet, Lark knows she's a goner.

Dante looks side to side, combing the area for any sign of the Banksy. He ventures down their aisle. Lark and Clash moan and purr as they unabashedly grope and fondle each other, surrendering themselves to the moment. Irked, Dante steps over them canoodling and continues his quest rubbing his eye.

The stairwell door opens, and Darbie emerges parched. Despite being an avid runner, the stairs had done a number on her once again. They work her muscles in a vastly different way than Savannah's flat terrain. Her thighs are burning, and her calves are a little tight. She glances in every direction, but alas, there's no trace of Lark. However, Darbie does see a water fountain to quench her thirst, but she decides against it due to the cootie factor. In the ninth grade, Misty Bobo claimed she caught mononucleosis drinking from the gymnasium's water fountain. Although, Darbie always suspected Misty more than likely contracted mono from locking lips with Griz Goddard in the janitor's closet. Suddenly, Darbie smacks herself on the forehead, annoyed with the realization of just how bad all her phobias have gotten. She makes a solemn promise to herself to work on these issues, starting first thing tomorrow.

Endless rows of dusty reference books surround her. Unsure where to begin, Darbie whispers, "Lark," but only silence fills her ears. Entirely focused on her quest to locate Lark alone, she misses her entirely. Darbie uncomfortably traipses by the twosome stuck together like a couple of love bugs. Not wanting to identify her accomplice, she uses Lark's code name. "Psst, Anna," she calls out louder. She extends her search, walking down the aisle in the opposite direction.

Lark pulls away from Clash, plucks the gum out of her mouth, and puts it back in his. "Darbie."

Darbie turns around, outraged when she recognizes Lark. She's in no mood for her shenanigans. Sometimes she thinks Lark is about as useful as a white crayon. Her eyes land on Clash's face. "Not you again." Darbie defensively steps between them, separating them. "Lark, what the H are you doing?"

Lark glances from Darbie to Clash, wondering how they know each other. "Number fourteen, make out in the periodicals," she declares, batting her eyelashes.

"Periodicals are newspapers and magazines. They're located on the second floor next to the microfilm," informs Darbie.

"In that case, I will meet you, snookums," Lark wiggles her finger on the end of Clash's nose, "downstairs," she says, pointing at the floor, "in five minutes," she instructs holding up five fingers.

"Splendid," Clash all too eagerly complies, letting his less than honorable intentions be known. The chemistry between these two is steamy.

"Don't hold your breath," advises Darbie. She puts Lark's backpack on and pulls her down the aisle beside her like a defiant child. Lark yanks back, refusing to budge another step.

Lark warns, "Dante is up here."

"What? Where?" whispers Darbie.

Speak of the devil, Dante appears at the end of the bookshelves holding his gun point-blank. "Give me the Banksy. It's mine!" he demands, twitching his eye. "And no funny business." Following his orders to a T, the three of them put their hands up. "Oh, and you're going to pay for this." He motions to his infected face and neck with his bloody hand. And then he stomps his foot, shaking his damaged leg. Regretting the last action, he briefly closes his eyes in misery. "And this," he says, holding up his shirt, revealing his shiny nipple piercing, a fish hook.

"Wow, now that's what I call a boobytrap," whispers Lark, praising Darbie.

The girls exchange an amused glance, and Darbie releases a small chuckle. Missing the joke, Clash looks confused.

"You won't be laughing when I'm finished with you," declares Dante.

Darbie and Lark lose their grins.

The elevator door dings and out steps Tony with his gun drawn. Tony's sporting a fresh fat lip to complement his taped up broken nose and black eyes. "I'll be takin' that Banksy with me now. Roll it over here." He points his Glock .45 directly at Dante's mangled face.

Dante narrows his eyes. "Drop your gun," he says, waving his pistol from the girls and Clash to Tony.

"Nah. I'm not doing diddly-squat. You're gonna drop your gun," counters Tony, standing his ground as he too continually waves the aim of his weapon of choice from Dante to the girls and Clash. Trigger happy, his Glock accidentally discharges which sends a bullet sailing past Clash and out a windowpane. Everyone ducks except Dante, who laughs, pointing his gun at Tony. Embarrassed, Tony's temper rises, causing his face to redden. "Reach for the sky, people," he bosses. The beads of sweat forming on Tony's temples, his unsteady hands, and his jittery voice are dead giveaways of his ranking amongst career criminals like Dante.

Watching him, Darbie compares his behaviors to that of a baby copperhead snake. This is due to the fact that they can be just as much, if not more, dangerous than a full-grown copperhead. Adults are capable of controlling the flow of their venom. However, when babies bite, they dump out all of their venom. In other words, he's a loose cannon waving that Glock around. One wrong move could set him off. He's capable of emptying his entire magazine and wiping them all out without much forethought. Terror-stricken, the group extends their arms. They raise their hands from shoulder's height all the way up as far as they can reach. Dante and Tony face-off, gun to gun.

Deflecting, Darbie fishes with a quivering voice, "Pardon me gentlemen, but before you kill each other, which one of you knows where Rufus is located?"

"Who the hell is Rufus?" questions Tony.

In the heat of the moment, the elevator dings and the doors spring open. Both Tony and Dante ready themselves to fire upon the occupants. The aloof female student from the bus with headphones on stares down at her cellular device lost in frivolous texting. She's entirely oblivious to her immediate environment. She meanders around everyone, never once looking up and acknowledging the precariousness of her imminent danger. Captivated by her, they all watch confounded as she moseys off.

Once she's gone, Dante picks right back up where they left off. "Drop it, or I'll make an example out of you, kid."

"You left me no choice. Ma said I can't come back home. I'm a disgrace to my family. I'm an embarrassment. This is all your fault, really. You ruined me!" barks Tony on the edge of some sort of mental breakdown. He examines Dante's fierce eyes as they stare coldly in his direction. "Do as I say, Dante, or so help me, I'll shoot you. I swear it! I'm gonna be the one to take the Banksy back to Simmons. Step aside, and I'll let you live."

"You gotta save face now, don't ya?" Dante ascertains in a sympathetic tone.

"Yeah, man. That's it exactly."

"Family," says Dante, shrugging.

"Yeah," agrees Tony, relaxing. "Family," he sighs.

Dante drops one of his crutches posthaste, swings the other one up, and knocks the gun out of Tony's hand, disarming him. Then, he fires a single round into Tony's foot. Tony's face distorts as he screams incoherently. Pale, all of the colors drain from his cheeks. "You shot off my big toe," Tony cries feebly as his lips quiver, staring in shock at the visible hole torn through his sneaker. He grimaces as his shoe puddles with the warmth of his fresh blood.

"Yeah, your balance don't look so good," Dante spits, lacking even the smallest shred of benevolence. Dante twists back, pivoting towards the group, staring them down, his eyes blazing. "Don't move a muscle," he barks, bending over to fetch the gun, holding one firearm at the group and another at Tony. "I suggest you beat it before I pull out my knife and make good on my last promise," states Dante.

White as a ghost, Tony wipes his tears on his sleeve. Hurrying along, he hops on one foot over to the elevator leaving a trickling crimson red trail behind him.

"Don't ever let me see your face again!" growls Dante.

Tony resembles a bobblehead doll, nodding his head up and down repeatedly. "Never," he promises low and raspy, weeping so hard he struggles to speak, he fumbles with the elevator buttons.

Just before the doors shut Dante calls out, "Hey Tony."

"Yeah?"

"Snitches get stitches." The doors close.

Unable to hold both guns with his injuries, Dante dumps Tony's weapon's magazine. It clanks to the floor. He kicks it under a bookshelf and tosses the gun in a trash can. All the while, he keeps a close eye on the group and fetches his crutches.

Thinking it's now or never and knowing they have nothing to lose because either way he's going to hurt them, Darbie instinctively snags a book from the shelf, and with extreme force, she catapults it striking Dante in the crotch. Doubling over, he writhes in pain, cradling his man parts. Lark cheers, "Never bring a gun to a book-fight. You'll be outsmarted every time," as she tackles him to the ground, sending his crutches flying, while Clash attempts to restrain him without causing any actual bodily harm.

"Look, bloke, I'm really against violence, so please don't resist," pleads Clash.

"Don't tell him that, dingbat!" lectures Darbie.

Lark pins Dante's hand to the ground and starts prying his fingers off the pistol, one by one. Assisting Lark, Clash tries to locate Dante's tickle spot, hoping it will force him to release his grasp on the weapon. Lacking one, Dante frees himself, and a rather sad one-sided fight ensues. Dante immediately regains the upper hand with ease. The girls flinch at every one-two, bell-ringer, and uppercut punch Clash submissively endures. Dante kicks his British bum.

Meanwhile, Darbie reads the label on a can of mace she removed from Lark's bag. Impatient, Lark snatches it from her and attempts to spray Dante, but the nozzle on the canister is facing the wrong way. She winds up aimlessly spraying Darbie instead. Darbie erratically falters around blind as a bat, screaming like a banshee.

"Whoopsy." Lark rotates the spray nozzle on the mace canister and aerosols Dante in his good eye. He winces in torture, cupping his face, blubbering vulgarity. Half-blind and fully deranged, Dante waves the gun in Lark's direction. She instinctively tilts the Banksy on its side. He fires his weapon at her. The bullet ricochets off the manhole cover and hits Darbie square in the back. She staggers forward and collapses to the ground lifeless.

The sound of the thud echos in Lark's head and an overwhelming feeling of dread washes over her. "Noooo!" she yells. In an instant, tears swell in Lark's eyes, and utter despair fills her tormented heart. Pushed to the breaking point, she's so inflamed she has only one thing on her mind, avenging her friend and ending this personal vendetta once and for all. Lark valiantly faces Dante. A wild and frenzied look fills Lark's eyes as she fixes herself on him. "I don't want it anymore!" she roars, trembling with rage. Her heart is pumping at warp speed, and her body temperature rises. On an adrenalin rush, she summons her raw emotions, surges them into super-human strength, and releases a warrior's yell. She effortlessly picks up the Banksy and runs at him with it, clocking him in his gut. He falls over, and his head whacks the ground hard with a sickening crack, knocking him unconscious. He lays motionless under the weight of the Banksy. "It doesn't belong to any of us!" she screams.

Stifling a sob, Lark rushes to Darbie and flings herself at her lifeless side. Time slows down, and Lark begins bargaining with God. She'll stop drinking, pay off her debts, start parking on the correct side of the road on street-sweeping day, whatever it takes to save Darbie. In reality, she reaches her in seconds, but, for her, it feels like minutes. Clash is already there, hovering above Darbie, checking her wrist for a pulse. A fluorescent light directly above them blinks, and a chillingly somber feeling sweeps over the room. The solemn look on his face reads utter despair.

"Oh, Darbie. Please don't — die. I'm so sorry," Lark cries, clinging to Darbie's limp body. Clash and Lark exchange a look, full of sorrow and regret. Something inside Lark crumbles; she begins to tremble out of control. Her whole childhood, her entire life, every memory touched by Darbie flashes before her eyes. With perfect certainty, she knows she'll never get over the loss of losing the only person who ever fully knew her and loved her, faults and all.

This one evening, this one decision, the sheer magnitude and the ripple effect of it have irrevocably shaped and altered the trajectory of their lives. Darbie's earlier words, "you'll be the death of me," echo in Lark's mind.

Lark is now pleading, begging God to spare her friend's life. To date, this is the first time she's prayed to God since she was a child and asked him to bring her mom home. She prayed to be part of a loving, happy family. Hurt and angry, Lark turned her back on God when he didn't fulfill her prayer. But presently, as an adult, for the first time, she sees that she was better off without her mother. God had, in fact, answered her prayer. He'd given her a family, the Harrington's. Clinging to Darbie, she asks God to spare her life. She promises that she'll never ask for anything ever again.

Lark and Clash roll Darbie over, revealing her discombobulated face drenched in snot and tears. Clash initiates the first breath of CPR, tilting her head back, his mouth blankets hers. He can feel her faintly breathing through her nostrils. Darbie's eyebrows crease. She forcibly zips her lips shut. Resistantly shaking her head side-to-side, she frees her mouth from his and moans a disgruntled whisper, "Get — him — off of me."

Elated she's alive, Lark shouts louder than a Southern preacher at a revival, "Thank you, Jesus!" She expeditiously removes the backpack and frantically feels Darbie's back. She lifts her shirt. "Where is it? Where's the bullet hole?"

Clash opens the backpack, extracts a small metal canister with a slug stuck in it, and smiles. Darbie moans lightly with her eyelids glued shut. Lark withdraws a water bottle from her backpack and pours it on Darbie's eyes. She instinctively winces as her eyes painfully flutter open. Her vision is blurry, and the burning sensation is so horrific blinking hurts. Unfortunately, not blinking hurts too. "Hold still," coaxes Lark. She gently pries Darbie's eyes open one at a time and dumps more water over them.

Clash opens the canister; pot smoke fills the air. Lark quickly dumps the remaining water on the capsule and protectively shoos the smoke away from Darbie's face. Lark's new soul mission in life is to vigilantly safeguard Darbie from any further harm or distress caused by her reckless behavior.

Darbie cracks a small smile. "Number twenty-five," she declares weakly, squinting her eyes. The girls embrace warmly.

Lark recognizes now that she totally lost sight of things somehow. She just wasn't ready to give up. It wasn't merely about the money; a big part of her simply wanted to see something through for once. But she almost lost her best friend in the process. Embracing Darbie, she gushes, "I love you like a sister."

"Sisters," Darbie concurs. "I love you too," she reciprocates. Lark squeezes her harder. "Ow. Can't — breathe," whispers Darbie.

Releasing her, Lark apologizes, "I'm so sorry — for everything. You were right. I'm done. The Banksy belongs where he created it."

"I'm sorry too." Darbie agrees. Taking ownership, both are fully aware that this thing got out of hand, and thus, the weight of their irresponsibility weighs heavily on their consciences. Greed, violence, and selfishness — they'd become the embodiment of what Banksy's art preaches against. "You were right, earlier. I am scared; I'm scared to move forward." No doubt about it, she knows she's been living in the past. "One of the things that I admire about you is that you embrace each moment. You're good for me, Lark. When we're together, I'm forced to live in the present too."

"But it's time we both start thinking about the future, isn't it?" finishes Lark, standing.

Darbie nods, "Mm-hmm. "Do you know why I love Isetta so much?"

Clasping Darbie's hand, she pulls her into a standing position. Then, she throws Darbie's arm over her shoulder and guides her to the water fountain. Darbie shuffles along beside her, barely able to distinguish objects. Her head is pounding; she could go for an Aleve right about now. Presently, she settles for water out of the fountain; desperate times call for desperate actions. "Because she's the cutest car ever made," Lark finally responds, holding down the nozzle as Darbie repeatedly splashes the water over her eyes — flushing the mace out.

"Wrong answer." Darbie grins. The vision improves in her bloodshot eyes. The pain diminishes. "Because you and Daddy made her for me. That summer, you both worked on Isetta; all I did was provide the music and refreshments. Building stuff — mechanics — that was never my thing. It's yours and Daddy's. I love Isetta because she was created by two people I love."

Clash starts to cry.

Annoyed, Darbie glares at him. "You're still here?"

Not wanting Clash to leave, Lark promptly changes the subject. "Darbie, how are we gonna get Rufus back from the art thief if we don't exchange the Banksy?"

"Ladies, I think I might be able to help you out there. I too desire for the piece to be returned to where it rightfully belongs."

"Not you too," states Lark, taking a step backward.

"Is all of Savannah trying to steal this thing tonight?" asks Darbie. "Wait, do you have our dog?" she drills before he can answer her first question, glaring at him like she's ready to pounce.

"Dog. What dog? Like I said. I too desire to return the piece to where it rightfully belongs," he repeats. On his cell phone, he shows the girls a photo of his motorcycle's sidecar. Inside sits a replica of the Banksy.

Darbie analyzes it closely. "It's an exact match."

"If you can do that, then why not just make a new one in the same location?" inquires Lark.

Clash shrugs his shoulders. "Because I'd know it wasn't the original." He lifts Dante under his armpits. "Give me a hand. I know what to do with this dodgy wanker."

***

Dante sits passed out in Clash's sidecar. Behind him, the Banksy is ratchet strapped to the bike's spare tire. Clash flags down a carriage ride operator. He loads the fake Banksy manhole cover onto the old fashioned horse-drawn carriage. Tapping on the replica, he says, "Just remember, it's rubbish. I used temporary chalk paint. Its purpose is just for the swap. I don't want anyone trying to make a penny off it. Handle it with care. I sprayed a fixative on the piece, but it'll smudge easily or wash off if it gets wet. Your time at the ball is minimal. You've got one hour until midnight."

Darbie eyes Clash. "Listen... I-I really appreciate your help. I'm sorry for the way I treated you before. It was a misunderstanding."

"Horse shite!"

"Yeesh! Look, I'm trying to apologize here."

"No," Clash clarifies, pointing to the ground. "Horse shite. You're about to step in it." A fresh, steaming trail of horse manure lines the asphalt.

"Oh, yeah, okay. Thanks. I'm just gonna go now." Darbie hangs her head, cautiously steps over the pooh, and climbs in the horse-drawn carriage. Clash gallantly offers her a hand and assists her as she takes her seat.

Turning his wholehearted attention to Lark, she leans in and whispers, "Shite. Never lose that 'e'. I just love it when you talk dirty."

Clash winks, lingering on Lark as he gently offers her his hand; he assists her as she climbs into the carriage. "Yeah well, I admire your moxie, foxy lady," he whispers in her ear. Lark's heart goes haywire. She grabs a handful of his shirt and yanks him towards her planting a smooch on him and then releases him.

"Off you go, love," she says with a simulated British accent as the carriage rolls forward.

Clash steps backward, dizzy and immensely satisfied.

Clip-clop. Two magnificent Percheron horses begin to pull the gently swaying wagon with the girls off into the dark stretch of campus. Lark turns around to find Clash standing under the streetlight where she left him. "Cheers," she yells. A strange and unfamiliar ache fills her chest as the distance between them grows larger with each gallop. Lark faces forward on the bench and releases a long sigh.

Darbie stares at her with several hard blinks and shakes her head in disbelief. "Why, I do believe you've gone soft, Lark Kingsley."

"Huh?" Lark asks not really paying attention.

"I've never seen you like this."

"Like what?"

"All googly-eyed. You've got heart-shaped emojis for eyeballs."

"Whatever," Lark denies, blushing and unable to hide the hearts in her eyes.

"Please, the eye contact between you two was so intense. I was afraid you'd get pregnant right then and there and before you two love birds had a chance to close on the sweet little house with the white picket fence you'd picked out together in the suburbs."

In a daze, Lark releases a giddy giggle and gives Darbie a misaimed air swat.

"What's that guy's name anyway?" asks Darbie.

Drunk on love, Lark shrugs. "We didn't do much talkin'," she sighs again, all dopey eyed, three sheets to the wind.

CHAPTER 17

Dressed to impress, Darbie and Lark dazzle in their evening gowns. They sneak in the back door to the Banquet Hall, holding Mardi Gras style masks up to their faces. Once inside, they ditch them on the name tag table. The vibe of this soirée is quite different from the roaring party they frequented earlier tonight. Here, the majority of attendants range in age from nearly thirties to barely forties. Instead of getting smashed, everyone looks smashing.

"Nice party," declares Darbie, reviewing the progress the volunteers made radically transforming the drab to fab space in a short amount of time.

"The tunage could use a little work. This schmoozefest sounds more like a snoozefest. I'm gonna work my magic on the DJ and crank things up a bit," states Lark.

"Hang on. Before you get this party started, we've got work to do."

"Yes, ma'am," submissively responds Lark, saluting Darbie like she's her no fun drill sergeant. "It's go time."

The place is relatively crowded with the hired DJ playing upbeat classic rock music. A full house of guests dance and socialize. The girls walk around, snapping selfies and jumping in group shots. Lark photobombs otherwise perfectly posed portraits. Darbie heads for a glass of punch at the well-stocked refreshments table. Her lilac chiffon gown beautifully sweeps the floor with her every step. Clay, Darbie's ex, the bee's knees and too big for his britches, hands her a glass. "Hello, Darbie. I've been watchin' you. You're even more gorgeous than I remember."

A rush of nervous energy hits Darbie like a lightning bolt. Her legs turn to jelly, and her throat feels as if it is closing in on itself. "Uh. Hey, C-Clay."

"I thought about you a lot over the years. This isn't exactly a chance encounter; I was hoping we'd run into each other tonight."

"Really?" Darbie anxiously gulps.

Clay runs his fingers down her arm and clasps her hand. "Sure. I remember everything about you," he reveals in his sexy voice.

Clementine, Darbie's ex-friend, pretty as a peach and mean as a snake, approaches. Little Miss Priss does an exaggerated clearing of her throat. Clay drops Darbie's hand.

Darbie can't believe the nerve of this guy hitting on her when he's still with Clementine, who is presently standing right there. She questions her own sanity for ever falling for such a misogynistic pig. Clay's proving the premise of the saying, 'If someone cheats with you, they will cheat on you,' true. Now Darbie feels dirty and like an accessory to a crime she never committed.

"C-Clementine," greets Darbie in a tizzy. The path carved into her arm by Clay's cold fingers still lingers.

"Darbie," acknowledges Clementine. She flips her hair and smiles, but it doesn't touch her eyes. "Are you here alone?" Clementine inquires, looking around pityingly. "Sad," she says, rubbing it in.

Rocking backward on her heels, the force of Clementine's words hit Darbie like a slap in the face. In the past, when it came to the choice between fight or flight with these two, Darbie had chosen flight. Rendered unable to form coherent thoughts, much less articulate words, she's speechless and leaning towards flight. Distracted by all the heist preparation, she'd been remiss in planning for the possibility of this dreadful confrontation.

Darbie breathes a sigh of relief when Lark saunters up in her slinky, yellow, high slit, satin gown which sensuously clings to her every curve. She swiftly snaps a picture of Clementine and shows it to her. "Yep, resting witch face still the same."

"As I live and breathe, Lark Kingsley." Clementine glares with an evil eye, assessing her threat. "Don't you look — desperate."

"Oh Clementine, I hardly recognized you." Lark gestures to the refreshments table, leans in, and whispers, "FYI, I think this is a one-trip buffet."

"I'm pregnant!" Clementine rubs her basketball-sized belly. Flanking Clay, she links arms with him.

Lark shrugs and inhales a deep breath. "Oh dear. That's the second time tonight."

"So, you two are still together?" asks Darbie, sickened.

"True love never dies. I'd never let this handsome devil slip through my fingers," declares Clementine in an abhorrent sugar-sweet voice.

Scrunching her nose, Lark mimics her fake sugary sweet voice. "I guess that makes you Satan's mistress."

Clearly masking her discontent that her man's wandering eyes are looking a little too intrigued with Darbie for her taste, Clementine sends a dreamy gaze up at Clay as he towers over her petite form. "You know, Clay and I were best friends first, and the foundation to any great and long-lasting relationship is friend-ship," fabricates Clementine, daring to offer unsolicited relation-ship advice.

"Pshh... Best friends! Listen to yourself. I mean honestly, do you even believe the meadow muffins you're shoveling?" asks Lark.

With Lark by her side, Darbie gets her bearings. She steps back into the ring of fire, looks them both up and down, and dishes out fictitious pleasantries, "Now Lark, it's plain to see that there's just no denying it; these two belong together."

Clementine misses the sarcasm. "Thank you."

"Clay, you're just all charm," proclaims Darbie.

"Oh, well-," Clay swoons, flattered. He straightens his already straight tie.

"No, I mean that's it. There's nothing beneath that odious charm." Darbie surmises that if she cracked it open, it would be a barren wasteland of nothingness. "It's just a facade, like Clemen-tine's friendship."

Lark swings her forearm side to side snapping her fingers. "Emm-hmm."

"I used to envy you, Clementine," confesses Darbie, realizing she's been looking at her memories of Clementine's beauty and success with rose-colored glasses.

Clementine bats her eyelashes. "Bless your heart."

Lark snags a tortilla from the buffet table and takes a bite. The filling shoots out the back onto Clementine's cleavage. "Oops. Happy accident," smarts Lark. Clay hands Clementine a napkin.

Darbie uses a simulated sexy voice and enticingly plays with his tie. "As you said, Clay, I've thought a lot about you over the years too."

Clementine unlinks arms with Clay and sends him a dirty look. Lark sneaks a deviled egg off the table.

"Both of you, actually. I'm just so thankful I received the opportunity to soirée with y'all again, because I see things so much clearer now."

"Darbie, Clay has moved on," insists Clementine, unnerved she's losing face.

Steadfast, Darbie dials into a higher level of confidence, a stark contrast to the meek, mild-mannered girl they once knew, and continues, "You've perpetually been this unattainable utopia that I've built up of in my mind, but there's no foundation to it. Clay, the reality is that you had one foot out the door long before you got in line for Clementine. We just weren't right for each other." She contemplates why she didn't bounce back faster. There certainly were missed opportunities to do so. In the end, she determines it's okay; it just means that unlike Clay, she didn't fall for the first pretty picture that came along.

"Now, Darbie, we're all grown-ups here, and Clementine thinks it's best to let sleeping dogs lie," chirps Clementine, speaking in the third person.

Looking Clementine in the eye, Darbie says, "Okay, well, I'm not sure which personality I'm speaking with, but when you see Clementine will you please tell her I couldn't agree more..."

Lark busts out laughing. Even the corner of Clay's mouth twitches. Clementine gives him a look that says he'll pay for that later.

"...And not to worry, I don't have any aspirations of derailing your relationship." Darbie decides not to even bother spitting out any opinionated or heinous comments because she realizes she wouldn't trade places with Clementine for all the money in the world. "This little reunion solidifies what I think I've always known, that you two belong together because I deserve better," finishes Darbie, pleasantly surprised to find her initial anxiousness has fizzled out. Feeling confident that she's officially bored with their past together and excited about whatever her future holds, she turns and sashays away.

Lark pats Clay on the back; unbeknownst to him, she smears the egg yolk all down his back. "No hard feelings, Clay," she states, happy as a clam. Glancing at Clementine, Lark adds, "Good luck. You're gonna need it." Catching up with Darbie, she praises her, "Well done."

"Like old times," replies Darbie, recalling the long-ago gum incident with Gena. Grinning at each other, they bump hips and snap their fingers.

***

The moonlight shines bright tonight, spreading beams of opal light, illuminating the translucent fog as it weaves and snakes its way across Bonaventure Cemetery's 160 acres. A maroon sedan drives through the gate and winds down a dirt road, meandering through the pitch-black night air of the 1846 hauntingly beautiful, Southern, Victorian cemetery. The sound of the tires crunching and sending sand and small rock sinking or sailing awakens the otherwise deadly quiet graveyard. The car's headlights shine on striking statues, stunning monuments, crypts, and headstones casting elongated shadows. The sedan, lying low, waits under an oak tree near the swift-moving Wilmington River. Spanish moss drapes the front windshield. A blackbird lands on a wrought iron fence, lining a dearly departed's resting place and crows. Rufus lays on the backseat of the sedan with the window cracked, trembling and whimpering. The dashboard clock reads *11:16 p.m.*

***

Exuding confidence, Walker approaches from behind and gently touches the small of Darbie's back. He relishes how soft and smooth her skin feels, like silk. "I was hoping to steal a dance from the prettiest girl in the room," he states, looking dapper in his structured suit.

"Walker? Aren't you dashing. What are you doing here?" asks Darbie, pleasantly surprised. Smitten, she resists the pull of her body's magnetism towards his.

"If I'm not mistaken, the event is an open invitation to all alumni. And please call me Jack."

"Sorry, your name badge said 'Walker.' And I didn't realize you graduated from here."

"Yes, an error by HR," he explains. "Class of 2009," he proudly declares.

Chrystal comes bouncing up, carrying herself like a posh soap opera villain. Exquisitely dressed, impeccably poised, and annoyingly flawless — not a single hair on her perfectly symmetrical head is out of place. She steps between Lark and Walker, entitlement oozing from her mannerisms. "Jack Walker, as I live and breathe," she gushes, extending her hand. He gently shakes it. "My, my, my, you sure grew up nicely. Where have you been hiding?"

"Shut the front door — Jack Walker? Jack Walker, of course! I can't believe I didn't put that together the other night when you dropped off Darbie's car. I remember you! Long hair. Skinny. Braces. A real smartypants," beams Lark, nudging Chrystal over a smidge, so she regains her position in the circle of conversation.

All at once, his name rings a bell and resonates with Darbie. She remembers he also had glasses and a goatee. Astounded she didn't see it before, Darbie gasps. "Stick? You were Clay's roommate freshman year!"

"Assigned roommate. And nobody's called me Stick in a long time."

"I would think not," surmises Darbie, biting her lip as she gawks at his muscular physique.

Chrystal, growing bored that the attention isn't on her, wishes to flee with her muse. "Jack, dear. Why don't you come join our private party at the VIP table for a slightly more intimate and vastly more stimulating conversation."

Before Jack can respond, Lark nips the idea in the bud. "Chrystal, darling. I just spoke with Hudson. He's been looking high and low for you. He said the sitter called; Junior has got the runs."

Chrystal's face drops, "Oh dear, I told her not to let him have ice cream. He's lactose intolerant."

"Good help is just so hard to find," smarts Lark.

"Isn't it though," agrees Chrystal. "Please excuse me," she requests, addressing Walker exclusively as she dials her phone.

"Of course," nods Walker.

Darbie's reeling from this revelation. "Jack Walker. You were such a sweetheart," she recalls fondly.

"So sweet, I'm getting a toothache just thinking about it. You followed Darbie around like a puppy those first few weeks." Lark unties a purple balloon and sucks a small amount of helium out. "Chrystal's correct about one thang, you've certainly been taking your vitamins," she asserts in a squeaky high pitched voice.

Lark releases the ballon, and it sails aimlessly through the air deflating. Empty, it inadvertently lands in a lady's lobster bisque. Disturbed, the woman fishes the choking hazard out, sets her spoon down, and slides the bowl away. Her eyes dart around the room seeking out the guilty culprit. Lark looks away, pretending to be innocently sipping on her wine glass.

Still wholeheartedly engrossed in Walker's disclosure, Darbie breezes past Lark's careless mishap. "I wouldn't have passed Medieval Art if it wasn't for you," recollects Darbie.

"Yes, well, you wouldn't have started dating Clay if it wasn't for me," he reminds.

"That's right. You and I went back to study in your dorm room one night-"

Lark elbows Walker. "Bet studying wasn't on your mind. Am I right?" nudges Lark. Walker agreeably smirks.

The events are somewhat jumbled up in Darbie's mind, but they're coming together in spurts. "You introduced us."

Walker vividly relives that moment. "He introduced himself. Allowing that to transpire was the biggest mistake of my life," he confesses, looking Darbie squarely in the eyes. Darbie's cheeks flush.

"Aww. That must have been torture." Lark touches his bicep. She squeezes it and not so subtly mouths 'wowzers' towards Darbie.

In her mind, Darbie hits replay on Walker's last words, "Allowing that to transpire was the biggest mistake of my life." Then, she bounces around the idea that he had followed her around like a puppy. Was he pining over her? She's experienced crushes before. Who hasn't? But she'd never imagined being on the receiving end of one. Much less the possibility that anyone non creepsterish would pine over her for well over a decade.

"What happened to you?" inquires Darbie. Like a lot of youngsters in love do, she'd made the rather catastrophic mistakes of casting her friends aside for Clay at the beginning of their relationship. All except for Lark, who'd sunk her talons in. Lark, incidentally, never approved of Clay. From the get-go, she trusted him about as far as she could throw him.

"Well... After graduation, I got my masters. Then, I became a Marine. After I was discharged, I moved to New York, went to work for the FBI, and made agent last year. When the Banksy assignment came up, I saw your name on the file, so I requested it."

"Destiny. That's hot," says Lark.

Darbie's alarmed. "Wow. I thought you were just extra security. FBI?"

"Yes, we have reason to believe an art thief might be in the area, targeting the Banksy."

Darbie makes eyes with Lark. "You don't say."

Walker motions to the dance floor. "So, how about that dance?"

"Uh, well. I don't kno-"

Lark shoves Darbie. "She'd love too!"

Taking the initiative, Walker grabs Darbie's hand. "Great!" he bellows, intertwining his fingers with hers. His hands are big, built like a lumberjack, and the skin is thick like a man who uses them often should be. They are the opposite of Darbie's long, thin, soft, perfect for piano-playing hands. Yet somehow they complement each other perfectly, magically fitting together in such a way that Darbie doesn't know where hers end and his begin.

***

Walker had omitted one key element from his story about what happened in his time apart from Darbie. About two years ago, by chance, he'd met a girl, Riley Davenport, one night after visiting a friend in Brooklyn. They were both standing on the same corner in the pouring rain. Being the gentleman that he is, he offered to share his cab ride with her.

Riley's an Occupational Therapist, who at the time, was returning from a year-long stint working with Doctors Without Borders in Zimbabwe. Both had traveled extensively and enjoyed swapping stories about their experiences abroad. The attraction was instant, and the two fell hard for each other over the next few months. Walker almost popped the question. He'd even bought a ring and carried it in his jacket for nearly a month, waiting for the perfect moment. Walker wanted the proposal to be spontaneous, but the ideal moment never happened. When one month led to two, he realized something was missing; they weren't right for each other, so he broke things off with her instead. She'd taken it pretty hard, which made him feel awful. He'd cared deeply about Riley and never meant to hurt her.

A few months later, Walker and Riley ended up bumping into each other on the subway. Much to Walker's surprise, she had a ring on her finger. She and the guy she'd dated several years ago had gotten back together. They'd initially broken up when she'd left for Doctor's Without Borders. But as fate would have it, on a trip back home, they'd run into each other at an early morning church service. They spent the afternoon hiking on familiar trails and rekindled things right where they'd left off. Riley's fiancé said there was absolutely no way he was going to let her slip through his fingers again, so he put a ring on hers. She said she was relocating back to North Carolina at the end of the month. Her face positively glowed when she spoke about him. Walker had never seen her so genuinely happy.

***

Walker and Darbie stroll out onto the dance floor, hand in hand. Lark briefly chats with the DJ, and "Jessie's Girl" by Rick Springfield starts to play. Walker and Darbie smile. Lark joins them on the floor, making a spectacle; she's dancing like a fool with the school's uncoordinated mascot, a sea turtle.

Darbie studies Walker as he moves. She adores everything about this man. He's ruggedly handsome with his strong rough hands, strapping physique, hypnotizing deep blue eyes and the pièce de résistance, his distinctive Southern drawl. Walker's natural scent, his pheromones are indubitably intoxicating. The man oozes sex appeal. Darbie melts every time she looks at him.

A slow song comes on, and Walker pulls Darbie close to him, encircling her with his muscular arms. She molds into his firm body, a perfect fit. Darbie ardently rests her head on his broad shoulder as they sway to the beat of the music. With their bodies entwined, her oxytocin or as scientists call it, her "cuddle hormone" levels rise. This causes a reduction in her stress and anxiety which in turn improves her overall psychological stability. That may sound scientifically dull to some, but for Darbie, it is exceedingly titillating. This man makes all her perplexities and idiosyncrasies disappear.

There is also something oddly familiar and comforting to his embrace. Something Darbie's only felt when she tasted her Nanna's Southern cooking or watched her daddy creating a masterpiece. She feels it when she smells her mother's sweet floral aroma, looks into Rufus's big brown eyes, or hears Lark's wild, childlike cackle. When he holds her in his arms, he too feels like home.

Euphoric, Walker drinks Darbie in. He's enraptured with the way she feels in his arms. Walker's always dreamt of holding her like this. He yearns to touch her soft lips with his again. Staring at them, he recalls how they tasted like sweet nectar under the stars in the sanctuary of the garden. Walker wishes there was a courtyard so he could steal her away.

Darbie wonders how she could've been so blind to his affection before. Walker is everything she has always longed for in a man. Besides the fact that he's deliciously sexy, he's incredibly ambitious, funny, immensely empathetic, a dang good dancer, and a heck of a kisser. This guy is the real McCoy; Walker's just so genuine. When he looks at her, there's a longing in his eyes she'd never captured with Clay. She feels truly seen and safe. She knows with every fiber of her being that he would never hurt her. At this precise moment, any remaining fragments of her past relationship with Clay disintegrate, and a new much more vivid quintessential picture materializes. This one's sharp as a tack. The strumming of her heartbeat quickens and falls into perfect rhythm with his. Darbie can feel a sudden jolt as their heartstrings tie an unbreakable knot.

Luckily, the pendulum swings both ways. As far as Walker is concerned, Darbie's every bit as alluringly beautiful as he remembers. He can't believe his opulent luck that she's still single. The other night when they were alone together, Walker had felt a scar where Darbie's kidney should be. He'd read in her file that she'd taken a leave of absence to be her father's organ donor. That kind of selfless sacrifice was a reflection of God's love. She'd never shined brighter to him than when he read that.

Head over heels, heart and soul, without question, he's endlessly devoted to this woman. Walker is grateful that divine intervention has aligned the stars to bring them back together again. Thus, allotting him this second chance with her.

Holding her, Walker knows why things never felt right with Riley. Riley wasn't Darbie. When he looks into Darbie's green eyes, he sees his whole future, a life, a home, children, them growing old together. Without question, Walker sees her, the woman of his dreams by his side every step of the way. At this moment, he too feels the tug on his heart made by their unbreakable knot.

"I wish you could've met Daddy," Darbie whispers.

"Me too," he replies, squeezing her a little tighter.

CHAPTER 18

L ark and Darbie power walk towards the Banquet Hall's rearmost obscured parking lot, out of sight of cameras. "Alright, Darbie. You head to Winnie. I'll grab Isetta."

"Dante butchered her."

"Now, Now. There is still hope. I can resurrect her," comforts Lark. She opens up her bedazzled clutch, halfway removes a small tool kit, and shows it to Darbie before releasing it back down into her purse.

"Only you!" squeals Darbie happy as a clam.

"Go ahead and get the ramp ready," instructs Lark. Darbie nods, and they part ways.

***

Dante lays shirtless, slumped over in the sidecar of the motorcycle, looking like he's knocking on death's door. Clash holds a stencil homage to a Monopoly board space with the image of Dante behind bars that reads *IN JAIL, JUST VISITING.*

***

Watching the minutes tick by while she anxiously drums her fingers on the steering wheel, Darbie readily waits in the RV's driver's seat. Her watch reads *11:43 p.m.* The instant Darbie hears Lark pulling Isetta in, she cranks the RV's engine and raises the ramp. Lark climbs in and takes her place on the passenger seat. There's nothing fast about driving this beast. Praying slow and steady will win the race, they pull out of the parking lot. It's bumper to bumper traffic. Undeterred, they bypass the main drag and take a short cut, turning down Greek Road.

Daisy and Caroline, the girls from the dorm, sit in a blue handicap accessible minivan, which emits loud music and booming bass. They're wearing neon yellow and green glow jewelry. The minivan loads the wheelchair, and the door closes automatically. Darbie stops the RV. Lark leans out the window. "Hey, girls! Sorry about that, Daisy. It ran out of juice."

Daisy sits in the driver's side window. "That happens. It has LoJack."

The interior light is on in the back of the van. Kenny leans forward in his seat and gives a friendly smile.

"Did you get a new fella already?" pries Lark.

"Met him in the dorm parking lot five minutes ago. Someone stole his crutches. Poor thing is starving to death," says Caroline, thrilled.

"Yeah. Kenny needs to borrow my chair. We're headed to Tasty Biscuit for a bite. Care to join us?" asks Daisy.

Out of nowhere, Gator over eagerly jumps in the minivan. "Count me in," he responds, inviting himself.

Lark and Darbie laugh. "Can't. Wish we could. You kids have fun!" encourages Lark.

"You too," says Daisy.

"See you later, alligator," Darbie yells at Gator, beaming.

"After 'while, crocodile," finishes Gator, happy as a clam, not taking his eyes off his prize, Daisy.

"Thanks again," says Darbie to Daisy and Caroline.

They all exchange waves. Darbie and Lark drive off.

"You get that we could've just borrowed that minivan in the first place, right?" evaluates Darbie.

Steadfast, they exit the campus into Savannah's booming downtown after hours gridlock. It's a madhouse of bar hoppers, homecoming attendants, and local event traffic. The rubberneckers have them packed in like sardines, bumper to bumper. The RV is utterly impossible to navigate.

"This is hopeless. Go right," instructs Lark, outsmarting the tourists.

They enter a sketchy area. Dilapidated housing and run-down, dark, abandoned buildings with broken or boarded-up windows line the street. Winnie creeps along down the dimly lit block. A woman seductively dressed and ready for business leans in a prospective client's car window. Darbie drives under a pair of sneakers with its laces tied together flung over an old power line. Cautious, she manually locks her door. Without looking, a grown man on a kid's freestyle bike, covered head to toe in body art ink, including a teardrop tattoo under his eye, swings out ahead of them. He exchanges something with another unsavory character standing on the sidewalk before cutting between a building's back alleyway. Darbie and Lark cross over to the next sketchy block.

"Stop. Park it here," instructs Lark undeterred.

"Here?" The dreary shotgun-style house to their left has a busted washing machine turned on its side, sitting in the yard with overgrown shrubs. A loud and highly aggressive pit bull chained to the front porch barks profusely at them. Three large overflowing garbage cans with trash bags stacked so high the lids can't close, sit on the curb, surrounded by even more half-open foul-smelling bags blocking the front walk. Broken glass litters the sidewalk. This desolate street is a far cry from the affluent neighborhood where they grew up. "I don't know. We're on the wrong side of the tracks," mutters Darbie, taking in her environment. "It looks pretty rough. This is a high crime area. There could be dangerous criminals lurking out there."

"Yeah, us. In case you've forgotten, Darbie, we are the criminals."

"Oh, right."

"Park over on this empty lot."

Trespassing, Darbie follows her orders. The ramshackle house next door to the empty lot sits crooked on its cement block foundation with peeling paint. The screen door is ripped and hangs loosely from one hinge, looking like one well-delivered sneeze would finish the job. The interior side of its windows are all covered with newspaper. Several bicycles, a skateboard, and a torn recliner lay scattered and abandoned on the unkempt lawn. Lark fetches the skateboard out of the yard.

Darbie lowers the ramp, and Lark jumps in Isetta's driver's seat with the commandeered skateboard in tow. "Get in," orders Lark.

Darbie hops in Isetta, and Lark hands her the skateboard. "Huh... Thief!" accuses Darbie.

"It's on loan."

"I'd feel better if you let me drive."

233

Lark ignores her, ready to lay some serious rubber, she announces, "Ladies, start your engines." She makes sound effects imitating a race car revving its engine and peeling off as she steps on the gas; they putter off. Picking up speed, she heads back out towards the main drag, weaving in and out of traffic using parallel parking spaces and the wrong side of the road. Darbie buckles her seatbelt. With traffic at a standstill, Lark hops the curb onto the sidewalk. She takes a hard right and lands on the road but not before sideswiping a newspaper dispenser. The tail end grinds metal on metal. "Eeek," cringes Darbie.

"No worries. I'll fix that," reassures Lark.

She cuts through several parking lots, takes a sharp left, fishtailing, and then right again back onto the main drag. A police car turns on its lights and speedily pursues them. Darbie looks back. "Oh, no!"

"I'll lose him." She runs a red light. He does too. "We'll take Bull Street." She turns right. He follows. She runs another light, swerving to avoid getting t-boned in the intersection. The cop slams on his brakes and narrowly avoids impacting the same vehicle she just dodged.

Darbie tastes the bile rising in the back of her throat and swallows hard. Lark wrings the steering wheel and makes a tight right turn. Darbie looks back again. "I think we lost him," she says, feeling sick.

A police car seemingly appears out of nowhere up ahead. Lark looks forward. "Nope."

Darbie looks forward. "Reverse! Reverse!"

Lark backs up. A police car emerges behind them. "Oh, jeez."

Darbie looks back and then swiftly catches sight of their only escape route. "Alley."

"Suck in and think skinny thoughts," Lark bosses as she inhales a deep breath and reverses down the smooth irregular stone paved alley. It's such a snug fit the car has mere inches between it and both walls flanking them. Sick, Darbie closes her eyes and clutches her stomach. Unable to fit, the police cars go around the buildings. Lark pops out onto the 200-year-old hand-laid cobblestone River Street. She puts Isetta in first gear, cuts the wheel hard, and heads east riding the former streetcar rails. The ride goes from a loud and bumpy road surface to a quiet and buttery slick surface. The cops tail them. Darbie rubs her forehead. "Dead end," she groans. The police car closes in and pulls up beside them. The piercing sound of the sirens reverberates in their eardrums.

"I'm gonna be sick," Darbie announces. She opens the leather-grain vinyl sunroof, which takes up the majority of the micro-sized ceiling. The roofs on these cars are designed in such a manner because the body is equipped with just the one front end door. If heaven forbid, there is a collision, and the occupants became entrapped; they can escape through the sunroof, so basically, the sunroof doubles as an emergency exit. Darbie determines that this, without a shadow of a doubt, qualifies as an emergency. She twists into a semi-standing position with one knee bent on the bench seat, clearing the roofline, and retches off to the side. Vomit spews on to the squad car's windshield. He turns his wipers on smearing it. Unable to see, he swerves and collides into a light pole. The police car behind him rear-ends him, blocking the narrow road. Both officers get out of their squad cars, quarreling with each other about who is at fault.

Squeezing the steering wheel, Lark drives up a wheelchair ramp. The side mirror strikes a handrail and falls off. Darbie cringes. "I'll fix that too," promises Lark. She makes a hard left onto River Street Boardwalk, looping them back in the same direction they just came. Pedestrians jump out of her way. Lark tears through the stand of a lady making Confederate Love Roses, sending palm fronds everywhere.

She drives down the stairs, returning to River Street. The bottom of Isetta sparks as her undercarriage scrapes the brick stairs. "I've been thinking a lot about what you said earlier — about working on Isetta with your dad. Tricking out cars has always been a fantasy of mine. I only did the culinary thing because I cooked for my father and me all those years, and I was good at it. But I don't enjoy doing it all day long for rude picky strangers." She cuts back down the same alley and sweeps left.

"Perfect fit, and you'd make great money customizing cars."

Lark lets go of the steering wheel. "Hold the wheel."

"Huh?" Darbie's eyes swell. She grabs the wheel in a panic. Her eyes focus on the road in front of her.

Lark slides her heels off and tosses them behind her on to the parcel shelf. Then, she seizes the steering wheel from Darbie. "A lot of technical colleges offer classes so I could get certified."

"You could intern at Jersey's Big Pimpin' Rides."

"Shut your pie hole!"

"What? You could."

"You really think so?"

"Sure! That is if we don't end up cellmates in the big house," states Darbie, holding on for dear life.

"Lord willing," agrees Lark. "Jersey's Big Pimpin' Rides," she mutters, "I love that show!"

A blanket of blue lights in the distance rushes towards them. Lark cuts the headlights, jumps a curb, and tears through Emmet Park. She weaves around benches, a ghost tour group holding flashlights, and does a u-turn around a fountain. "Watch out!" exclaims Darbie. Lark slams on the brakes so hard Darbie almost hits the front windshield. The Associate is standing directly in front of the car. Unfazed, he taps on the window's glass. At once, Darbie recognizes him and wonders how he seems to be around every corner. Even a talented stalker isn't that gifted. Consumed with terror, she squeals, "It's him! Go. Go."

"What are you talking about?" Unlike traditional automobile designs that feature windows that open by rolling them down, Lark presses a release hinge and slides open the driver side's tiny bubble window. "Sorry about that, Hollis!" Hollis smiles forgivingly, reaches in the car, and hands Lark a handful of pecans. "Thanks, man. I'd love to hang out, but I've gotta go see a man about a dog," she explains. He nods, steps away from the car and waves. The blue lights are long gone. "Here." She shares the pecans with Darbie, dumping them in her lap, flips the headlights back on, continues driving, and takes a right out of the park. The car makes two loud thumps as it drives off the curb. The girls jostle about, knocking shoulders. Lark imagines the tires laying rubber as she makes the sound effects of them peeling out. In reality, they accelerate as fast as Isetta will handle without blowing her motor.

"You know him?" asks Darbie.

"Hollis? Sure, who doesn't? Locals refer to him as Pecan Man. He doesn't talk much, but he knows the location of every pecan tree in Savannah. The man is practically a celebrity. Honestly, Darbie. You need to get out more."

"He's the Associate. That's what the guy on the phone told me. He's been following us all night."

Unable to fathom the absurdity of what Darbie is saying, Lark chuckles. "Hollis? No way. He's a Savannah nomad — hangs out all over town. He's harmless, wouldn't hurt a fly."

***

Wishing he hadn't consumed that second cup of coffee, Officer Tripp Stevens straddles his motorcycle while waiting on a red traffic light at a congested intersection.

"Officer Stevens, what's your 10-13?" requests police dispatch over the radio. "We have a 10-25 on a red and white Isetta BMW, over."

"10-4. All clear on Skidaway Road and Pennsylvania Avenue, over," responds Officer Stevens after scanning the area. The light changes to green. His bike thunderously rumbles and crackles as he takes a right. Discharging a small trail of exhaust in his wake, he rides off. The Mini Cooper that sat beside him pulls away seconds later, revealing the previously obscured cunning little Isetta BMW. What Isetta lacks in speed she more than makes up for in agility. The girls breathe a sigh of relief, Lark flips the headlights back on, and they proceed to East 36th Street, free as a bird.

CHAPTER 19

Intense heat lightning flashes vivid and expansive electric light across the distant horizon as Lark zooms through the Bonaventure Cemetery gate. Darbie rides shotgun holding her cell phone to her ear. "Yes, officer. I just got home, and it was gone... Yes, sir. She's a beauty. I'd hate for anything to happen to her... You don't think someone would sell her for scraps, do you?... A car chase? Oh dear. I hope not... I'll come down there first thing tomorrow morning and file a report. Please let me know if you hear anything else... Thank you." She presses 'end call' and drops her phone into her lap.

A car parked up ahead flashes its headlights. An ominous figure and Rufus stand beside it. Hazy fog permeates the dank air. Lark parks and leaves the lights on, casting amber light on the area. Darbie grabs the skateboard and situates it into position. Lark and Darbie carefully place the bogus Banksy on the skateboard. Then, they duck down behind a set of large headstones. The figure fires an arrow from a crossbow and impales Darbie's passenger side door.

"Jeez. Was that really necessary?" yells Darbie. The arrow has a note attached. Darbie shines her flashlight on it. The letter reads:

GIVE ME THE BANKSY, AND I'LL RELEASE THE MON-
GREL.

Lark hollers, "You first!" Crouched next to a dwarf palmetto, she gives Darbie a series of hand signals which indicate her next course of action will be to sneak around towards the figure. Darbie shakes her head 'no.' Defiant, Lark valiantly follows through with her strategy and disappears into the dark desolate unknown. The figure fires another arrow. The arrow passes so closely, Darbie can hear the whoosh as it zips by her head before puncturing her esteemed German car. "Use your words!" she hollers. Darbie unfolds the note, and it reads:

SEND IT NOW, OR THE DOG GETS THE NEXT ARROW!

A hot mess, Darbie's eyes widen with fear. Doing her best not to allow her raw emotions to hinder her actions, she steadies her shaky hands and fervently pushes the skateboard down a narrow path. The figure stops it, shines a flashlight on the man-hole cover, and grins satisfied. Rufus gives it a sniff and begins to lick the phony artwork, smearing the paint and unveiling their operative bait-and-switch tactic. The figure's head snaps up. He releases Rufus, but then points the crossbow towards Darbie.

Calm and collected, Lark sneaks up behind him, reaches down, and grabs a concrete vase filled with clover. She smacks the figure on the head with the pot knocking him out cold; his body collapses, succumbing to vanquishment. Darbie rushes to Lark's side. Elated, Rufus wildly wags his tail, thumping it on every surface in its path. He frantically vaults himself on both of the girls, springing and pouncing like a large hairy bullfrog. Exceedingly enthusiastic, he licks their hands and faces. Covered in sweet Rufus slobber, they bask in their reunion, buoyantly petting and loving all over him. "Sweet boy. We've missed you so much," gushes Darbie, rubbing him behind his ears.

"Who's the man? You are. Yeah, you are! That's who." raves Lark, patting him on his tush.

They study the demobilized art thief's comatose physique. "Check it out. He's wearing the first outfit you tried on at the thrift store," points out Lark.

"Whoa. Well, I'll be. He sure is."

"And now for the sixty-four-thousand-dollar question, who the heck is this?" asks Lark, using a mock game show host voice.

"I'm dying to know!" proclaims Darbie.

"Would you like to do the honors?"

"You bet your sweet cheeks I do!" Darbie leans over the body.

"Drum roll," says Lark drumming her hands on a headstone.

Darbie surreptitiously removes the mask off his face, beams her flashlight on his face, and gasps. "It's-It's Bernice!" she stammers, stepping backward, away from her.

"Behold your future," taunts Lark.

Dumbfounded and feeling rather betrayed, Darbie gazes down at Bernice. She contemplates just how long Bernice has been masquerading as the dutiful gallery coordinator, all the while plotting and setting Darbie up for a criminal's demise. This is by far the most valuable work of art the gallery has ever had on loan. All at once, the scheme begins to unravel in Darbie's mind with crystal clear recollection and razor-sharp imagery. "Of course. The day I got the call — Bernice was fiddling with her cell phone. She waited until Walker had stepped out the back door. She knew I'd be alone. I never actually saw her leave for her lunch break. She has full access to the security camera footage on her computer. She knew my every move because she was spying on me via the gallery's security video feed, and her window over-looks the same view I have at the reception desk. It was just a co-incidence that Hollis was there doing his thing. She made up the whole elaborate 'associate' bit," Darbie relates. "But what about Rufus barking? He couldn't have been there," she thinks out loud. She'd thought the condescending tone of the caller's voice sounded obscurely familiar.

Lark rummages through a bag, pulls out a recorder, and presses play — *Barking*.

"She knew I'd take the magnetic strip the day she had to fire me. She practically handed it to me."

"She's an amazing actress and a master manipulator, isn't she? She totally set you up."

"Precisely. She used me," agrees Darbie, rocking on her heels. She gazes down at Bernice with a disgusted expression.

Rufus releases a low growl, circles Bernice, lifts his hind leg, and urinates on her. "Good boy," praises Lark. She forages through Bernice's bag some more. "She had no intention of pay-ing you anything. There's no money in here."

"What is in there?" asks Darbie.

Lark reaches inside again and withdraws a voice disguiser. Darbie and Lark exchange a puzzled look, and then Lark holds it to her mouth, testing it. "Hello (manly disguised voice)." Lark snickers. Holding it back to her mouth, she serenades Darbie with Twenty One Pilots, "Stressed Out." Darbie's stiffened expression melts away into a giddy giggle.

***

In Bernice's car, the girls and Rufus pause at a stop sign. Hollis rests on a bench snapping his jacket closed.

"Look who it is," points out Darbie.

"That's three times in one night."

"It's a sign. Give the man some cash."

"Okay, but we're seriously down to our last five bucks," Lark explains, unzipping her backpack.

"Give him all we got," she decides, rolling down her window.

Lark digs in her bag and pulls out a roll of Banksy bills with a phone number scribbled on a piece of paper. "Whoa," says Lark, showing them to Darbie.

"Clash!" they both exclaim, staring at the graffitied money.

Darbie unfolds the wad, fanning it out. "Do you know how much these are worth?"

"How much?" eagerly asks Lark with dollar signs in her eyes. She pauses for a moment, overcome with greed. Suddenly, she begins rapidly shaking her head side-to-side, snapping herself out of her money-hungry state. "You know what, on second thought, I don't wanna know," Lark declares. "Hey, Hollis!" she calls out, waving him over to Isetta.

Darbie beams a welcoming smile as he approaches the car door. "Hey. We have something we wanna give you," greets Darbie. She uses a gum wrapper to jot down a name and phone number. "Get in contact with this appraiser. She's a highly esteemed expert in her field, and she'll be able to set you up with a buyer's agent. Don't take less than 1,500 dollars apiece for these," she discloses, handing the Banksy bills to him. Lark nearly chokes on her gum.

Hollis lays his other filthy hand on top of hers. "God bless you," he whispers with tears in his eyes.

"You too, my friend," says Darbie.

"Do something great with that," encourages Lark, leaning over Darbie. He nods, and they drive off.

"Here you go," says Lark, offering her a hand sanitizer bottle.

"No, thanks."

"What? You don't want any?" asks Lark, shocked.

"If by God's grace, I can survive tonight's preposterous rampage, I don't think a handshake is gonna kill me."

"Who are you?" asks Lark with a grin.

"What can I say? This evening has been cathartic," reveals Darbie, returning an enthusiastic grin.

A few minutes later, Darbie parallel parks Bernice's car in a seedy neighborhood. They leave the car running with the driver's side door open and walk off. Two teenagers approach the car, laugh, jump in, and take the sedan for an off the cuff joy ride.

Darbie, Lark, and Rufus return to the RV on foot. Lark chunks the skateboard back down next to the bikes on the lawn.

Entering the RV, Lark collapses onto the couch. Lark's so worn out, she can hardly keep her eyes open. Darbie opens a water bottle and fills a bowl for Rufus. She grabs a Sprite for herself and chugs half of it. "You know, we could just stay here for the night," proposes Darbie.

"In this neighborhood? No way! Leaving Winnie here was one thing, but I'm not staying here."

"It's quieter here than out on the lake. That is if you don't mind the sound of the occasional gunfire," jokes Darbie.

"Wow, you really aren't a country girl, are you?" laughs Lark, deliriously tired.

"You got that right."

"And here I thought you were starting to acclimate."

"Not even close." Darbie tenderly pets Rufus while he's nuzzling up next to her with his head resting in her lap. "I was only joking. We gotta get out of here. This thing will stick out like a sore thumb come morning."

Lark nods and tosses her the keys. "Mind driving? I'm so spent; I can't even see straight anymore." Her exhausted eyelids are about to succumb to sleep deprivation.

"Really? I'm catching my second wind."

"Darbie Harrington outlasts me. I never thought I'd see the day."

"Ah. The student has become the master."

CHAPTER 20

SGT. Patterson leads Darbie and Lark over to a dual-sided desk. Stacks upon stacks of files and endless paperwork sit in heaps and lie strewn haphazardly about the office space. Moments earlier, Darbie and Lark were elated to hear their names called after waiting for well over thirty minutes in a packed vestibule. Two unsavory men flanked them; one smelled like BO and cigarettes, and another reeked of whiskey and soured milk. Overworked, SGT. Patterson slouches in his seat opposite of them, shuffling paperwork. "Darbie Harrington?"

"Yes, sir."

"You're here to report a 10-41, auto theft. Is that correct?"

"Yes, sir. Last night, we were-"

"I'm gonna stop you right there, miss. I need you to fill these out," he orders in a firm and authoritative voice, handing a clip-board over to her. "Are you," he pauses, sliding his glasses down his nose, studying a form, "Lark Kingsley?"

"Yes," she hiccups.

"Agent Walker will be handling this case from here on out as it's linked to a much larger crime spree. He requested to speak directly with you both upon your arrival. He's been tied up putting two assailants through the wringer this morning, gathering intelligence and whatnot. I'll just let him know you're here." He gets up and exits the room. The police station is bustling with chatter. Everyone seems to be claiming to be either wrongly accused or a victim.

Darbie starts tediously filling out the paperwork on the clipboard. "This morning, I got a message from my contact at the New York Banksy Gallery. She heard I was let go at the gallery. She absolutely loathed Bernice and always insisted on collaborating with me. She mentioned that they're looking for an art curator," shares Darbie, anticipating Lark's reaction.

Lark beams, unselfishly recognizing this good fortune to be precisely what Darbie needs right now. "Perfecto. Sounds like a great opportunity for you. You should totally seize that."

"Really?"

"Really. I'm happy for you. And hey, your mom's nose can finally return to normal size. Win, win."

SGT. Patterson returns with a powdered donut. A layer of confectioners sugar sprinkles his chest. "Make sure to fill out the back too. I'll need to get a copy of your license, insurance, and registration," he instructs with a mouth full of donut, white dust spraying from his thin lips.

"The registration is in the glove box," explains Darbie.

Walker enters the office looking as deliciously intimidating as ever wearing an FBI jacket. "SGT. Patterson, I'll take over from here. Ladies..." He ushers them towards the interrogation room.

***

The girls take their seats on one side of the table. Darbie crosses her legs and nervously shakes her foot. Lark fidgets, repeatedly twirling her hair into ringlets with her index finger.

"Normally, I'd just speak with you in private, Darbie. But Lark, it seems there have been some allegations made against you as well, so I'll go ahead and question you both," informs Walker. He slides into a chair across from them.

"Accused of what?" utters Darbie uneasy.

He opens a folder and glides a photo of Clash across the table. "Have either of you seen this man before?" he grills.

"Nope," lies Lark, cool as a cucumber.

"Um. Yeah. I recognize him," affirms Darbie, uncrossing her legs and tapping her heel on the linoleum floor. Lark shoots her a quizzical glare, wondering why on earth she's spilling the beans. "He came in the gallery the day the Banksy exhibit went up," partially confesses Darbie. Confident the cameras would've recorded their brief interactions, she decides to pony-up and discloses it now as a half-truth.

"Yes, we have quite a bit of footage of him hanging out up at the gallery this week. For years he's been suspected as a possible Banksy conspirator, or he may, in fact, be Banksy himself," confirms Walker. Darbie and Lark gasp, realizing they may know the identity of the most wanted artist in the world.

Walker opens another folder and slides a photo of Dante across the table. "Have you seen this man before?" he probes.

"No," Darbie and Lark vehemently deny in sync.

"His name is Dante Capello. He is an extremely dangerous thief suspected in over a dozen multi-million dollar art heists.

He's been eluding us for over a decade. I apprehended him tonight passed out in your Isetta with Bernice Musko."

"What? They stole my car?"

"Looks that way. There were empty beer cans everywhere. Bernice smelled of urine. Not sure if it's hers or Capello's. They went through the gallery like two bulls in a china shop."

"What?" Darbie's eyes dart from his to Lark's. "How did that happen? I mean, what exactly did they damage?" she asks, horrified.

"Oh, nothing of consequence. It was all brassware pieces. Not a scratch on them."

Darbie exhales sharply, staring at Lark. "What a relief," she mumbles.

"A fake Banksy manhole cover was discovered in her car clear on the other side of town." Walker points to the photo of Clash. "We think this man intervened and switched them at some point in the evening as the Banksy was found returned to its original street location this morning."

"I'm speechless," insists Darbie.

"Shocking!" proclaims Lark.

Lark walks over to the one-way mirror and stares at it. She makes a couple of outlandishly silly faces. Then, she starts walking past it as if she is walking down a staircase.

***

Officer Varnell, a young hefty fella, munches on a bag of pork rinds as he walks by the viewing room and glances at the one-way glass. He sees Lark looking as if she's walking down a flight of stairs with Walker and Darbie seated in the background.

He chuckles, moves his head side to side to see if anyone is watching, and then enters the empty room.

***

Walker wrestles a smile. "They claim not to know each other. Although their body paint and the undignified positions we found them in would suggest otherwise..."

Lark snorts, which she rapidly disguises with a cough. She returns to the table, grabs a notepad, and starts fastidiously folding paper into origami puppets.

"...The surveillance footage, albeit blurry, does suggest two partners. While it's common for criminals to return to the scene of a crime, this is a bit of a head-scratcher. But Bernice and I are the only gallery employees whose thumbprints have been programmed into the new security system. And I was there when she gave the new hire his key-card. He wasn't able to use it because the security strip was missing from the back. The system shows last night's scan as his key-card strip. Bernice was the only one with prior access to it, plus it was found stuck to her forehead."

"Unbelievable," declares Darbie.

"And yet completely believable," counters Lark.

"Is Isetta okay?" ascertains Darbie.

"She's got some body damage. Nothing that a trained professional can't repair, I'm certain," Walker rests his hand on top of Darbie's, comforting her for a fleeting moment before regaining his professional composure.

"Thank heavens. It couldn't have been much of a car chase. Isetta has less horsepower than a riding lawnmower," responds Darbie.

Lark returns to the one-way mirror, squats on the ground, and with her hands raised above her head, she starts performing a puppet show.

"Lark, there's nobody in there," assures Walker.

"Sure. Sure. I bet that's what you tell everyone."

***

Officer Varnell watches Lark with child-like wonder as she performs her amateur puppet show from the other side of the one-way glass. Reclining his chair back on the two rear legs, he props his feet up on the wall immediately below the glass. Cackling, he shoves pork rinds in his mouth, nearly choking on them.

***

Darbie dismissively shrugs, encouraging Walker to continue.

"They were heavily armed — two duffel bags full of weapons. A paintball gun used in the heist was found on their person. In an odd twist, we also recovered a 9mm pistol used to shoot up a bus stop. They led police officers on a high-speed chase. Regrettably, we were unable to ascertain any witnesses to corroborate our story as they were all too distract by the rarity and uniqueness of the little car to pay attention to the driver. We believe the thieves were intoxicated at the time as one vomited during the pursuit."

"It would also explain the urine," equates Darbie.

"Been there, done that," relates Lark, returning to her seat beside Darbie.

A very disheveled Bernice and Dante shuffle by the door in shackles and handcuffs with multiple officers leading them. "You're making a serious mistake. It was them. I'm innocent. I swear!" cries Bernice, making a desperate last-ditch plea. Walker gets up, closes the door, and sits back down, all the while maintaining his professional composure. "I will be exonerated!" yells Bernice. Her voice fades out as they proceed further down the hallway.

Lark leans in and whispers in Darbie's ear, "I knew she was in the building. The temperature just dropped twenty degrees." Darbie's eyes fix on the table as she pinches her lips together, hiding her inner chuckle.

Walker, missing the joke, continues, "Darbie, we also believe they stole your car in a rather far-fetched attempt to frame you and Lark."

Darbie and Lark bust out laughing.

"Us? Art thieves?" cackles Darbie.

"Can you imagine?" chimes Lark.

***

Bernice stands in her underwear sweatin' like a whore in church. An officer hands her the orange prisoner's uniform. Another inmate and the officer cover their mouthes snickering. Her back is spray painted with a Banksy stencil of a crooked, framed Mona Lisa wearing coke-bottle glasses. Underneath it reads *CROOK*.

***

Walker gives Darbie and Lark a dismissive wave and responds. "We ruled you both out immediately. Darbie, you reported your car stolen around the same time as the chase. Both of you have solid alibis for the entire evening. You're all over social media in several photos setting up at the Banquet Hall and attending the actual alumni homecoming party. We have countless eyewitnesses who saw you partying at a frat house, streaking, and skinny dipping."

"Wait, how do you know about that? Please tell me there aren't photos," Darbie cries.

Lark smiles devilishly and reaches for a folder. "Please tell me there are photos."

Walker slides the folder away. "I'm one of the eyewitnesses."

Darbie turns beet red. She wants to crawl into a hole and die. "You were there?"

"What a coinkydink," chirps Lark.

"Once a brother, always a brother," smirks Walker.

Mortified, Darbie crosses her arms, slumping in her chair, wishing it would swallow her whole. Lark beams with pride.

Walker sports a sinister grin. "I saw everything. And I do mean everything."

Ruth, a plainly dressed secretary, enters the room. "Pardon the intrusion, Agent Walker. When you wrap up this debriefing, Detective Hayes requests a moment of your time. I'm afraid it's rather urgent, sir."

"Ladies, please excuse me. I'll be right back. Once you complete that paperwork, you're free to go."

Ruth and Walker depart expeditiously.

Darbie and Lark wait for the door to close. They both breathe a sigh of relief, feeling slightly worked over. Lark watches as Darbie's face shifts from intensely pensive to evenly placid.

Elated to pass Walker's relatively watered-down third-degree session, they each use a folder to obscure the camera and the mirror's view of their profiles. Turning to face each other, Darbie sees Lark smiling from ear to ear and mirrors her expression. Rejoicing, their first order of business is performing their secret celebratory handshake under the table.

"Ohhh. I almost had you that time," claims Manuel, Hector's middle child.

"Almost doesn't count," retorts Hector, with a smug grin.

"Let me have a turn," whines Margo, Hector's only daughter. "You've been hogging it all morning," she huffs, folding her arms, sulking.

"Have not."

"Have too."

Manuel and Margo sit side by side on a brown suede sectional sofa pulling back and forth on a controller to their game system. Hector is lounging on the floor, stretching out his aching back. His angelically beautiful wife, Maria, sits at the table, helping Juan, their youngest, construct a solar oven for his science project.

"Papa, Manuel just hit me," tattles Margo.

"Did not!"

"Did too," she cries. "It's my turn, and he knows it!"

Hector and Maria's oldest, Javier, snappily walks into the room from the kitchen, holding an empty box of Little Debbie snacks. "Who ate the last Zebra Stripe? Confess now, and you'll live to see tomorrow."

Ding dong. The doorbell rings. Javier starts to head towards the door. Hector heaves himself into a sitting position. "I'll get it. You never know who it might be," grumbles Hector. Pushing down on the armrest to the sofa as he stands up. It's Saturday morning, and Hector is still in his comfy pajama pants. Stepping in front of Javier as he wobbles slowly to the door, hoping it's not someone with a complaint, maintenance repair, or even worse, a rent excuse. "This better be good," Hector gripes. Reluctantly, he opens the door and discovers no one is there. It occurs to him that it's probably just another ding dong ditch scenario; frequent pranks are an unfavorable side effect that comes along with being a landlord. Looking down at their front *Hey y'all!* doormat, he finds a gallon size glass jar with an envelope taped to it. He grunts, bending down to pick it up. It's a jumbo jar of pickled eggs. Cradling the container like a newborn baby, he opens the envelope and pulls out a small piece of carefully folded yellow legal pad paper. The note reads:

Heya Hector,
    Condolences, they're still out of pickled pigs feet.
Here's the money I owe you. Sorry, it took so long.
        No hard feelings,
        Lark

Peeking inside the envelope, he discovers a check for 2,250 dollars. Grateful to rightfully receive the money he's been due, he waves the check in the air at the kids. "Who wants to go to soccer camp?"

The kids all gleefully yell, "I do!"

Then, Juan stops grinning and stares at his project. "How about space camp instead?" he timidly asks.

"You bet. Everyone happy?"

"Yes." Smiles light up the room.

"Bueno. Get dressed. We're going out for breakfast."

"Yay!" The entire family cheers.

CHAPTER 21

A lot can happen in a year. Sawing logs, Rufus naps on a plush rug beside Darbie's swollen ankles. She's seated at a desk composed of recycled scrap metal in a stunning office space decorated with upscale furnishings. Her desk, which formerly belonged to her daddy, showcases the picture frame of the two of them on the Tybee Island beach, flying a compound kite alongside the photo of Rufus. Her face glows, exalting in her good fortune while she arranges a few additional frames. There's one featuring Lark with her coworkers at Jersey's Big Pimpin' Rides and one of her momma and Ada Mae wearing red hats. Darbie gazes at her newest addition, a framed newspaper clipping highlighting Hollis with his pecan food cart, voted Savannah's most successful entrepreneur this year.

Darbie's laptop beeps and she smiles pleasantly at an incoming Skype call from Lark. Lark and Clash pose on camels in front of Egyptian pyramids featuring Banksy Graffiti art on the back of a porta potty trailer. Darbie goads, "Hey, trouble!"

"Sorry. The signal is a bit sketchy. Anyways, I figured it out," proclaims Lark.

"What?" asks Darbie.

"You know. The answer to your big question. What's it all about?"

"You were listening?" questions Darbie.

"Always," affirms Lark with a humongous grin plastered across her face.

"Really? Well, I can't wait to hear it."

"Yeah. So, I woke up suddenly in the middle of the night last night, and it hit me like a ton of bricks."

"Wow."

"Yeah. I sat straight up in bed and grabbed a piece of paper and pen off the nightstand. I jotted it down so I wouldn't forget." Lark flashes a receipt with notes scribbled on it at her phone's camera.

"Impressive."

"Yeah, I remembered how you kept that dream diary in college. I can't tell you how many times I woke up to the sound of your pencil scribbling down tidbits from your dream state to analyze later," recalls Lark.

"Well, if I didn't record them right away, I would've forgotten them later," Darbie defensively explains, embarrassed. "Anyway, you figured out the meaning of life," she reminds.

"Ah-hmm. And then, I ate the rest of a piece of chocolate cake I ordered for dessert at dinner. Huge mistake, by the way. It was so rich. I couldn't go back to sleep after that. I was so hopped up on sugar."

"Alrighty then." Darbie inhales a deep breath. "Lark, honey, I'm gonna need you to focus. The anticipation is killing me. The meaning of life — Let's have it already."

"What?" inquires Lark.

"Seriously?" exasperates Darbie, frowning.

"No. I'm just messing with you. It's about love, faith, helping each other, hard work, and maybe a little dumb lu- "

The signal cuts out. Darbie stares at her black screen. Shaking her head, she presses the 'return' key several times to no avail. "Typical," she smirks.

Rufus's ears perk up when Walker enters holding a cardboard box, which he sets down. "Last one," he announces. Walker walks up behind Darbie, leans over her, places a wedding picture of the two of them down. He interlinks his hand with hers; their wedding rings touch. She turns and slowly rises, revealing her full baby belly. Darbie opens the door, welcoming the bright, beautiful, warm sunlight. They all exit the Winnebego, which has a large Banksy spray-painted on its facade. Walker throws Rufus a tennis ball down an embankment in Central Park. A sign staked in the ground reads *Moving Exhibition*. It's positively heavenly outside with blue skies and vibrant greenery delighting the senses as everything is in full bloom. Walker gently plucks a ladybug off of Darbie's shoulder. The ladybug takes flight sweeping over the park. Relishing the moment, Darbie and Walker kiss.

EPILOGUE

Nightfall descended well over an hour ago. A crowd of tourists gathers on the sidewalk in front of the SSAI Art Gallery. A waning crescent moon hangs aglow above them in the glimmery, starry sky. The air is still, and the sand gnats are out feasting with a vengeance. A tenderhearted woman in her fifties, donning a green and white polka-dot sundress, extracts a canister of bug spray from her woven tote bag. She generously sprays the repellent on her and her husband's ankles. Then, she hands the bottle over to the circle of strangers to pass around because she was brought up with the philosophy that if you have something good, you share it. The group stands, intermingling, and engaging in idle conversation as the canister circulates amongst them.

A tall thin man clothed from head to toe in all black, including a black trench coat and combat boots, appears from seemingly nowhere under the eerie glow of a street light. "Greetings all. My name is Trigger, and I'll be your guide tonight. Together we'll stroll past Savannah's most spine-chillingly haunted locations. Please, don't let the daytime beauty of our fine town fool you; Savannah's reputation as America's largest city portal to the spiritual world is more than a legend. Have your cameras and mobile devices readily available because inadvertently catching a glimpse of an apparition or orb is not uncommon, especially on a night like tonight. Just yesterday, I had a guy text me a photo he snapped on our tour last week. He'd rapidly fired off his camera at the scene of every grizzly tale. A few days later, he was weeding thru and editing his pictures. He was about to delete one in particular because, at first glance, the photo quality appeared to be pixelated and overexposed. Upon closer examination of what he originally hypothesized was a granulated blur, he discovered, without realizing it at the time, that it wasn't a photo defect at all but a ghost," he tells the group in an omniscient tone.

Trigger pulls out his cellular device, and with a few clicks and a scroll, he finds the image. "I see that look of doubt in your eyes there, young lady. Here you go." He hands the device off to a disgruntled teenage girl with a stripe of bright purple hair and a nose ring. The temperamental girl, who's been making snide comments and pouting all evening. She's being forced against her will to endure tonight's events, events that are clearly beneath her, by her conservatively attired parents who stand adjacent to her. "Take a gander for yourself. Study the area to the right of the doorway, and you will discover the faint but distinct outline of a woman," he directs.

Her miserable grimace washes away, revealing a genuine look of intrigue, registered with a satisfyingly wicked smirk that showcases her rarely seen set of metal braces. "Whoa!" she says captivated. Her parents lean in closer to her. Her dad raises an analytical eyebrow while her mother releases an audible gasp surprising the rest of the onlookers.

"Kindly pass that around, so everyone can have a chance to see for themselves the supernatural sight," instructs Trigger. As it makes its way through the group, he begins. "If you will direct your eyes straight ahead, you will see the SSAI Art Gallery. This postmodern architectural structure houses a small collection of classic and contemporary art. In stark contrast, the infrastructure stands in juxtaposition to Savannah's historic buildings. The gallery is also home to one of Savannah's most notorious crimes, the Banksy art heist, by the outlaw Dante Capello and his inside woman, Bernice Musko. While no one perished on this long ago dreadful night, a small child named Billy initially believed he'd witnessed the ghost of Jebediah Pucket's horse searching for its master. The boy grew into an old man who passed away in 2104. On his death bed, he spoke of that frightful night when he was just four-years-old. Billy claimed that once the apparition crossed the street, he'd noticed it wasn't a ghost at all but two masked, female assailants. The dying man insisted that the real Banksy thieves were never apprehended as no one in his family would listen to the conflicting testimony of such an imaginative young child. The event plagued his dreams his entire life. Every year on homecoming night, you can witness the ghost of little Billy tugging, in vain, on his mother's skirt. Don't believe me? Listen closely. You'll hear his shrill cries echoing throughout campus."

ACKNOWLEDGEMENTS

The creation of this book generated a bunch of laughter and, to be honest, a few tears. It's been a calling I least expected, as callings often are. One which I embarked on feeling downright inept and quite out of my comfort zone. Fortunately, the creative process proved blissfully rewarding. I wouldn't have attained the courage to undertake such a project without my husband and editor, Ben, cheering me on, right out of the gate. He believed in me when I didn't believe in myself. I will always love him for that. I'd also like to thank my talented daughter, Skyla, who helped me design the cover for *The Banksy Exchange*. It exceeded my expectation as everything she accomplishes does. And of course, I want to express gratitude to the folks who brought me into this beautiful and strange world, my amazing parents. They selflessly forked over their hard-earned money so I could get an Art degree and learn about artists, such as Banksy. Additionally, I want to acknowledge all my friends and family who encouraged me along this wild and unchartered book journey. Also, a special thanks to Banksy for reminding us all to think outside the box and choose love over anger, fear, or violence. Lastly, thank you to all my readers. I hope you had as much fun reading *The Banksy Exchange* as I had writing it.